Wild Things

Wild Things

Stories

Jaimee Wriston Colbert

BkMk Press
www.umkc.edu/bkmk
University of Missouri-Kansas City

BkMk Press
University of Missouri-Kansas City
5101 Rockhill Road
Kansas City, MO 64110
www.umkc.edu/bkmk

**Missouri
Arts Council**
The State of the Arts

Financial assistance for this project has been provided by
the Missouri Arts Council, a state agency.

Executive Editor: Robert Stewart
Managing Editor: Ben Furnish
Assistant Managing Editor: Cynthia Beard
Cover: Michael Mayhugh

BkMk Press wishes to thank Marie Mayhugh, Anders Carlson, and
Cameron Morse.

Library of Congress Cataloging-in-Publication Data

Names: Colbert, Jaimee Wriston, author.
Title: Wild things / Jaimee Wriston Colbert.
Description: Kansas City, Missouri : BkMk Press, 2016.
Identifiers: LCCN 2016038783 | ISBN 9781943491056 (alk. paper)
Classification: LCC PS3553.O4384 A6 2016 | DDC 813/.54--dc23 LC
record available at https://lccn.loc.gov/2016038783

ISBN 978-1-943491-05-6

Acknowledgments

"We Are All In Pieces" – *Isotope*, winner of the Editors Fiction Prize and a Pushcart Prize 2010 Special Mention

"Wild Things I—Ghosts" (as "Ghosts") – *The Gettysburg Review*

"The Man Who Jumped" – *Jane's Stories IV: Bridges and Borders*; winner of the Jane's Stories National Fiction Prize

"Things Blow Up" – *Hawai'i Review*, winner of the Ian MacMillan Fiction Prize

"Elegy" (as "You Will Remember This") – *Drunken Boat*

"Elegy" (as "You Will Remember This") *Deep Waters: Rivers, Lakes & Seas* (Outrider Press)

"Gravity" – *Paterson Literary Review*

"Dog Days" – *The Evolutionary Review*

"This Is a Success Story" – *Solstice*

"A Kind of Extinction" – *Green Mountains Review.*

"Wild Things II—Migrants" (as "Migrants") – *Solstice*

"Finding the Body" – *Tahoma Literary Review*

"Erosion" – *Natural Bridge*

"Suicide Birds" – *Fjords Review*

"Aftermath" – *Gargoyle Magazine*

"The Hoodie's Tale" – *Paterson Literary Review*

"The Hoodie's Tale" – *Home* anthology (Outrider Press)

The Author Wishes to Thank:

My perceptive manuscript readers (some of you multiple times!): Maile Costa Colbert, Ian Colbert, Joe Weil, Minrose Gwin, Leslie Heywood, and Libby Tucker. Maria Mazziotti Gillan, Chair of the Creative Writing Progarm at Binghamton University, and Binghamton University, for support that makes it possible. BkMk Press for its commitment to excellence, in particular Cynthia Beard for her meticulous editing and fast response to all manner of eleventh-hour requests; and Ben Furnish, editor extraordinarie, whose passion for literature, thoughtfulness, and insightfulness helped the early incarnations of this manuscript become a book I am proud of. Thank you for never giving up. And thanks so very much to Bonnie Jo Campbell, Jack Driscoll, Pam Houston and Christine Sneed for their beautiful cover endorsements. I am deeply honored. My publicist, Sheryl Johnston, for her wisdom, professionalism, and encouragement. And my family; without their love, none of it would be worthwhile.

In memory of my mother
Helen Pauline Wagner Wriston
1926-2012

Contents

Prologue

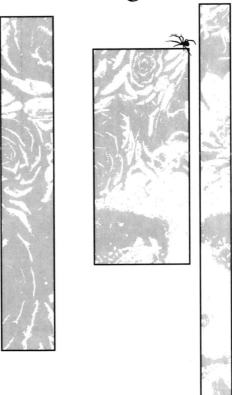

Elegy

The day the water sucks out of Kawela Bay is when the old poet confesses his love for you. He tells you *You're the beautiful one* and you tell him, *Oh, you say that to all the girls,* and a look at his craggy, saggy, grinning old poet face and you just know this is true. *Tell me something I don't know,* you say, *that I haven't heard before.* Meanwhile you see the water receding like there's a giant hand out there dangling from the clouds and reeling it in, like when you were kids and your brother's alive and the two of you holding out your hands, the crystal dark water of the 'auwai settling in, and you're pumping it fast as you can, onto the crabgrass bank in search of crayfish. What did you do with them when you found them? You remember a plastic bucket, your brother's lacy red net like a hooker's stocking, and crayfish the slick auburn color of hair dye scrabbling around in the bucket one on top of the other, looking for the way out.

Your nipples are like pencil erasers, the poet says, and you say *OK, that's a first.*

But since he's a poet and an old one at that you'd expect him to make up an elegy of sorts on the spot as more and more of the pale water draws back, revealing a gum line of sand and rock and pastel-colored coral heads, a long stretch of reef, then more rock, and the humps of dead fish like they're tiling the sea floor, belly up and shining all silvery in its wake.

Last night when you brought the old poet back to his hotel he stood on his tiptoes in the elevator and stuck his tongue down your throat, then when the elevator doors sighed open he marched out in front of you like this was his due, into the velvet wings of his wife, head cocked, hair feathery as a bird's. *Perhaps one day he'll write a poem for you*, she chirped, winked, then fastening the leash around his ankle, black leather with sequins glistening like grains of sand, flew her husband back to their room.

Now though, instead of an elegy, the old poet makes a sound like *ohhhhh* wrenched out of the hole of his mouth, and he grabs his flabby chest, sinking down on his knees in front of the vast expanse of beach as the water shrinks back and back until it's a blink on the horizon, like he's praying to this new waterless world. And you can't not remember it, clutching the koa urn with your brother's ashes against your chest in the back seat of your father's Plymouth, your mother up front and she's asking you who you are with, over and over until you name it, your brother, grit and bone and the dry little chunks of him that later, the funeral done and everyone gone, you would drizzle into this ocean, his name on your tongue unrelenting as a song that keeps replaying, a rerun whose images will never again be new. The taste of this absence like everything and nothing at all. Fly *now*! you whisper, remembering the Hawaiian crow tattooed on his shoulder, iridescent wings inked into a permanent liftoff; the 'alalā, which means *cry like a child*, nearly extinct.

Stories

When despair for the world grows in me . . .
I come into the peace of wild things
— Wendell Berry, "The Peace of Wild Things"

I hope you love birds too. It is economical.
It saves going to heaven.
— Emily Dickinson

We're in a giant car heading towards a brick
wall and everyone's arguing over where they're
going to sit.
— David Suzuki

Gravity

Vito picks me up, and I swear he's dressed like the honest-to-god stereotype of his given name, a Mafia-wannabe guy, only check this out—he's not even Italian. Vito Smith, I mean really. His uncle's name, he'll tell you, like that explains it. He's wearing a beige coverall with lots of pockets and black wingtips gleaming like poured tar—kind of a cross between a carpenter and a pimp. He's taking me to my waitress job at the Red Door Inn, which isn't really an inn, since it doesn't have beds, and as far as that goes it doesn't have a red door. At one time it did, at least the signs are there, a door that's faded to a pinkish brown like the color of a bloodstain, like everything else in this piss-poor little upstate town of ours—you got to grudgingly admire it, I guess—faded but here. We haven't hit invisible yet.

The big news at the Red Door is Mel Gibson's coming to town, and we think he'll eat at our inn because, OK, there isn't much else. Our parkway like parkways anywhere has the chains, so I suppose he could grab a lobster at Red Lobster, but if you're a famous Hollywood guy scouting for a movie location do you go to Red Lobster? I can't imagine the movie he'd film here, maybe a depression something or other—he seems big on the ones where people live tortuous lives, endure all manner of pain, and then they die. But whatever, the Red Door Inn is it. One side of the dining room has a river view of the Susquehanna so that's where they'll put him. The problem though is it's not my section, and I have something important I want to ask Mel.

I had that section when I first started this job, but they changed me to the one I'm in now, which is our buffet. The issue was serving chicken dinners, or worse, the little squabs. They'd sit hunched on the plate, surrounded by wild rice and veggies, kind of the way a cat sits curled into itself when it's waiting to pounce on something. But no pounce left in those squabs, that's for sure. I got to thinking they were staring at me, reproachfully too. I'm not ignorant; I know you don't leave their eyes in when you cook birds. It's metaphorical, which means a kind of supposing. In other words, they *would* stare at me if they could. *Who makes these rules?* Their eyes would ask. *Who says the life of a squab is worth less than the fat woman you're serving me to?* And in truth I couldn't answer that. It got to really bothering me, so I asked Genny with a *G*, the Red Door manager, if she could put me in the vegan section. She gave me her put-upon look, pained arch of her furry eyebrows—I swear she slaps those puppies on with glue, like those fake mustaches you get at the Rite Aid around Halloween. "Birdie," she bleated, "you think this is Frisco or LA? We don't *have* a vegan section." And then she put me in the buffet room, which is less work because you're not schlepping peoples' plates so you're not serving the reproachful poultry, but it also means you're not getting a whole lot of tips. You fetch folks their cocktails and little extras, like if they want a dessert from the regular menu, and that's about it.

Bird eating is just not something I'm comfortable with. You might say I have bird envy. I've always wanted to be one, because I've always wanted to fly. I don't mean *United* with its jet engines and wings that only imitate. I'm talking about the real deal, three milliseconds of up, up, and away, into the sky, which if you're like me and get a little panicky in crowds, this is a homerun. The sky is the freest place in the world. It's the hollowness of their bones, makes them almost as light as the air they liftoff into. Have you ever held one? Sometimes on our frosty fall mornings before the humming birds leave for the southern sunshine you can pick one up—the cold makes them sluggish—and it'll warm in your hand then whoosh, off it goes.

Last year I biked down to our community college on registration day, and I told the lady sitting behind all her files and whatnot that I wanted to be a person who studies birds. She looked at me kind of funny.

"You mean an ornithologist?" she sniffed, sounding like she was trying to suck marbles down her throat at the same time.

I said, "Not exactly. The person who studies what birds can teach us—to fly."

She didn't have much of a response to that. "Basic English, basic math, that's what we're about here," she said.

Vito is all about explosions, though he'll tell you *implosion* is his specialty. It's like you explode from the outside in, he said. He talks about blowing things up, particularly his wife and the fag (he calls him that) she left him for, but I think that too is just a metaphorical way of speaking—though he does have quite the interest in dynamite.

"Dynamite?" I said. "I didn't think anyone used that anymore. You don't hear much about it anyway, as far as things that can make other things blow up. It's like it's been updated, car bombs, plastic explosives and suicide vests are all the rage these days, what with terrorists and all."

He clucked his tongue at me. "Birdie," he said, "let me give you some stats. What was the biggest building ever imploded?" I shrugged. "J.L. Hudson Department Store, Detroit, Michigan, 1998. Dynamite," he added. "What was the tallest man-made structure blasted?" I shrugged again. "Nineteen ninety-eight, a radio tower in Argentina, dynamite."

"So when did terrorists bomb that Oklahoma building?" I asked him.

"I don't remember," Vito said. "But you get what I'm telling you here? There's dynamite history under our feet, Birdie. In 1901 two trains crashed in Vestal, and the car carrying dynamite exploded killing five people. They were finding body parts a quarter of a mile away, maybe in your back yard."

Vito knows about dynamite because he's a demolition man, which means he explodes things for a living. Not explosions per se, he told me. "Implosions, a falling-down instead of a blowing-up. It's a beautiful thing to see a building go down," he said. "Angles go all curvy and brick, concrete, move together like a wave, like its fluid, and then it all folds in on itself." Vito is proud of what he does. He says anything man's built he can take down. "It's a cleansing," he said, "a cleaning out of something old so the new can take its place."

His biggest problem is that there isn't enough demolition work around here. You'd think there would be, what with everything coming apart. Our town and most of upstate New York has been crumbling away ever since America stopped being about manufacturing—old steel mills, factories where they made things, left to rot. "The issue," Vito said, "is people are so fuckin' poor they don't want to pay to have it taken care of. They just let gravity do it, slow as you please. Demolition," he said, "is a way of helping gravity do its job." He said Nobel, the peace-prize guy invented dynamite from nitroglycerin, which is super-explosive and hard to control, so he called it safety-blasting powder. "Which proves it's a good thing," Vito said. "Because he also invented the peace prize."

Vito is really pissed at his wife for leaving him, even though they fought all the time and swore to each other's face they hated each other. "She's my wife!" he said when I pointed this out, like that answers something. He knows where the fag lives, he said, and if his wife doesn't call it quits pretty soon and come home— "Boom! I'll show you what it looks like to fly," Vito said. That's because I told him I want to learn how to fly, but what he said he knows about is dynamite.

We don't have *sex* sex together, because Vito figures if we go all the way in the biblical sense, then he'd be cheating on his wife, so he could hardly implode her for what she's doing, now, could he? Vito likes to talk this way, like he has a moral order to things. But I think it's because he can't get hard enough. Today, on the way to the Red Door, Vito pulled a shot kit out of the glove compartment.

"Do you slam?" I asked, thinking maybe he was getting into shooting drugs, and he gave me a sick kind of look.

"I'm not about *that*," he said. "You know this about me, Birdie. Whiskey is my thing. And if whiskey ain't around I'll swallow whatever has alcohol in it." He said the shot was for his prick, so he can keep his hard-on. Then he explained how the woman—and he looked at me significantly here—could inject him in his privates and it would be kind of like foreplay. He reached over and squeezed my hand, grinning that Mafia grin of his.

"Count me out," I said. "I don't do needles."

"Well I don't do pills," he said. "Viagra's for fags."

What we do is rub each other's parts, as Vito calls it. I'm not really keen on this, but I look at it as a kind of barter, payment for the taxi which Vito is when he can't find demolition work, when there's no buildings in his immediate future that require blowing up, and since I can't afford a car, this way I don't have to dip into my scanty tips and minimum-wage paychecks. I'm saving to maybe buy a parrot. They're good company. They talk to you, but they only say what they've learned from you saying it first. So, as an example, if you don't want them to call you a bad name, like *slut* let's say, then you don't teach them that word. They can also squawk out the sound of the doorbell or the toaster, if they hear a doorbell or toaster. I went into Pet Mart the other day to talk to the guy about parrots— pet stores are sad places where everything is behind wire and glass, hardly a place for a bird that can't ever lift off into that sky. He told me some types of parrots are so moody and depressed you have to put them on Prozac. It's no wonder, I thought, looking at his cages. Having a depressed mother who developed her own habit with pills

made me wonder if there was room in my life for two pill-poppers—
though Pearl isn't in my life much anymore since she changed the
locks on me.

Here's how that went. I won my first thing ever in my entire
life, a trip to Hawai'i! WSPG, our local radio station, sponsors this
call-in competition about movies, and this time I knew the answer.
They asked what animal was present in the final scene of *The Passion
of the Christ*, and it was birds! You could hear them chirping when
they dragged away the boulder that was across Jesus's tomb. It was
a trick question because most people remember birds plucking out
the eyes of the thieves crucified with Jesus, not twittering around
the tomb. But my mother and her boyfriend and I watched that
movie three times after it went into DVD. It was something we
could do together.

So I was all hyper—I mean who wouldn't be! A trip to Hawai'i!
And I did invite my mother, but I knew she wouldn't do it, because
it's not like we ever had *that* kind of money, as she pointed out. She
was sure I couldn't afford it either, even though they paid for the
plane and the hotel, since I'd have to feed myself. But I figured I
could catch fish. "What will you do, fish?" Pearl sneered, and I
grinned. We used to always read each other's thoughts, my mom
and me, though that was mostly before she got into the pills, which
began after she lost the baby. My little brother Sammy, born the icy
blue of a glacier, three months too soon. Pearl needed Valium
afterward to calm her down, and then Vicodin for some pain or
other, Xanax for anxiety, anti-depression pills of course, and then
she had no energy from all of it, so she's doing uppers to help with
that, then downers to counteract the uppers, sleeping pills so she
could sleep, and so on.

One day I came home from work early—the kitchen closed
because of a grease fire—and my mother and her boyfriend were
sprawled on the couch with a bunch of pill bottles spread across
the coffee table like appetizers.

"Happy hour," Pearl said when I pointed this out.

"What kind of a mother would you be to him!" I hissed, which was nasty, but I mean really—they're doing mixed-pill cocktails.

Pearl shrugged. "The thing about babies," she said, "is they love you anyway."

I worried about leaving her, but I figured her boyfriend was there, and since Sammy was his baby too, shouldn't he be helping her? So I go to Hawai'i for the week, and the hotel isn't on the beach but it's at least in walking distance, which is good because as it turned out I loved body surfing and did little else, just a drive on a tour bus up the Pali, a steep green pass through the Ko'olau Mountains. Now there's a place where you'd want to be a bird, lift off into that glittery blue air, the towns of Kāne'ohe and Kailua gleaming below like jewels, all the way to the sea. But body surfing! If you close your eyes you can almost imagine it, caught in the lip of a wave, and for just a moment, inside its curl, you're airborne.

On the way back I stopped off in LA where my best friend from high school moved; she's the only one of us that actually got out of upstate in any permanent sense, so she's kind of like a hero. By the time I was home, just two-and-a-half weeks later, my mother had changed the locks. "You're just not part of this anymore, Birdie," she said at the door, opened only enough to stick her head out, her hair scraggly, her pupils thumb-sized and black as rocks. I'm standing there with my Walmart flowered suitcase on the concrete path I used to sweep for her, begging her to let me in, and Pearl's just staring off over my head into the dark line of woods beyond. The house was silent but in a ghostly kind of way, like you could almost hear it, little Sammy wailing from somewhere inside.

So I camped out in the yard, sleeping in the shed, waiting for my mother to come to her senses and open that door. Surely she would open that door. Where was her boyfriend in all of this, what things could he, should he have done? Who knows? I never saw him. I kept thinking I heard that baby cry, and sometimes I would sneak around the living-room plate-glass window and peer in—Pearl passed out on the couch, not even dressed. The shed overflowing with gardening tools we never used, boxes of stuff we'd long forgotten, cobwebs, smell of some sort of rot, and I'd hear the cheery sing-song of the ice-cream man which made it seem all right somehow, me being where my mother didn't want me, a sense of some kind of normal. One day I poked my head out the broken slats of the shed's wooden window just to see him and discovered it wasn't the ice-cream man after all, but some Department-of-something-or-other golf cart filled with cables, power tools, spark plugs, things to fix other things and a scruffy bearded driver in a blaze orange don't-run-me-down vest, the ting-a-ling music a warning for people to keep clear.

I pictured myself breaking in late one night, garbed in black, Batwoman—which is almost like a bird—soaring up to the second floor window that was open just a little, hoisting it enough to slip inside. What would I have found there? Prescription bottles, all of them empty, strewn across the floor? Pearl slumped over in the bathtub, the girth of her belly like a ledge propping up her unconscious head, keeping it above the rising water, the faucet she *forgot* to turn off.

WHAT KIND OF bird would I be? Maybe an American crow. They're not the prettiest, and their song isn't sweet, but those smart eyes of theirs, like shiny black frog's eggs set in a face sharp as an ax, are attracted to things that gleam, like cash. A survivor bird. Or those drab little sparrows, *bitch birds* Pearl called them, when she used to put out feeders, and they were the ones that mostly would come. They're tough, gnarly, and aggressive. They know nobody's interested in them, and they can't get by on their looks, so they natter and shriek at each other—there's power in numbers—and pretty much take over the feeders. The sweetest are the mourning doves. If you want to know what love looks like take a look at them. It's sure not my mom and her boyfriend, I'll tell you. It's become pretty obvious they only stayed together because she was pregnant with Sammy, which is so 1950s. The boy and the girl dove sit together on a tree branch making out, no reason except they like each other. She's not even doing that fluttery thing female birds do so the male will feed her and then they can nest. That's just a process, the way humans generally have a date before sex. Doves kiss and nuzzle each other because they want to, and if one of them dies, the other stands sentry over the body. I guess that's why they're called mourning doves.

Here's the clincher though. The dove, supposedly, is the Holy Spirit, the big guy, we're talking G-O-D here! OK, *symbolizes* the Holy Spirit, which is kind of like a metaphor, but it's something. They didn't pick a dog or a turtle or a cow. A dove, a thing that flies! When Jesus was baptized the Holy Spirit appeared as a dove, the Bible says. And in *The Passion of the Christ* the dove appears in the Pilate scene. Makes me think the chirping when they rolled away the rock to get into Jesus's tomb was a you-know-what.

Which is what I need to ask Mel about. Mel Gibson is like an authority on things Catholic. In the movie you hear that chirping, and I know this is true because I won that trip to Hawai'i. And we know that Jesus rose into heaven. If you're a Catholic you believe that, or even if you're not but you need to believe in something. It took six hours for Jesus to die once they nailed him to that cross, and in the movie Mel uses these hours well, there's no downtime— they're torturing Jesus from the get-go, flaying him, scourging him, whacking him with mallets, piercing him with spears—there's no doubt this will end bad, and when it does the earth shakes, the skies go dark, and he's a goner.

When they open the tomb in the next scene they pan to the empty burial robe. But then we see Jesus alive again, and we know it's him because, OK, this actor's pretty hot so there's no mistaking him for someone else, plus he has nail holes in his hands. This is three days later and in between the time he's dead and the time he comes back again he went to heaven, right? I want to ask Mel how he got there. Because I have my own theory. I think God turned him into a bird and he flew! So, if that's the case when Jesus claimed he was the resurrection and the life, does this mean that believing in him when we die, we too will fly? It's what *I* want to believe in. That when all is said and done, in the end I'll fly.

THE HOUSE SITUATION has not improved. Once I managed to catch Pearl in the driveway in between schlepping take-out cartons from her Ford and her rush to get inside, and I pleaded with her to let me in too, but she just kind of looked at me like she wasn't entirely sure who I was, and she had this sour-chemical smell like she had swallowed too much of something, and it was leaching out of her skin. My mother is living on the edge of her own life, like she's one foot in it and one foot God knows where, and I have yet to see that boyfriend of hers since I've been back from my prize-winning trip. One night I heard a car pull in late and thought maybe it was him, but when I peeked through the wooden slats it was a man with a briefcase. A man and a briefcase in the middle of the freaking night? He left pretty quickly so probably it was a delivery, more pills for Mom. Vito told me the ingredients to make dynamite and what struck me was that one of them, ammonium nitrate I think it was, is also used to make crystal meth, which for all I know Pearl might be tapping into. It's a kind of toxic speed, and the way she's been dragging since Sammy, you can almost see her justifying that one too. A while back I saw on the news how another meth lab exploded taking out the house and the people inside; the woman who owned it was older than Pearl.

I decide the thing to do is to build myself a nest right here in the shed so I can keep an eye on things, all comfortable and snug, scraps of clothing I find poking about in the Dollar Store and Goodwill, pine needles, hay, bits of plastic, Pearl's old wool coat I pulled out of the trash after she had downed too many Vicodin and crammed it in there, cardboard boxes from the Red Door, shiny bits of this and that like a crow would snag, and of course my prints, Audubon's birds, taped to the sides. I don't totally approve of Audubon, since he slaughtered his birds to draw them, but I appreciate that he wanted to get them right. Anything that can fly and sing and look as drop-dead gorgeous as so many of them do, deserve to be done right if you're going to do them at all. I figure if I nest in the shed long enough Pearl will get used to the idea of having me here and maybe when winter comes and most birds go south or they freeze to death, she'll unlock the door and let me in.

Unfortunately that's not what happens, as one night I get home from working a damn-near double shift and the lights in the house are all blazing, so I sneak over to the windows to peer in and it's empty! Not a stick of furniture, no pan or plate or even an ashtray, a sweater, a scarf, no lost earring lying around to confirm there had ever been my mother in there. Not even an empty pill bottle rolling about on the floor. Nothing. She even packed up the stuff I still had inside and took it wherever she went. I don't get a good feeling about this.

I ask Vito if he thinks I should call the police and he says, "So what are they gonna do, arrest her for moving?" He offers to blast out the front door so I can go in, but I say no. Something about the house sitting empty doesn't invite me to enter it. It doesn't feel like home. And it's a rental anyway. What made it home was my mother there.

It's a stifling July afternoon, chattering of the cicadas and crickets, but everything else is still as death, and we're sprawled on my air mattress inside my nest rubbing each other's parts. Suddenly I don't want to do this anymore and yank my hand back. Vito offers to let me suck him instead and I shake my head.

"Feed me!" I tell him, and flutter my arms and legs.

He frowns. "I'm not the feeding type," he says, and tugs his pack of cigarettes out of his coveralls slung on the floor, lights one, inhales, then starts bitching about his wife on the exhale.

I swear if we're not rubbing parts or he's not imploding a building, this is the only thing Vito has to talk about. "One day, ba boom!" he says, and I have a vision of that old TV show *The Honeymooners,* and how Jackie Gleason would threaten he was going to pound his wife—but you knew this wouldn't happen because Alice would never allow it and you laughed. My mom loved that show, something else we could do together, reruns. And anyway blowing up someone with dynamite is a step or two up from a punch in the nose. I realize there are men who do this, strong-arm their women, but the kind I know are my dad and my mother's boyfriend, such lightweights that one day they just float away.

SOMETIMES I TRY to picture how it would be if Sammy had lived. But he can never grow up, not even in my mind, because I can't picture Pearl anymore without the pills, the kind of mother she would've been. *Imagine this. She puts the little boy into the Volvo, kisses the new husband goodbye like she was just going shopping, the movies, out with her friends and their children, a play date, with lunch foods packed by the mothers. Perfectly normal, though my mother is hardly normal. But imagine it. A play date. But she never shows up. The other mothers wait and the children play and then the ladies stop waiting and dig into the food—hmmm, PB&J sandwiches, white bread with the crusts cut off, a favorite of the kids. Everyone stops waiting. They know better. They know Pearl. Even though, reality check, she wouldn't have had any friends. No play dates for Sammy. No movies, no shopping. Now imagine the Volvo (safest car, her new husband would've insisted,* Consumer Reports *said so) as it plows through the Pali guardrail. What would she be thinking as it takes to the sky, Kāne'ohe and Kailua glistening below like in a dream, the day blue as the sky and the ocean in the distance bluer than that. Would she believe she could make it? Flying all the way to the sea?*

Except, of course, Pearl never went to Hawai'i. Should I have insisted, used up what little credit we had, promised the Red Door I'd be their buffet-slave for life if they floated me a loan? Would it have made a difference, my mother, the boyfriend, all of us still in the little house?

THE NEWS IS that Mel Gibson comes in two days! He made an honest-to-god reservation and at the Red Door everything's a whir, tablecloths washed, windows scrubbed, the wood floor buffed and shined, and the cook is thinking up new dishes, or at least renaming the old ones: *Lethal Weapon* Lasagna. Genny with a G is giving us all our posts, our scripts—what we're to say, do, and who we can say/do to. Only Luanne will be allowed to speak to Mel once he's seated, since he'll be in her section. Genny will seat him and his entourage. Caroline our hostess will seat everyone else. We are warned that he's much shorter than he appears in his films (Genny's been reading the kinds of magazines that tell you these things, along with that most actors and directors prefer their movies be called *films*), and we're not to stare at him.

I consider talking privately to Genny, explaining how important it is that I take five minutes to ask Mel my question, maybe less— three, I could do it in three. I consider a bribe, that I'll do the dishes, work extra shifts, clean her house, do her laundry, mow, weed, paint, power wash the siding, whatever she needs if she'll let me serve him his coffee and dessert, just that. But before I can get much further down a litany of offerings she gets *The Phone Call*. It turns out Mel Gibson won't be coming after all, Genny tells us, her lips pinched almost as white as one of those newly washed and ironed tablecloths. She shakes her head, her helmet hairstyle holding forth. He won't be choosing us at all, she says, not the Red Door, not the town. His agent said he wants a place more damaged, something *quasi-apocalyptic* (the agent's very words, she says), and he'll be scouting one of Pennsylvania's abandoned steel-mill towns.

For a couple minutes it feels like the air has been sucked out of me, like drawing in a breath at all is going to be a struggle, let alone not being able to ask Mel whether he thinks God turned Jesus into a bird and he flew to the sky. I think about that movie, how my mother's boyfriend rented it, and we watched it those three times; Pearl even made us popcorn. This before her boyfriend disappeared, though I recall now the way he would stare past the TV out the window. Was he looking into the distance of his leaving, even then? And now my mother's gone too.

I think about Mel's Jesus, how he just stood there and took it, all the horrors people could dish out, whips, floggings with chains, lashings with cat-o'-nine-tails, hangings—good grief if they smoked cigarettes back then they'd have been scorching him with these too—and I figure he must've dreamed of flying away well before they shut him into that tomb. If he could have, just turned into that dove right then and there, risen up over all that hatred, those poor arms nailed to that cross become wings, feathers, hollow bones light as air, lift off into that sky.

THE NEXT DAY I decide to abandon my nest. Let it be a shed again, and maybe I'll put my parrot money down on an apartment, something with a genuine doorbell instead of a parrot squawking the sound of one. How sad is that anyway, a parrot imitating the doorbell when it should be in a jungle somewhere, making like the wind. This is what birds do: they use their nests and when it's time to go they're gone, *outahere*, and the nest collects snow in the winter, or it blows away, or bugs take it over. The bird doesn't miss it because she'll build a new one next year.

I call Vito and tell him I want to go someplace and he takes his taxi out of commission and picks me up. I tell him about Mel choosing an abandoned town in Pennsylvania because of its apocalyptic promise, and Vito says he knows where we'll go. We cross over an ancient iron bridge into Pennsylvania, the tree-lined roads, the mid-day heat shimmering off the leaves, bright green roll of the hills on either side, the Endless Mountains these are called. He drives off the pavement onto a dirt road then onto even more of a dirt road, stones, tree branches, pockmarks, huge ruts in the ground like navigating Mars, then he pulls up in front of what looks like an old factory of some sort, steel girders, concrete walls, and broken-out windows, exposing what once must've been floors, rooms, work places, a business, a life, all surrounded by

long, waving weeds and an emptiness so huge even the crickets
have stopped purring.

"Where are the people who had jobs here?" I ask.

Vito shrugs. "Moved on, wherever people go." He says what
he'd really like to do is take this sucker down. "I have faith," he tells
me, "in just one thing. Gravity," he says, "and the power of dynamite
to do what gravity will do anyway, only a hell of a lot faster."

We crouch in the weeds and I watch Vito stare at the wreck of
a building, almost with a reverence of some sort.

"You want me to tell you how I'd do it, Birdie?" he whispers.

I shrug, and a shadow plays over his face so I nod. "Sure," I say,
"OK."

He grins, puffs his chest out a bit and I think of the male dove,
the way he displays for his girlfriend, his gray, fluffed-up breast.
But Vito's no dove. For one thing he wears a chain around his neck,
and his top two buttons unbuttoned so you can see it sliding in and
out of his chest hairs like a little gold snake. No self-respecting bird
would do that.

"The bigger ones you've got to do in stages," he says. "Planting
the dynamite into holes in the basement and detonating, then the
building drops a few floors, then more dynamite, and it drops a few
more until it's down. But this one is just the right size," he says, "to
get all at once, the whole enchilada."

So then he's explaining to me about the dynamite, how it comes
in sticks and you pack it into the hole and you connect it to another
stick that has a detonation cord. The real danger isn't the explosives,
he tells me, but the other stuff, booby traps inside the building—
loose concrete, floorboards, even waste people left. "It's hazardous
work," Vito says, "but the explosion itself is clean. It's all about
knowing what you're taking down," he tells me, "because once you
detonate, dynamite moves through the walls at the rate of sixteen
thousand feet per second, history undone in the time it takes to
push that button."

I whistle appreciatively. "Would it make someone fly, a blast that powerful?"

Vito scowls. "Birdie, listen up. Just because they named you that don't make you a bird, you know?"

I think about telling him the secret of my name, how really it's *Bertie* for Roberta, my grandmother's name, but my dad couldn't spell worth a damn, according to my mother, and he wrote *Birdie* on my birth certificate while she was still passed out from having me. Instead I close my eyes and remember her telling me about a friend of hers who had taken some kind of drug and was hallucinating that he could fly. "Only," said Pearl, "he had a rope around his neck, perched on the garage roof ready to do it, let the world fall away."

"Imagine it," Vito whispers, his breath hot in my ear.

So I do, the giant bang like a clap of thunder, a roar as it sucks the oxygen out of the air, the air gone purple, the ground trembling, a roiling cloud. The walls cave in, a wave of liquid concrete, like in the beginning when this is what there was, water, sky.

Wild Things—1

GHOSTS

And Max the king of all wild things was lonely and wanted to be where someone loved him best of all.
—Maurice Sendak

Sometimes when Jones stares at the girl what comes to mind is the time he left this place, years ago and still living with his mother, who one gray and sodden spring, his thirteenth, decides to send him to the man his mother claimed was his father, all the way out to the West Coast. So she puts him on the Greyhound, packing him a lunch like this should do it, only it's four days and nights of worn brick cities, towns with their crumbling bus stations, hauling his backpack off and on buses, the roll of the land opening up to a great flat swath, pimpled with barns, cows, fields of things growing he assumed were the source of the food in the cans his mother served him, popping them open and sometimes not even taking the contents out but simply handing him a spoon or a fork. He figured at some point that food must've been rooted somewhere, must've been fresh and growing. After the farm lands, the fields, came the mountains, ragged, snow-struck giants, and Jones felt like he had entered a new land, one that had no relation whatsoever to where he had come from.

He had thought of it as a kind of trial, that he was on trial with his father who had looked him up and down when he got off that final bus in Portland, Oregon, his eyes a sinewy blue and watery as mouthwash, staring at his hair, which needed cutting, neck too thin with the bloom of new acne, right down to the shoes he wore, his last year's boots. His father hadn't said much, just hoisted Jones's backpack into his pickup truck, told him to get in with it. Whatever the trial was, the test, he must've failed, as he hasn't seen or heard from his father since. "Margo always did have her whims," his father said, the only thing he mentioned about his mother sending him there. He didn't say he was Jones's father nor did he deny it. But his father's last name was Jones, and Jones figured this was probably why his mother had named *him* Jones, which had nothing to do with her own last name and his, which was Robert, one of those names that people always wanted to turn around on you, make it Robert Jones instead of Jones Robert. He babbled nervously about all this to his father on the way from the bus station, but his father didn't have much to say about it. "Call me Bruce," his father said.

Bruce managed a motel across from the beach on Highway 101, and Jones spent a lot of time walking that beach, the waves thundering on one side and the cars, the giant logging trucks, roaring past on the other. He remembers the gulls, *flying rats* Bruce called them. A dead one on the sand, picked apart, its feathers everywhere. His father said probably its own did it. "You know," Bruce said, his eyes a kind of gray then, like the waves that had a line of oily, churned-up sand in them when they broke—"that bird probably was born weak, maybe something wrong with it like a crippled wing so the others took care of it. It's called mobbing," his father told him. Jones thought about that, the squalls blowing in and the wind sweeping across the sand, rain slashing down, and the gulls rising in bird-clouds above him, squawking, fighting just to stay in place, to not get blown away.

It's the razor-clam shell though that the girl makes him think of. When he saw it lying near the shore on the silvery wet part of the beach he picked it up carefully, noting it was empty of its animal. The pale yellow and lavender parts of its insides still had the muscle attached holding the two halves together—he guessed the muscle was part of the animal and maybe one of those birds had torn the rest of it out—what did he know about sea things? It had lain there pristine beside the cartilage and claws of a crab. It was beautiful and so fragile, and he was overcome by a desire to rescue it, to keep it whole. It seemed to him then that the world conspired against such things, that the way things were was more about brokenness.

For the couple weeks he stayed with his father at the Sleep Inn Motel, Jones stared at that shell every night, lying on the scratched bureau-top his father said he could use for his things, though not much else would fit there since it also had a TV on it—the shell and a couple magazines he had found on a Greyhound station bench, *Sports Illustrated* and *Popular Mechanics*. He thought maybe they'd impress his father seeing them there, men's magazines, but Jones was more interested in the shell. Its colors, the membrane of thin seaweedy stuff coating it and when that peeled back you could see the pale checkerboard of golds and lavenders and pinks, in a kind of blurred plaid like Easter eggs when the dye ran just a little. It reminded him of a particular jacket his mother wore a lot—she called it a *duster*—and when she was gone through the long nights (she was a waitress at the Night-Owl diner and didn't get home until dawn sometimes) he'd ferret it out of his mother's closet and put it on. He liked its touch on his skin, cool like his mother's hands, and her scent—a mixture of Lucky Strikes and Ambush perfume, clung to its fabric. Bruce would've probably called him a pussy if he knew, which was what he called one of the motel guests who couldn't figure out how to work the TV remote, though not to his face.

When his father said it was time for Jones to go back home he wrapped the shell in toilet paper from the motel bathroom and placed it in a brown paper bag, carrying it on the bus like it was his lunch, though his father wouldn't have thought to do this, fix him a lunch. Bruce asked if Margo had given him money for food, and Jones said yes, figuring that she hadn't was something to be ashamed of. Jones had scavenged enough coins from around the motel, under couch cushions, behind washing machines, to buy snacks from the bus station vending machines to last him to Chicago. After that if he got hungry, he'd just think of other things. He'd done that before, when his mother pulled a double shift at the Night-Owl and there was nothing in the cupboards to eat. All those miles back with the jagged mountains on either side, then the land flat as the backs of his hands he kept the bag safe on his lap, but somehow the shell broke apart anyway into two halves.

On his better days Jones reminds himself that the girl is here so he can keep her safe. A hank of her hair lifts in the breeze from the window he has her tied up under; hair the color of winter birds, he thinks, those juncos that hop dizzyingly about on the snow, trying to uncover things to eat below its surface. He thinks how he had borne that shell through all the flatness, at least four different bus transfers in grungy stations before he noticed it was no longer whole. He thinks about the waves, the wind on them and how they looked like scraggles of toothpaste from his father's motel windows across the highway. When he walked, those killer gulls, rising and drifting on the currents of wind like there's nothing else in the world, nothing but him and those birds, snakes of sand writhing and wriggling and blowing by him and then he was running, his heart smacking against the inside of his chest, his father fixing a broken toilet in one of the rooms and Jones alone, the wind so fierce and him in the hollow of it. Jones understood then that his father was right about how it could happen, the one on the beach, dragging a broken wing maybe, a leg, something where it couldn't rise with the rest of them. Done for, his father said. He remembers the sneaker waves, Bruce called them—you're walking along the beach and suddenly there's water up to your waist and it's tugging at you, and when it retreats it takes you with it. The gulls a brigade of soldiers lining the shore, and a dead fish on the beach, gutted.

He hadn't wanted it to be this way with the rope, told the girl it didn't have to be except that when he let her loose she kept trying to bolt from the trailer, and if ever she made it to the highway God only knows what could happen. You'd think he was going to hurt her, the way she acted, when it was him who rescued her in the first place.

HER MOM TOLD her about some poisonous frog, was it in Arizona? Some desert toad, a horny toad she said, and something in its skin would make you see visions, prepared a certain way. You euthanize it in chloroform, her mom said, then you slice its back off and you cook that. Her mom was what they used to call a wild child. Loulie thinks about the stories her mom told her so she doesn't have to think about her own, moment to moment, don't think what might happen tomorrow or the day after because the man doesn't give her much to go on, just a shower twice a week which isn't enough to get the grime from the window sill out of her hair, or a time she made a run for it, squeezing into the shed and hiding there up against some oil cans; then he comes howling after her and one of them fell, coating her hair, her neck, her clothes in black goo. He looked the other way when she got out of those clothes, stepping quickly into the shower, which wasn't hot enough, worrying all the while he might peek through the gap in the disgusting shower curtain that was sticky and spangled with mold. He gave her a flannel shirt of his to wear and some pants that didn't make it to her ankles so her feet are always cold; he took her shoes away after that botched escape. She figures she must be taller than him, but she doesn't want to stand close enough to know this for sure. He said he wants to help her, but she can't think what that would be, what it would look like. He hasn't hurt her, but he hasn't set her free either.

She remembers this: arguing with Troy-boy in the parking lot at the former IBM plant and maybe she sort've remembers another car there, but mostly nobody went there anymore since IBM pulled out, and something about them having left contaminated ground from the chemicals they buried all around their plant. The argument went the way it always did, just louder this time. "BUT I LOVE YOU." "NO!" "HOW COME, IF I LOVE YOU." "NOT YET!" "PLEASE? YOU DON'T LOVE ME THEN." "I DON'T KNOW. I'M JUST NOT READY!" "YOU DON'T GET HOW IT IS FOR A GUY. IT HURTS US YOU KNOW." "NO!" "YES." "NOOOOOOO." "IF YOU LOVED ME YOU WOULD . . ." And so on. Would've bored her to tears if she hadn't of been wasted. Though probably if they hadn't of been wasted they would've for sure seen the man's car. But the argument escalated, and before this they had smoked the splif laced with meth, which was pretty good, she had to admit, though she'd been hesitant about it the first couple times, didn't want to become an addict like some she knew who just couldn't seem to have enough of the drug and were doing crazy things to get it. True, it made her want to do stuff, but she was just not sure the stuff she wanted to do was best done with Troy-boy. She wanted her first time to be special is all, to mean something though she couldn't say what, and what was love anyway? When Troy-boy said it to her, what did that mean? The words were as easy as any: *pass the catsup; I'm so tired; I love you.* Three-word sentences, a simple sentence, Ms. Hendricks her sophomore English teacher would tell them, a subject and a verb.

He'd been giving her the meth, and he told her most people had to pay. She liked the buzzing, electric feel of her skin when she smoked, how it made her feel happy and excited like something good was coming her way—like Christmas morning, before she went out of her room and there was still that hope, when she used to believe in Santa and she'd ask him to bring her a dad, and if he couldn't do that, then a dog. Not that she ever got either, just that hope. But here's the thing: Loulie wasn't sure yet who she was or was supposed to be when she smoked the drug, just that she felt pretty good. Would letting Troy-boy do her, as her friend Josie called it, change any of that, make it more solid or sure? She doubted it. And then when he clamped her neck in a choke-hold and forced his tongue down her throat all the while glomming on to her boob like it was some kind of life-line, well that freaked her out. So she kneed him where her mom said you go for a guy if he's being fresh, and he let go of her, groaning, curled up like a question mark, and she bolted out of his car, straight into the arms of this man who hoisted her into *his* car—was it really sitting there in that parking lot the whole time?—like she was a slab of something, forcing her down on the floor, tying her up like a trussed turkey, a wad of some stinky material—maybe a sock? in her mouth so she couldn't yell and he drove her to this place. Beyond that she doesn't remember much, just the terror like a hot white light filling her from the inside out, thinking maybe she died, that maybe this was the light people talked about at the end of some tunnel and there she was, already on the other side.

The man has been muttering about some beach in Oregon, and she almost feels, listening to him, like she too has been there. But it's her mom's stories, one when her mom was the wild child, eighteen years old, and she and her friend are hitchhiking down the coast from Longview, Washington, where they lived, running away from home, her mom told her, for no good reason, just the adventure of it. It's late, the fog coming in, so when the hippie-man stops they don't even hesitate about getting into his beat-up hippie-van with the peace and flowers decals (which made them think the ride was safe, he's one of them). He promises to take them as far as Astoria on 101, and since they're heading down to California, well that's a little closer, anyway. Her mom was pretty, prettier than Loulie (her mom's face is rounded and symmetrical whereas Loulie's has a sharpness to it, a slight raggedness like it had been jabbed a bit around her cheek bones and chin, the father's side of her gene-pool no doubt); but not pretty enough, her mom told her, not as pretty as her friend. Then it's dark, a moonless night and the man starts talking crazy, claims he's seeing butterflies, so they suspect he's dropped LSD and make him pull into a deserted picnic area with giant redwood trees hanging over it creaking and moaning in the wind like ghosts. Figured maybe a little sleep would do them all good. They climb into the back of his van and a couple hours later Loulie's mom wakes up choking with a blanket over her face and the man pressing it down, trying to smother her so he could have her prettier friend to himself. Needless to say, her mom said, she didn't sleep again for the rest of the night.

Later the next day on a Seaside, Oregon, beach her friend is searching for a whole sand dollar and Loulie's mom finds one but the animal is still inside, so she shags it into the ocean so her friend won't boil it out or some such thing. Loulie's mom told her about the aquarium on that beach, since 1937 the sign said, one of those ones that advertise freaky things like some poor ancient octopus, and little spiny creatures in cages. But it's the seals Loulie feels bad about, sea lions her mom told her that live in the sea in front of the aquarium and they kept a few of them inside, in a small pool with rocks in it. Loulie imagines how sad they must have been, those sea lions, hearing the roar of the ocean just beyond the wall and not being able to get to it.

Think minute to minute, Loulie tells herself, how her scalp itches because he won't let her shower more than twice a week, and even at that she does it so quick just in case he's watching her from a peep hole somewhere he's poked into the wall—she's seen that kind of thing in movies—and with her hair as long as it is she can't really get it clean in a short rinse. She's thought about asking the man for scissors to cut it off but no doubt he'd look at her like she's crazy, being she's all trussed up and wouldn't she use the scissors to cut the ropes instead? Well no, she's thinking about her greasy hair, but she'd hardly convince him of that, especially since she made the decision not to talk to him at all. Don't talk, don't speak, don't let yourself hear your own voice in the room forming actual words because if you do that makes it real. He hasn't touched her so far except to tie her to this window crank, the window with its frosted glass where she can't see out—why even put in a window if you're going to do that? At first, whenever

he would leave she tried yelling and shrieking through the crack
he keeps open for air, but nobody came and she never hears any
neighbors, nothing but the cars on a distant highway—probably
Route 17, it's not like there's much else going in and out of this
town—so she figured they must be pretty isolated.

Her mom told her the things men can do to girls, told her these
days it's not safe to be a wild child and if ever Loulie thinks about
running away she should talk it out with her mother, that Annalee
would listen. *There's nothing you can't say to me,* Annalee's told her,
and now because of the drugs and her mom suspecting Loulie's
gotten into them ("No!" Loulie squirmed when she asked, of course
not, she'd never do that...), Loulie is afraid this is what her mom
thinks: that because of the maybe-drugs, maybe Loulie was hanging
out with the wrong crowd, ran away with them, and won't be coming
back. And they'll stop looking for her.

She's got her eyes on the man, just in case, forces herself to stay
awake (she wouldn't want to wake up with a blanket over *her* head,
for instance!) until he falls asleep on the couch across from her, and
only then does she lie down on the mattress he keeps her on, stinking
of duct tape and some ancient spoiled food, and still she pries her
eyes open as long as she can. Moment to moment, minute to minute,
inhale, exhale, think only the breath, in and out, in and out, in and
out, the rhythms of the tide on a far away beach she'll never get to,
as long as there's breath she's alive.

HE HEARD ABOUT some tribe of Indians who believed if you put a
Sawfish over your door it would keep ghosts out. Jones would like
to get himself one of those, but where? Surely not the Susquehanna.
His father had told him about the salmon in the Northwest swimming
upstream to spawn and even as they're doing that they are already
dying; they don't bother eating, no nourishment, no idle twitching
about, just fighting the current to get to the top of wherever they
had to go to lay their eggs and replicate themselves, make sure they

keep on—except now this strikes Jones as a strange thing, since recently he heard the salmon out there had all but disappeared.

He thinks sometimes he sees her in his trailer, once at the little Formica kitchen table built into the wall and another time just standing by the couch like she was considering sitting on it but couldn't make up her mind, sort of hovering there. She hated that couch, a rat-brown color and torn at a couple of its seams, one of the few things that came out of the fire unscathed, though it still stank a bit of the smoke. His mother, whom he really did love and he wishes she hadn't gone and done that crazy thing, getting into those dangerous drugs like she was some teenager again instead of a sixty-five-year-old woman; and just what was she doing in her house, anyway, when it blew up? The police said they were cooking crystal methamphetamine and showed him the emptied bags of fertilizer for the anhydrous ammonia, paint thinner cans, acetone, crushed Drano bottles, scooped out and charred batteries and burnt, crumbling Sudafed packages found on the property, to prove it. It's damn flammable, the police said. When Jones shook his head one of them snickered, "I don't suppose your mother used anhydrous ammonia to blow the clogs out of her pipes when the Drano didn't work?" The others roared like this was some joke. It seemed to Jones that the world outside this piece of land with his broken-down trailer was in peril. He had hauled it here when his mother's house burned down with her inside it, after living in a trailer park that a guy he used to work with managed. Now the trailer rattled in the wind that swept across the valley, rain slashing against it like knives.

So save the girl. It's the thing he can do. In the parking lot, late afternoon the color of shale, a storm brewing with rumbles of thunder and she's writhing, sobbing, doesn't fight much when he pushes her into his car, like a part of her recognized this was the way it needed to be. He considers it fate. He hardly ever went to that parking lot, no reason to, but something made him want to pull off the highway that day, to a quiet place and just sit awhile. Jones thinks it must've been a sign.

He had lost the first one, the one who sat down beside him on the city bus when he still had his job at the Giant food store, stocking their shelves, mopping the floors, culling through the vegetables for ones a little too bruised to sell, checking for out-of-date milks and yogurts in the dairy section, whatever they needed until they didn't, what with the economy and all they told him. They gave him two weeks. Coming home that day, his second-to-the-last paycheck in his pea-coat pocket, he thought how he'd never seen her before, the way you recognize regulars whose bus routes and schedules are the same as yours, even though you don't know where it is they go when they get off. Fair haired, her freckled hands clutching two giant white lilies, their cloying scent getting to him like something you couldn't quite shake off. Her father's funeral she said when he asked her where she got them, and her face didn't budge, didn't turn to look at him, just stared straight ahead. He told her he was sorry and she shrugged.

Then he couldn't help it, followed her off the bus two stops ahead of his, figuring she'd disappear into the neighborhood but instead she slipped into Moe's Place, a dim looking bar behind the laundromat, and she began drinking pretty heavily, crouched on a bar stool, one beer after the other. The men perching on stools around her started buying her more, margaritas and a Bloody Mary when she said she was sick of the suds, and one of them snagged a cucumber from the bartender's vegetable bin, carving it with the bartender's knife into a fish of sorts—a shark he told her, as he passed it to her —and she laughed uproariously like this was some joke, then tipped her neck back, the man pushing the cucumber inside her mouth and she's sucking at it. Looks like she's felatin' it! the man cried, and the bartender laughed, and the other men laughed too and Jones slipped back outside without even finishing his drink. Not that he's a drinker. But he might've at least enjoyed the Coke he bought, if only he had figured out something he could do for the girl. The girl never even swiveled around on her bar stool to notice him there, hunched at a table behind her.

THE HEADY SCENT of those flowers stuck with him, getting to him days, weeks, months since he saw that girl, but what was it he could've done?

Jones has mostly avoided anything to do with sex. His mother said it ruined her life. "It's a sword you learn to swallow," she told him. His mother was in love with Sam Shepard, ever since she saw him in some movie saving his family from a raging river, though he lost the farm and everything else. "He had his principles and his priorities set straight," Jones's mother said. She said the great tragedy of her life was never actually meeting Sam Shepard, because she was pretty sure if she had, that he would've fallen in love with her too. "It's the way things work," she told Jones. "We are destined to go through living a parallel life apart from the one we should be living with." She pointed out that Sam was just a little older than her, which was perfect for a relationship, and that he had a craggy, handsome sort of face that managed to look kind too, and he had a good sense of humor. She too could enjoy a clever joke now and then, and men thought her pretty, the ones who came to the diner anyway, though not in a conventional sense, his mother told Jones—just like Sam. She watched every movie Sam Shepard starred in, sometimes five or six times! And she took out his books, his plays and stories from the library. Jones's mother had never been much of a reader, but she put the books on the white wicker night table by her bed so he'd be near her when she slept.

Once at the Night-Owl she even replaced a picture of Jesus with a picture of Sam Shepard (Reggie Ernest the manager had taped Jesus inside the cash register drawer), but Reggie made her put him back again. She had nothing against Jesus, she told Jones, it's just that whenever the cash register popped open, that chinging sound, his filmy blue eyes were staring up at her from under the quarters, sort of accusatory, Jones's mother felt.

Jones had tried sex, but it didn't take: once with Stella from school (rumored to be "easy") in the woods behind, but before he had even climbed on top of her he heard the thrash of footsteps in the dried-out leaves, and he quickly zipped himself back up and ran, not even checking to make sure she followed. Then another time with a cashier at the Giant market, but when he wasn't sure exactly what to do and was fumbling just to peel off her pants, she laughed at him and so he left then too. He didn't know what those men did with the girl whose father had died, who when he left was sucking so hard on the cucumber shark, like she would have to learn to swallow that too.

FOR A WHILE there were posters up all over town with her picture on them, stapled to telephone poles, on Giant's bulletin boards, in the post office, and he even saw one on the bus, which he started taking again just in case someone equated his car with having been seen where she last was, in case the boy she was with had noticed anything. The car, a nine-year-old Chevy Malibu, had become Jones's after his mother died, and he wasn't all that attached to it, just something that was hers and now his. Jones studied her picture, while sitting on that bus. She was smiling in it, a crooked kind of teenage smile with just the hint of good front teeth (maybe the photographer caught her unaware, like she really didn't intend to smile for the camera but he startled her into it). She looked friendly enough, like she'd grow up to be the kind of person who's invited to Christmas parties and to friends' houses for dinner and she'd smile and smile and smile; not once has she smiled at him. A flurry of newspaper articles with yearbook shots of the girl and the boy she'd been with (Jones didn't like that, seeing their faces side-by-side in the same frame), and a TV appeal, local news, a woman whom he assumed was her mother, pretty like her though older and worn looking, a kind of rubbed-out version of the girl, offering a reward for her return. Like she was a lost dog or something, Jones thought, and then he stopped putting the television on because the girl began moaning after this, carrying on all night. Since she wouldn't talk to him he couldn't get her to tell him what was wrong, but he figured it had something to do with seeing her mother on the TV.

He thought maybe he had scared her into silence, when after she tried to run away the first time, getting as far as the backyard in the rain before she slipped in a puddle and fell, so of course he had to tie her up—he explained this to her—and then when he tried to help her take her wet shirt off, figuring he could slide it over her head even with her wrists bound, the girl shook and wailed so he thought it might be better to just toss a blanket over her shoulders so she wouldn't catch a chill. Since then she had tried another escape, getting as far as the shed. Now her clothes are smelling, and he'd wash them for her only he's afraid she'll wail up a storm; and these aren't even the ones she came to him in, which were splattered with oil from the shed that wouldn't come out, not even after he soaked them in detergent. He felt sorry for her, showering and having to get into smelly clothes—he offered her more of his but she refused, shaking her head in defiance he thought, and couldn't help but remember again the girl in the bar, the way her head tipped back, her long freckled neck, sucking that cucumber with the men laughing all around her. He remembered one of them tugging at her arm, yanking it toward him like it wasn't even attached to her.

Jones didn't have a daily bus schedule anymore since he lost his job, but he did have his regular appointments at the unemployment place, so he could prove to them he was trying to find a new job. Which he was, but there was nothing. Soon his unemployment would run out, and Jones worried about feeding the girl without it, even though she ate next to nothing. A couple spoonfuls of macaroni and cheese, which he fixed most nights to fill her up; wouldn't even touch the cans of spinach he gave her for her vegetable. Eventually the posters about her became tattered and rained on and nobody was replacing them anymore. Jones started putting on the TV again so the girl wouldn't get bored, sitting there all day—there was nothing about her being missing on it. Most likely they figured she ran away. Girls did that around here and boys too. And fathers. His father struck out for greener pastures, his mother used to tell him and until he visited Bruce out on that beach, Jones had a literal picture of it: his father becoming a farmer or a ranch hand, working in the fields, pastures with animals, a clean, green, bright sort of life that had little to do with the one they led here, business after business failing, padlocking their doors, factories with their boarded-up windows, just another has-been town slowly shutting down.

LOULIE'S MOM CAME here all the way from Longview, Washington, to work for IBM. It was her ticket, she told Loulie. A data-entry job, but her plan was to finish college at the local SUNY campus, a business degree, and then she would be promoted to Systems Analyst. A new life, Loulie's mom told her, a real job that she could dress up for, a college degree. Coming from a family of smelt fishermen and paper-factory workers, why this was something! She stopped her wild-child ways after she had Loulie, whose birth name is Louise-Annalee after her Great-Grandma Louise and her mother's own name, but Loulie's mom said trying to say it was a mouthful—too many *i*'s and *e*'s, so she crammed it all together and *Louise-Annalee* became *Loulie*. Her father could've been one of four guys, and what her mom said is she loved Loulie more than the four of them piled together, and that's what mattered. One of them she barely knew his name! "Just a one-night stand," her mom said, as if this should be a comfort. "Things are different now," Annalee told her. "It's not safe to be a wild child anymore."

Now IBM is gone and her mom is out of work. They stole her best years, Annalee said; she'd put roots down and they yanked these up like they were pulling weeds and left.

Her mom wore white gloves when she was fifteen, and little white heels, *pumps* these were called, and a lacy camisole that you could see its outlines inside her white blouse, like under the florescent lights of classrooms. Her mom ran away when she was eighteen, but that's the kind of thing a wild child does, her mom told Loulie. Loulie wonders if the man and his father were at that Oregon beach he talked about, the same time her mom was hitchhiking there.

Maybe they passed them, Annalee and her friend hitchhiking by the side of the road. Maybe the man's father muttered something, like, "Those girls shouldn't be hitchhiking, they're asking for trouble."

Her mom will be ashamed of her for lying about the drugs, and that's the thing Loulie regrets most, disappointing Annalee. A vision of Annalee before Loulie existed, Annalee in her white gloves and her white pumps and her lacy camisole, and let's put a white lacy thing on her pretty head too like the bride of Jesus. Brides of Jesus do not hitchhike or run away from Longview, Washington. They are not wild. They stay with their smelt-fisher family and their children are born there and live there and the rest does not exist. Inhale, exhale, inhale.

Here's what Loulie is thinking now: vampire finches. She heard about these in her science classroom, she'd been daydreaming about something or other and Mr. Delgado says that name, *vampire finch*, and voilà she's tuned back in again, huh? What's this? She wanted to ask him where these are, these finches that suck blood from... who? What? But that would have been admitting she wasn't listening, which is what she needs to do now: do not listen, do not think, do not think about what the man is saying to her or what he might say or do in the future. There is no future. There is no past anymore, not hers anyway; those vampire finches, sixth period life science, last class of her last day and when the bell rings she hurries to Troy-boy's car, his Toyota Corolla, which he loved more than her, and they head to that almost-deserted parking lot where her mom used to work, the curl of smoke as he lights the spliff (*ice*, he called the crystal meth), curling over their heads.

He can sense her disapproval, that sour-jawed, tight-lipped way she had of looking at him when he wasn't the man she thought he'd be, is how his mother used to put it. Even when he wasn't a man, just a boy, she'd say it that way, shaking her head, sour-jawed, tight-lipped, "You're not the man I thought you'd be." Though this wasn't often, as mostly Jones behaved on instinct and his instincts were usually good. Like with this girl. She is so good that every time he passes her, shuffling from the trailer's little living room to its even littler kitchen—she's hunched over on the mattress, her head between her knees, he wants to lay his hand atop her head, that long tangled hair of hers, maybe stroke it a little, work the kinks out, his fingers inching through them like parting morning-glory vines. Jones doesn't want to scare her, but he does feel something irrevocable here. He can't return her; she's not a purchase with a warranty. Admittedly he hadn't thought it out this far but, he reminds himself, he's protecting her. That boy was going to make her do things. The world is like that, forcing you to do or be who you don't want to become. Always in a state of becoming. With Jones she can just be.

His mother's ghost told him he can't earn love from a tied-up girl, and he told his mother the ghost he didn't mean anything by it, only to save her. "She's fine-boned," he told his mother the ghost, "delicate as a teacup, or a pearl necklace. She could've been hurt." What should he do now? he asked her.

"You made your bed . . ." his mother the ghost told him, and he pointed out that *his* former bed burned up in the fire, speaking of beds. His mother the ghost gave him that look again, those lips tight as bobby pins, which he could just make out as she drifted past him, her face sort of blurry and wobbling like a balloon on a string, her face like a mask. It occurred to him then that maybe his mother the ghost is really his mother in a mask, sneaking in and out of his trailer *pretending* to be a ghost? The remains they found were so badly incinerated from the house explosion the coroner couldn't make a positive identification, and Jones figures they could've been the other meth cookers (who nobody claimed or even admitted knowing), or all of them, now crammed together for eternity in the wood urn he put them in, digging a hole for it under his mother's favorite oak. Which meant that the other two might show up in his trailer as well. He really must get that sawfish! He hopes the girl won't notice his mother the ghost, though the girl doesn't look up much; he asked his mother not to speak unless the girl was asleep—*out of sight, out of mind*, as she herself used to say.

"They were paying me to let them cook that stuff in my house," his mother told him. "You try pulling double shifts at the Night-Owl to stay on top of the bills when you're as old as me. Everything ached," she said.

That much, Jones figured, was true enough. He's having a hard time just managing the taxes on his mother's land. Luckily her house having been destroyed took care of the mortgage, along with the small life-insurance policy his mother had from the Night-Owl; homeowner's insurance won't cover methamphetamine labs exploding on the premises. This got him to thinking though, if it *is* his mother, and she isn't a ghost, why would she slip in and out of his trailer wearing a mask? Was she hideously burned in the explosion and she's embarrassed? His mother always was a little vain. Or she wanted Jones to collect on that life insurance? Worn out from paying all those bills, all those years and this, a way to hide? None of it made much sense to Jones. If his mother could do either of these things, survive the explosion and come back, or not survive and come back, then maybe he could expect other impossible things to be possible too. Maybe God himself could show up in his trailer one day, at his kitchen table, let's say, and Jones would serve him some macaroni and cheese, and he would make everything right. Perhaps he could even make the girl love him, just a little—or *like* him, Jones would settle for that!

Jones could ask his mother if she's really a ghost, but here is the root of the problem, the deeper thing that runs under it all. His mother doesn't listen to him and she never did. If she *would* listen to him, what he would tell her is this: It goes back to that beach; she shouldn't have sent him there, to a man who didn't give a damn about either of them. Jones never got why she did, a *whim*, as Bruce said? His childhood undone on his mother's whim? It wasn't so much that his father didn't like him. Jones could've understood that, as that would have taken something resolute—energy, emotion, a feeling, at least, toward him. But Bruce was just not interested in him. Jones could've been anybody getting off that bus—worse, he *was* anybody.

Before that, Jones didn't know just how lonely loneliness could be. It's a void and if you're lucky you get one or two things your whole life that can even begin to fill it. He would tell his mother that theirs is a world where danger lurks and wounds don't heal and things get damaged, fall apart, even burn up; hurricanes, tsunamis, earthquakes—those are the ones everybody takes note of, but what of the smaller terrors that crack open your heart, don't kill you all at once like a raging flood, but slowly, a poison seeping into your blood, freezing up your lungs, slowing your brain, until one day the woman who loved Sam Shepherd, who slaved away her life just to pay for the roof over their heads, loses the roof, not to mention her life, cooking crystal meth. "You should've stuck to the canned food!" he would tell his mother the ghost.

But never mind. Jones has been thinking about this and he thinks he can do it, build his mother's house again or some kind of house anyway, on this land. Maybe unemployment would count that as something, a possible business building houses, and they'd cut him a little slack and extend his benefits for a while longer. Not that *he* needs them so much but he's got to keep the girl fed. He's figured out she'll eat, but only if he's not in the room; so he puts her food on the linoleum floor in front of her (it's okay, he uses a plate) then goes to the kitchen and eats his own meal, does the dishes, and when he returns she's done.

They can live this way. On this land with woods behind them and in front, where the property doesn't end so much as fade into the woods, where they can hear the constant tide of cars on Route 17 just beyond, but they can't see the cars and the cars can't see them. There are only the trees and birds and owls in the night hooting from the trees. Sometimes they can hear coyotes howling from the hills over Route 17. Todd, his friend from their former job who manages the trailer park, said the coyotes are returning and soon it'll be wolves, that the wild things are taking back the land after humans screwed it up, made a mess of it, lost jobs and dumped chemicals and houses foreclosed on, the people who lived in them gone away, so the wild things will return.

Jones and the girl can live in the house he builds with the wild things outside and them inside. Their windows will be like the river at night, clear as the stars, and new life will take root, the winds wailing from the valley in the winter and in spring the seeds bursting open, a jungle growing thick and green and sure around them. Maybe then he can untie the girl and she'll stop running, because there won't be anything left of the world they knew before to run to.

We Are All in Pieces

In 1875 the largest plague of locusts ever recorded in American history descended upon the Great Plains, a swarm about 1,800 miles long from Canada to Texas. They were the Rocky Mountain locusts, crawling out of river valleys, gnawing their way across the entire country. A humongous black cloud, glowing around the edges where a million lacy wings caught the glint of the sun, they fell like a blizzard, blanketing everything a foot deep: trees hunkering down under their weight, branches cracking, a howling like a hurricane as they devoured every piece of vegetation in their path.

I read about this in one of Jagger's nature books. Normally locusts live in a solitary phase, the book said, but if breeding conditions cause more young to hatch, resulting in overcrowding and not enough food, they become agitated, gather in large numbers and evolve into a single migrating plague. It talked about a Malthusian trap, populations of living organisms being controlled by their available food source. The Rocky Mountain locust is believed to now be extinct, it said.

MY MOTHER IS driving me to the abortion clinic, though she won't use that word. *Procedure* she calls it, like we're off to get plastic surgery, mother-daughter Botox injections, a bite of lunch, shopping, girls' day out. Last week we went to the clinic for the interview where they ask you if you're *sure*. We sat surrounded by the sort of feminine décor my mother, who's a real-estate agent, might point out to her clientele in an "updated" bathroom, a stencil of flowers near the ceiling and the walls a watermelon pink. Spacious cabinets, she'd tell them, cherry wood; though in an abortion clinic what's inside those cabinets I, for one, did not want to know.

"Of course we're sure!" my mother snapped. She's taken this thing to heart, a project. Amanda likes a good project, an A to Z contract with a *definitive* ending, she'd say.

The weather is suspicious today, midsummer, steamy yet cool, the kind of day my mother proclaimed impossible to dress for, though she dressed up anyway, her spaghetti-strap top with a linen jacket, denim skirt and high-heeled sandals. "I see no reason to look like a slob," she'll tell you. I figure we cancel each other out, me in my genuine faded and torn jeans—as in I would never buy them off the rack this way, with some designer's label stitched on to make imitation worn-out a coveted thing—and an oversized T-shirt that belonged to Jagger. I like to wear my brother's clothes, what I managed to salvage before Amanda schlepped the rest to Goodwill. I begged her not to get rid of his books and she agreed. Goodwill has no use for books, she said. When I wear his shirt, I like to imagine sometimes it's his skin brushing up against mine.

The ride feels endless—not exactly an abortion clinic on every corner in upstate New York. I shut my eyes and remember another car ride, how long ago? Jagger's still with us, a child in fact, which would have made me pretty little for this memory. But I can see it, my brother in the front seat and our mother explaining to him why she won't let him join the Cub Scouts. "They discriminate against gay people," she told him, tapping her manicured fingernails against the steering wheel for emphasis, and Jagger asked if we are gay. Amanda stared at him, that perplexed look of hers, that where-did-you-come-from, surely-not-from-me! withering glare. That's what our father called it, before he too was gone, searching for Jagger in every city this side of the Mississippi River, keeling over one day in one of them: "Beware of your mother's withering glare."

"What's *that* have to do with the price of milk?" she said.

Earlier this morning I told her in fact I wasn't so sure. "Nonsense!" my mother said. "You don't even know who the father is." I pointed out the odds weren't bad, a 50/50 shot, and anyway they both looked alike. Generic, I was thinking; that was the type who went for me, and the baby too would look like nothing special.

My mother frowned. "What's *that* have to do with the price of milk?"

"You know, Sadie," she starts now and I jolt awake, the hum of the Pontiac's engine an ocean tide, accelerate, decelerate, accelerate, decelerate—Amanda Lang's unique way of keeping to the speed limit. I wasn't asleep but I yawn and scowl at her for the startle. She sighs, oblivious. "In retrospect," she says, "if I could do things over again, maybe I wouldn't have teased your brother about it, but the fact is he *was* at our wedding, and probably there wouldn't have *been* a wedding but for him being there, the size of a bean inside me. Do you get what I'm saying to you, Sadie?"

"The point is . . ." she pauses, torching a cigarette with the plug-in car lighter, a habit she took up after Jagger was gone. "You just can't know, so you better be a hundred percent sure, you hear me? A hundred percent sure, because God only knows the anguish he will cause you. One day your life is one way, and the next it's forever something else." She exhales hard, spiraling her second-hand smoke into the car.

"I'm not supposed to breathe that gunk," I tell her, sniffing for emphasis. Being pregnant and all—but I keep that part to myself.

MOST OF THE *Hawaiian honeycreeper birds are also extinct, along with ivory-billed woodpeckers and the Carolina parakeets that John James Audubon drew to appear sentient, alive. Audubon, known as "the Prince of American Ornithology," killed birds to sketch them, even endangered birds; so he'd get them right. So they would look alive. Audubon's talent with a gun was legend. If he didn't kill at least a hundred birds between sun-up and sundown he considered it a waste of a day.*

THE DAY JAGGER went missing started out with the sound of gunshots down at the river, hunting season for waterfowl and every year it's the same man—we have imagined him old, snarly face, failed, Amanda figured, in some inexplicable way. Standing on the island in the middle of the Susquehanna, between one bank that is one town and the other another, over and over he fires his shotgun into the cloud of squawking ducks. My mother called the police, complaining about how the shooting began at dawn and continued all morning long. "Kids play down there!" she emphasized. They said there was nothing they could do because the island was in the middle—not their jurisdiction nor the other town's neither. Amanda marched into Jagger's room then, noting that the sheets were rumpled like maybe he had slept, or at least lain down, and probably she poked about his dresser (she doesn't tell this part), wanting to find his works but dreading it such that in the end she ferreted out a pack of cigarettes from his socks drawer, took them to the kitchen table, and while sipping the dregs of her morning coffee snipped the filters off each cigarette with her coupon cutting scissors, diced the pack into bite-size pieces with her paring knife, then chucked the whole mess into the trash. The night before she had dreamt of a mountain lion, she said, and the lion's teeth were stained with blood.

I READ THIS on the Internet about mountain lions: Starving females will eat their kittens and older males will kill younger males just to keep them from hunting in their territory. They control their own populations that way.

WHEN MY NAME is called my mother asks if she can come too, and the nurse says *yes*, and I say *no*, and we stare at each other until my mother, rolling her perfectly made-up eyes, mutters *fine*, and sits back down. "I'll be right *here*," she emphasizes, those beer-bottle green eyes a warning, the color of a storm. What does she think I'm going to do, escape mid-*procedure*, hurl myself out a window and flee?

As I turn to follow the nurse my mother leaps up, grabs my hand and smacks a kiss on my cheek. I'm startled, the normally reserved Amanda Lang, and I yank my arm away, even though I know she meant it to be nice. But really, what is this? The kiss of Judas? I rub the oily mark her lipstick made. Though I can't see it I know it is scarlet.

A FEW MONTHS after Jagger disappeared the police quit looking, and at the age of just eighteen he became yet another face on *The Missing Adults Website*. Amanda froze up. "Like a computer," my father said, "only there's no *force quit* on this one. Grieve, Amanda, goddamnit!" he shouted one night at dinner. She gazed thoughtfully at her plate, then lifted her fork and shuttled her untouched peas from one side to the other. Our doctor said, "Perhaps this is *how* Amanda grieves." Then my father too was gone.

NAKED UNDERNEATH A gown, a blush of rose buds all over it—to coordinate with the color of the walls?—I'm ushered to a holding room with two other girls and a woman around my mother's age. We don't look at each other. The time for any camaraderie in this thing has passed. We will bear our separate grief. Outside in the parking lot protestors rag us about killing our babies, their voices all outrage and hate, drifting in through a cracked window on a breeze that's not cool, not warm, but strangely damp, clammy—like it's carrying wet laundry, lines of it, shirts, towels, underwear wrung out; the sky through the window a weird, anemic green. Maybe a storm really is brewing.

I don't let myself think about the baby much, because really it isn't one yet, more like a miniscule guppy. And what would I do, a Mom at seventeen? Be one of those girls you see at the mall, eyes like empty plates, schlepping a stroller, popping her gum, a toddler clinging to her hip like a behemoth growth of some sort? That's what a lack of information will do to you. It's one of the reasons I like to read about nature, things that have happened or could happen, *the science of being alive*, Jagger called it. He liked it too, back when he was still reading. Got us thinking about things. Besides, I don't even like one of the could-be fathers and the other was just a friend; "friends with benefits" they call this, having sex with a friend. But let's get real here, it's not exactly a game of pickup or a stroll together to Starbucks for a latte. Afterward he told me he would've settled for a blowjob.

I tilt my head back against the waiting-room chair, pink as the insides of an ear, and think about my brother. The needles began about a year before he disappeared. I found him on the floor of his bedroom one night when our parents were out, and I'm still dumb enough to imagine he's hurt, sick, he's giving himself a shot. "Beat it little sister!" he roared and I fled. Later I woke to him sitting at the foot of my bed, his shoulders in the yellow light from the hall were slumped and shivering. A raw sound snuck out from between his clenched lips, and I pretended I was asleep, figuring he wouldn't want to know that I saw it, his despair.

After he was gone I had a dream about finding him in the field beyond our house, where we used to chase Pansy, his chocolate Lab, as she swam through the high grass, jumping over it like she's dodging ocean waves, submerged so that all you could see was the tip of her wagging, chestnut-colored tail.

In the dream I'm in this field, air swollen with the smell of rain even though it's dry as a stick and the sky the color of bleached bone, and I'm parting the long grass like Pansy did, like a deer might, poking my head and neck through, shoulders pressed against the fringy tassels. I come upon him suddenly, crouching down between the blades like he's trying to shield himself from the wind that whistles through, light a cigarette maybe. Only it's a needle—the silver glint as he punches it in between the webbing of his toes, pushes down then releases, rolling his eyes, his head lolling back. When he sees me standing there he grins, that slow sweet smile, tugs at my hand, pulling me down in the dirt beside him. *Little sister*, he calls me. Still holding my hand he rolls my arm over, places his other hand in the crook where my upper arm meets my lower and tap, tap, taps. "Great veins, little sister!" he tells me.

Joey was always attracted to risk, our father used to say. Even as a kid, an eight-year-old, he climbed up on our two-story roof and jumped, just to see what it was like. Marijuana, beer, the usual teenage pastimes—how could those have been enough? Even his name, Joseph, became tame; he began insisting we call him *Jagger* instead.

PASSENGER PIGEONS ARE also extinct. They used to fly in clouds, darkening the sky, their droppings so massive branches would crack and break like they were coated with ice. Their extinction was the result of one of the largest slaughters in history. In just one year over seven million were killed in Michigan alone, sent east as a cheap source of food. The last survivor of a species that once numbered over five billion died in the Cincinnati Zoo in 1914. She was discovered lying on the bottom of her cage at one o'clock in the afternoon. Her name was Martha.

IN CONNECTICUT THERE is a ninety-acre preserve dedicated to the Magicicada, a cicada that appears every seventeen years. My mother told me about a recipe she read for cooking cicadas that said you could boil them or fry them, that they are sweet, like a good venison. Not that she or I would know what venison, good or bad tastes like. We draw the line at eating deer.

Some people confuse locusts with cicadas, locusts are big grasshopper-like bugs, cicadas whine and carry-on, singing so insistently through the sultry nights, the yellow-hot afternoons, like they know something the rest of us don't, like their little hearts are going to break if they don't do this thing, *sing, sing, sing.*

It was Socrates or maybe Plato who wrote that cicadas were at one time human. I read this too in Jagger's book. When the Muses first brought song into the world, the beauty so captivated people they forgot to eat and drink. So when they died, the Muses turned them into cicadas. *Sing, sing, sing.*

In a bird's world singing is survival and it's the father who teaches his male young to sing. Males sing and the female chooses the best song, mates with the singer, and life goes on. Maybe our father never taught Jagger to sing? *Swallowed up*, they call it, when a drug addict disappears. As if the land, like a giant concrete mouth, just opened up and ate him.

After he was gone I spent most of my free time walking with Pansy in our field (I started calling it ours, Jagger's, Pansy's, mine), and I kept walking there even after Pansy suddenly died. A heart problem the vet speculated and probably he was right. Pansy was Jagger's dog and she was never the same after he left. I think she died of a broken heart.

It was in the field that I discovered I was pregnant, squatting to pee in the dirt, focusing on the orange globe of a pollution sunset and I smelled that smell. I read about this in a pamphlet from my mother's doctor's office. How hormones in flux can make some pregnant women's pee smell like they've been eating asparagus.

HAVE YOU HEARD? *Now it's the honeybees that are disappearing.*

DURING THE CAR ride back I start to cramp. They warned me to expect this, and I curl up like a shrimp on the front seat; I can feel blood soaking through the pad. "We'll clean you up when we get home," my mother says cheerfully. Like I've messed myself and a wet rag should do it. End of project, mission accomplished, scratch this one off the list—Amanda is satisfied. "You'll be fine," she assures me.

I stare out at the sky, the late afternoon light still too green, like the world has turned itself upside down somehow and the grass is above us and below is the emptiness of space. I think about those

locusts, scarfing clothes right off the farmers' backs, harnesses off
their horses, saddles, clothing off the line, fence posts, anything
that at one time was in any way organic and it's gone, digested,
yesterday's news. All that is left in their wake are pieces: wings,
exoskeletons, a shedding of what was.

I think about how really there isn't any cure for it, this loneliness:
my brother will not be coming home, and all that's inside me now
is a vast hollowness, like I swallowed the sky.

AFRICAN ELEPHANT, AMERICAN *Alligator, Asian Elephant, Asian
Lion, Black Lemur, Black-footed Ferret, Blue Whale, Bowhead Whale,
Cheetah, Chimpanzee, Common Green Turtle, Crested ibis, Dodo,
Eastern Cougar, Eskimo Curlew, Fin Whale, Flightless Cormorant,
Giant Anteater, Giant Armadillo, Giant Panda, Gorilla, Great Auk,
Grey Whale, Grizzly, Humpback Whale, Indian Rhinoceros, Jaguar,
Komodo Dragon, Leatherback Turtle, Loggerhead Turtle, Leopard,
Monk Seal, Mountain Gorilla, Orangutan, Pygmy Hippopotamus,
Sea Otter, Sei Whale, Snow Leopard, Tapirs, Tiger, Trumpeter Swan,
White Rhinoceros, Whooping Crane, the Yak.*

SHE HAD MY father's body flown back from the city he died in—was
it Minneapolis? Some northern city, a cold-white light, a too-big
sky. It was winter, and at first she said we couldn't bury him because
the ground was too hard, then one day she decides to cremate him
but still no funeral. His brother calls, says we need closure, and she
gets that tight-lipped look, her withering glare, and after that the
urn with his ashes disappears. One day when she is somewhere else
I creep into Jagger's room, and I find it in his closet, wrapped inside
the Yankees jersey our dad gave him, though neither of them much
liked sports.

"It hurts!" I whimper, and my mother reaches her hand across
the front seat, stroking my wrist lightly, my own hand clasped over
my stomach. She thinks I'm talking about the abortion. Am I?
Everything is aching. "I wanted to save him," I tell her.

"It's the cramps," my mother says. "They'll be gone in the morning. You were too young, Sadie. I'm supposed to save *you*. That's my job."

PIECE BY PIECE of him stripped away, like some kind of eating machine that stuff needled into him and he just became less and less. I dreamt of a mountain lion, she said, with blood on its teeth.

ONE OF THE 50/50 fathers, the one I liked, told me it's probably not true—starving mountain lions eating their kittens. "Males maybe," he said, "but not the mothers. Mother animals don't eat their babies". He said maybe it's a rumor started by gung-ho gun-types, the ones who want an excuse to extinguish a protected species, just because they've attacked humans. Later that day I looked it up on the Internet. "Mountain lions are protected, so attacks are on the rise!" touted one website. "Mountain lions look at just about any living thing as dinner," it said.

Last November I went to our field during hunting season, and it had transformed into a killing field of sorts, with wooden platforms erected in the trees so the hunters could track and shoot without even having to stand up. Kind of like golf-carts for golfers: low-impact sports, you don't have to move except to step out of the cart and knock the ball into the hole, or pull the trigger. There were beer bottles strewn below one of these platforms, a glitter of deep green and amber poking out between the wheat-colored winter grass.

A hunter garbed in head-to-toe camouflage leaned up against a tree with his shotgun poised. He was so still, so completely inanimate, at first I thought he was a mannequin, an imitation hunter made of wax, action-toy hunter, a decoy encased in flesh-like plastic—maybe the deer propped him there as a warning! I called out to him several times, checking for life. *Hey!* When he finally turned his head, I told him I needed him to recognize I'm human.

The property owner in an abutting field had seeded it with alfalfa to attract the deer, then killed them as they grazed on the bounty he served them. Another neighbor told us about watching a huge buck with an eight-point rack surrounded by does, chowing down the alfalfa, and suddenly the buck staggered forward, maybe twenty yards, then collapsed. There was no sound, just the wind through the trees, and he figured it out, he said. A bow and arrow. A lucky shot. "They breed like rats," he said, shrugging. "Cockroaches with tails. Long after we're gone they'll inherit the earth."

January, the end of the hunt, I came upon the survivors, a doe in the field with her two yearlings, the three of them backlit and golden in the setting winter sun. They stared at me and I at them, and then the young bounded off into the woods. The doe remained a couple more moments, gazing at me, almost defiant, I thought, until she too tossed back her head, that beautiful long neck, turned toward the ring of dark trees and ambled in.

I STARE AT my mother's profile in the waning light, her left hand clutching the steering wheel, bony knuckles white as eggs, her right hand resting on the seat beside me, those slender certain fingers that used to strum a classical guitar, play volleyball, *play*; that held my father's hand, back when there must have been love; that once grasped her son's shoulders, guiding him to safety crossing a street, when she could still do this—keep him safe, keep him, at all. I slip my hand into hers.

At first we will imagine it's raining and she'll tell me to close my window. Then harder, tiny pebbles flung against the roof, the windshield, and pretty soon it will be more like sand, dense, a storm of it such that the Pontiac's wipers can't move fast enough and it's piling up. Squish, squish labor the wipers as they drag across the glass, thick splotches in their wake. We will inch over to the side of the road where everything has stopped, the air blackened like a mid-day eclipse only it has wings, this air, and I know if I crack open my window we will hear it, the ravenous want.

A Kind of Extinction

$\mathcal{S}$ ometimes Fortune Hopewell still sees herself as *That Girl with the Leg Braces*, running down the hill to her house at the bottom of it and they're clunking and clanking, clankity clank, banging like cymbals as the knobs of her knees career into each other, and in all the other little broken-down houses she passes, faces pressed against the windows, laughing at her. They put them on when she was five years old for what the doctor called severe in-toeing but what Fortune knows was just another way to say pigeon-toes. And that's what the kids at school called her, *pigeon-toes*. Sometimes one still hisses it, *pigeon*, but not to her face or she'd smack him, and since she's a foot taller and thirty pounds heavier than most they're mindful of that. It's what she's got over them, she's a big girl. That's what Mum calls her. "You're a Big Girl!" Mum says when Fortune comes wailing into their room at night after one of her bad dreams, "Go back to bed." Like size has anything to do with being afraid.

Clanky, clunky metal torture racks attached to long, black witches' boots, snapped on and snugged tight with Velcro. Sometimes when she sneaks under the Beatnik's window to check on what he's doing she thinks she still hears them, clankity clank, and worries he'll hear them too and come after her. Mostly he's playing that shivery music on his saxophone, so smooth she imagines whipped cream and butter and globs of rich vanilla ice cream, thick and cold.

And she thinks of aquamarine, her color, swimming pools and oceans and icy glaciers, the sky on summer evenings and the best sea glass in the world. A friend of Mum's once said: "Fortune won't ever be a pretty girl, not even close, but she has those beautiful aquamarine eyes." The way the Beatnik blows into that horn, what comes out of it is pure aquamarine.

Fortune's dad calls him the Beatnik On The Hill and Mum says, "For crying out loud, there's no more beatniks, you think it's the fifties?" Then Dad points out that he *looks* like a beatnik, with those billowy white pants and his pointed beard, and "he wears *jewelry*," Dad says. Plus he's a jazz player, which as far as Dad is concerned is no kind of music and certainly no kind of work. Their property abuts the Beatnik's only his goes up the hill and theirs is flat downhill, which means the Beatnik gets the view of the river and the hills beyond while the Hopewell house is hunkered in the trees where not even enough sunlight beams in to melt the ice from their driveway in the winter.

Near the chain-link fence that separates their properties, the Beatnik has a giant maple tree that drops its leaves in the fall into the Hopewell yard and Dad rants, *Whose leaves are these?* Then he mutters that they are the Beatnik's because they came off his tree, so he should be the one to rake them. The Beatnik just nods and smiles and goes about his business, which isn't raking the leaves, and Dad won't rake them either, tossing refuse from his job installing windows and doors at their property line—old cracked window frames and busted doors from the houses he put new ones in, hissing, "*View* that! And anyway," he said when Mum questioned it, "schlepping that damn crap to the salvage yard costs a mint, and the old man who runs it is a bloody *kike*, if you get what I'm saying," his eyebrows flying up. "You think we're made of money?" he whined. "In this economy how many folks you suppose *want* new windows and doors? They want a job, that's what." Fortune's Mum just shrugged. She's got her own concerns, she'll tell you. First Officer of the local branch of the Tea Party, which is a spinoff from the bigger county branch, as in they're none too happy about that one's growth—"Soon it'll be just another kind of Big Government, you watch," Mum said.

Fortune wishes Dad *would* go to the salvage yard so she could poke through it for aquamarine things, china, toys, old machine parts—who knew what she might uncover? It's like digging for buried treasure. The last time she was there she found a set of four bright-blue wine goblets she brought home to her Mum, but Mum said they weren't worth the plastic they were made from. "And furthermore," Mum said, "drinking wine is what yuppies do, people who can afford to waste money on luxuries. This household shall be wineless!" she proclaimed.

The Beatnik has an aquamarine shirt Fortune would like to own someday. She's sure it's a luxury, silk or satin, something whispery smooth that he puts on when he's going out for the evening, Fortune peeking from behind the Christmas-berry bush snugged up against his bedroom window. She can almost feel the slide of it against her own skin; it would make her skin like his—sleek as a tiger's with the knobs of his shoulders poking through. Its color would be like wearing the sea.

The local branch of the Tea Party meets biweekly in the Hopewell living room, starting their meetings with the Pledge of Allegiance to the flag Mum props up in a Folger's-coffee can on top of the TV, then belting out the *Star Spangled Banner*, Mum leading with her deep, hard voice. Then they launch into how the bigger Tea Party movement is an embarrassment, whose founding principles the local one embraced but then decided its endorsement of giant corporal entities like Fox TV and even Glenn Beck ("He's become *so* mainstream," Mum said) was a threat to their commitments.

Their commitments, as far as Fortune can tell, involve being able to recite by heart at least part of the Constitution, the second amendment, the freedom to bear arms, and use phrases like *Big Brother* and *Newspeak*, the *thought police* and *doublethink*. The Bible and Ayn Rand are also important, and though most of the local Tea

Partiers are not readers by choice, they're literate and therefore instructed by Fortune's Mum to read everything Mrs. Rand wrote. Mum threatened to make Fortune read these books too, if she didn't behave, and given the heft of *Atlas Shrugged* Fortune does not want to be caught sneaking about the Beatnik's property.

The local Tea Partiers are stockpiling gold, survival gear, forming armed militias, building shelters filled with powdered food, ammunition, cleaning their guns, getting ready for the Big Show. "You're either with us or you're the enemy," Mum declared. The latest to be added to the Hopewell stockpile are really ugly flannel clothes to keep them warm after the Big Show, when the textile industries are all gone since they've hired out their workers in foreign places like India and China, so they're targets, Mum said. Fortune asked Mum to at least get her something aquamarine, even if it had to be flannel, but Mum said Fortune must not be picky. "It's pickiness that got us into this mess," Mum said. Fortune isn't sure what this means or even which mess her Mum is referring to, but asking would only prolong the conversation and it still wouldn't get Fortune a less-ugly stockpiled shirt.

One of Mum's enemies is Mr. Diaz, Fortune's sixth-grade, earth-science teacher, whom Fortune would spy on if only she could figure out where he lives. Not in their neighborhood, that's for sure. Every day when school is done he gets into his Toyota Prius and drives someplace, away from here. When Dad finally fixes Fortune's busted bike she'll follow Mr. Diaz home.

They're doing a unit on global warming, which Mum claims is a hoax started by Radical Leftist Environmentalists and perpetuated by Democrats for their political gain. Yesterday Mr. Diaz showed a film about Alaska's Columbia Glacier, how just this year it lost another half mile of ice, ten miles since 1940. "It's moving fifty feet a day," Mr. Diaz said, "and it's only a matter of time before Columbia withers away. Dead ice," he called it. The film zeroed in on a couple extreme surfers, surfing the waves spawned by the crashing ice melt, and Fortune thought how she'd like to do that one day, ride those roaring waves. She imagined herself in the lip of one, where everything inside is aquamarine and all you could hear would be the rush of the water tumbling down. When they get to the sea the breakaway icebergs are taken by the tide never to be seen again. "It's a kind of extinction," Mr. Diaz said.

He told them glaciers everywhere are dying, and with them go one-sixth of the earth's water, that glaciers are second only to the ocean for bearing our planet's water. "There's an ice sheet in Greenland that moves 150 feet a day," he said, "losing more ice each year than it gains in snowfall. Coastal folks will be goners; the polar ice melts will flood the planet."

Mum dismissed this *theory* with a violent shrug when Fortune told her about it. "Anyway it would be good riddance," Mum said, since the coasts are where the yuppies and liberals live, radical bike riders, people who condemn cars and plastic water bottles, want the world to drink from metal. Far as Mum is concerned the best thing that's come up the pike is the plastic water bottle. You can haul your lightweight water without wrecking your shoulder and when you're done you throw the bottle away, and it's guaranteed to stay in the world well over a hundred years from now. "You cannot outlive the plastic water bottle," she said.

"Glaciers are dynamic systems, always moving," Mr. Diaz said. "As the ice melts it forms an aquamarine lake, which can suddenly disappear overnight with massive cracks, booms, and pops like it's declared war on itself. The water rushes out and in less than forty minutes the entire lake is gone."

Blue is Fortune's color. Her eyes, and her pale skin too, are blue in some lights, like the one in their shelter with Mum's stockpiled stuff. It runs on a generator, hooked up to the concrete ceiling, a wide, thin light meant to illuminate the pure black of underground, or maybe the end of the world.

AT FIRST WHEN she began taking things it was anything goes, notebooks from the school supply closet, bottles of paste with their shiny black tops, handfuls of pencils, some already sharpened and others the size of cigarette butts, juicy-fruit candy and cherry cola lip gloss from the Rite Aid (which she picked for its flavor, not that she'd *ever* wear lipstick), even a tiny box turtle from Pet Mart. That one was tragic, as it managed to get itself lost before Fortune was able to steal a bowl for it to live in and turned up like a petrified turd behind the couch when Fortune's sister Miriam Meth-Girl shoved that out in the middle of the room one day, searching for drug money. After this Fortune decided to limit herself to aquamarine things: marbles from Toys R Us, blue, grass coasters from Home Depot, wind chimes from the Dollar Store and sea glass from the Crafts and Hobbies shop. The sea glass is the best. Even though it's just regular glass pocked and beveled to *look* like sea glass, she can stare at its rippled surface in the aquamarine color and imagine the ocean and those glaciers, far away from here.

Once she got caught trying to snag a globe from her world-history classroom—she liked its turquoise color from all the oceans and lakes and glaciers that covered its plastic surface. It was too big for her backpack though, and it certainly didn't fit under her jacket without making her look like she was going to have a baby. The principal called Mum in to talk about Fortune's *disturbing* behavior, but instead of getting angry at Fortune Mum discovered they were teaching global warming and evolution and she got the Tea Partiers to leaflet the school with websites for more accurate information on these things.

Fortune Hopewell. A name like they thought she'd be someone. Her oldest sister's name is Barbara, a practical name, but she was the golden one. Then the next is Miriam, who knew why. Mum chose Barbara and Miriam, so Dad got to name Fortune. Once upon a time, before their first-born daughter became something *else*, her Dad was the sort who would pick a name like Fortune Hopewell.

When they first learned of *The Great Betrayal*—the BMW Sport Maxi-Scooter bearing the school's two head cheerleaders on their way to a game, roaring down Kamikaze Hill, the Chenango River snaking below, only instead of taking the turn at the bottom to the stadium they shot straight onto 81 (rumored to have flipped the bird as they blew by) and three hours later were starting new lives as a *couple* in New York—Mum went to bed for a week and Dad hid in his basement shop, turning all the machines on, power saws, drills, things that whir and shriek and clatter. "Sorry Mum, but we're so *outathere!*" Barbara trilled, finally answering one of Mum's frantic calls, and when Mum asked her what she'd use for money because she wouldn't get a red cent from them until she came to her senses and came home, *alone*, and by the way, what about school? Alyssa Adams cut in, said not to worry, they'd try their luck at modeling. "We're tall, skinny, and willing," she said.

Then the Hopewells hardened, refusing the outreach from neighbors, their church, even entreaties from the parents of the *other*. ("It's the twenty-first century," Alyssa's mother said. "They're eighteen. We can't choose who they love.") "We'll handle this our own way," Mum announced. Eschewed all of it in favor of good old rage, at the school for allowing kids to travel on their own to sports events, too cheap to provide a bus, Alyssa Adams who was driving her dad's motorcycle, "without a lick of sense in that waste of a blond head," Mum said, and the county for championing football games in schools unwilling to fund them properly despite the criminal amount of tax money they get. Mum started the local Tea Party group, though she swore it had nothing to do with Barbara's (probably brainwashed!) *choices*; she was just so mad at what their country had become, hijacked by Democrats and environmentalists and Obama lovers and socialist professors, yuppies and people like the Adamses who would own a *German* luxury motorcycle in the first place in an area that can't even support its American Big Dog franchise for crying out loud, and invited others who felt this way—Tea Party people sick of how big and bureaucratic their county movement had grown, birthers and the like, to unite.

Dad's rage was more personal, erupting on whomever and whatever he came in contact with, from a driver who neglects to use his turn signal, to an unlucky squirrel choosing that moment to scamper across the street Dad is driving on, to a neighborhood kid's forgotten toy that he trips on at the side of the road while getting the mail, stomping on it until it cracks in two. *Whose leaves are these!* he roars in the fall; come winter he will shovel them along with the snow, flinging all of it over the chain link fence onto the Beatnik's driveway. Miriam and Fortune are left to their own resources, the older turning to chemical pursuits, and Fortune becoming a spy, which suits her fine.

It's finally summer and Fortune has a job of sorts, which is to walk the mile and a half to Grandma Edna's house, spying as she goes, the McGullys', the Farnsworths', Mister Blister, she calls the old man with the warty face and the blisters like bubble wrap on his nose, who refuses to recycle all his empties and they sit in a beat-up tin garbage can on the curb, a favorite stop for the county's homeless and drug addicts since wine and beer bottles are refundable. Some of the houses have *For Sale* signs stuck in their yards, overgrown weeds and unmown grass, ivy-smothered porches, the windows boarded up.

When she gets to Grandma Edna's she does things like help Grandma Edna pull her diaper pants up, which is the worst, because she doesn't like to look at her grandmother's you-know-what, Fortune down on her knees and it's staring at her like a vertical smile if a smile could stare—her grandma lost what hair she had there. Then she dusts Grandma Edna's billions of knickknacks, her *pretties* Grandma calls them, which is the best. "Grandma Edna is a hoarder," Fortune's Mum said, and Grandma Edna says she knows damn well that some think it's irrational, Mum can spare her the diagnosis, but she just can't bear to throw anything away, since she never could trust that somewhere down the line she might have use for the very thing she tossed out.

So Fortune takes a feather duster she found atop the stacks of this and that and dusts, because Grandma Edna has allergies and the dust gets to her after a while, and if she has a sneezing fit she'll also pee the diaper pants, which Fortune must then help her take off and place new ones on yet again, Grandma Edna using Fortune's shoulders to steady herself as she steps into the pants, Fortune tugging them up. Grandma Edna broke her hip and when she recovered it was like she had turned into a Lego toy that couldn't bend, could only be arranged into different configurations.

Fortune tries not to take much from Grandma Edna, but sometimes she can't help herself, slipping a particularly brilliant aquamarine glass egg, for instance—that was yesterday's haul—into the zippered pocket of her backpack. "Fabergé," her grandma said when Fortune asked her about it, "costs a mint!" Fortune knew that even though at one time the egg might have been worth something, it's not now because it has a chip in it from being at the bottom of a pile of folding metal chairs, mismatched china and cakes of old soaps, half-used bottles of laundry detergent and an ancient iron with rust and lime deposits all over it. And she knows Grandma Edna won't miss it, because on top of all her other ailments she can no longer see, with cataracts clogging both her eyes and no insurance other than Medicaid to do much about it. "She ain't going to the damn County Hospital!" (which would take her Medicaid) Dad declared. Grandma Edna is his mother so he gets to say what will happen to her, unless, says Grandma Edna, she is of a different opinion, in which case she'll do as she damn well pleases. They are in agreement on this: no state-run hospitals, and no state-supported nursing homes; Grandma Edna will stay in her own damn house for as long as there's breath in her body.

It's a hot summer, the kind where you can see the air, filled with the humming and buzzing of insects, and Fortune helped Dad drag Grandma Edna's bed right under the window so that if there's a breath of breeze to be gotten Grandma would get it. Now Fortune props the hippo pillow behind Grandma's back to help her sit up straight in the bed and Grandma rolls her cloudy, filmy blue eyes toward the window light.

"Gawd damn!" she whines.

"Son of a bitch!" Fortune replies, grinning. They like to swear at each other. It's their secret code.

Grandma Edna says she wants to feel the snow on her face one last time before she dies, though Dad said Grandma Edna isn't dying. "She refuses to," he said.

"Won't be long now," Grandma Edna says. "What do I got to live for? Now take me out so I can feel the snow on my face."

Fortune says, "It's summer and bloody hot."

And Grandma Edna snaps, "I know that but I'm pretending cause I can't see for shit, anyway."

"Gawd almighty damn," Fortune agrees, and she closes her eyes and imagines it, but what she sees is a grey, wet November, one of those *indeterminate seasons*, Mr. Diaz calls them, on its way to becoming something else.

"OK," she says, "what the hell, I'm opening your window so the snow will blow in on you."

Then Fortune climbs up on Grandma Edna's bookcase where piles of books, old telephone directories, ancient newspapers and magazines and file folders filled with crumpled clippings are stacked a mile high. She's made a sort of nest for herself, with an old ratty bedspread and some towels, and perches like a gawky bird, watching as her grandma tilts her chin into the hot blade of yellow sunlight blazing through the window.

"One more winter," Grandma Edna sighs, "and I'm done for."

FORTUNE HAS A secret fort in a huge oak tree just in from the edge of the woods, where if she climbs high enough she can see out of the woods, and using her spyglasses she can see into a trailer's windows, the trailer itself in an open space at the bottom of a long secluded dirt driveway. It's here that she discovered an even bigger secret, in fact could be the biggest secret in the world! What do you do with a secret like this? She looks about the age of her sister, Miriam Meth-Girl, but she won't tell her sister about it when she comes skulking around, sweeping her scabby hand under sofa cushions, chairs, behind bureaus, inside drawers, looking for money. And could be there's a ghost inside too—one day she shadowed the man who lives there. He's walking to the bus stop and Fortune scurrying behind bushes, slinking under trees, all the way up the road, him shaking his head like a crazy person, muttering about a ghost. Fortune isn't so sure about this, the man could be *touched*, is how her Mum describes mental people; for now she'll keep her distance from the trailer, just in case. She doesn't want any dealings with a ghost *or* a crazy person.

Fortune's Dad is mad at everything so she won't tell him her secret. Mum says, "Don't get mad, get even!" Not that she pays Fortune any mind either. After Saint Barbara swapped the family for Alyssa Adams and Miriam became a meth addict, seems her parents aren't much interested in Fortune's future, like they've already given up on her, out of leg braces and into Juvie. "Good thing you got those steel traps off," Miriam sneered, after Fortune was busted for shoplifting (just once!), "so you can run from the girl-rapers if they send you to the reformatory." She said at the reformatory the older girls gang up on the younger ones and rape them with brush handles, plastic forks, toilet paper tubes, whatever's convenient. "To show who's boss," Miriam said, sniffing and scratching her meth-sores.

The secret fort was once a deer stand for hunters. She knows this because a deer skull bleached white as the belly of a shark hangs over the rotting wood floor on a pulley rope, and there's always fresh deer poop below like they're making a statement of some sort. Every day after Fortune is done helping Grandma Edna, fixed her lunch then tucked her in for her afternoon nap, she slips away to her fort, climbing up, up, up the rickety ladder, the steps built right into the trunk of the oak, to where there's a stool at the top, a stretch of faded blue canvas with a hole cut in it and a plastic jug under it with the top slashed off—maybe for gun cartridges, Fortune thinks, or it could be a place for the hunter to stick his dick down and pee. Fortune knows that word, *dick*, because Miriam Meth-Girl called their Dad that when he wouldn't give her money and he went raging after her, so Fortune figured the word had muscle.

She tried it out on Grandma Edna for good measure and Grandma Edna cackled, said dick*wad* was even better. Then one day Dad made her look at his when he was very drunk in his basement workroom, and he pulled her inside, the sour stink of whatever he'd been drinking leaching out of his pores, mingling with the smell of sawdust and old rotten doors, Fortune just back from an exhausting afternoon of spying on the neighborhood. Dad wore only his boxer shorts with no shirt on, and he told her to feel his biceps, flexing them: "Come on, squeeze these puppies, feel how strong I am!" Fortune shook her head, tried to tug her arm away from him and he yanked her closer, whipping his dick out of his shorts. "Ever seen one of these?" he hissed. She glanced down for just a second, saw that it looked prickly as a pig's snout, then he told her to get the hell out of his workshop, covering his face with his hands. For weeks Dad wouldn't look at her, like something was Fortune's fault, playing Barbara's old Nick Drake CDs non-stop, which made Fortune want to kill herself. Miriam said Nick Drake committed suicide and Fortune could see why, the songs were so *wretched* (a word she learned in her English class, meaning very, very sad). Now Dad is just plain furious again and Fortune keeps her distance.

The first time she crawled up the ladder to her secret fort, the steps going shake-a-shake-a, the tree blowing in the wind even with the weight of her on it (Fortune isn't exactly a featherweight), she sat scrunched at the top to avoid the rotting boards, and she discovered a faded photo of a dragonfly stuck on a branch with a rusted tack. Fortune decided she'd call herself that, *Dragonfly*, the secret-agent spy. Dragonfly spies on the crazy man in the trailer with the tied-up girl, and she rubs the deer skull hanging there for good luck. Maybe if she gets really brave she'll sneak into that trailer one day and find something good to take, give it to Dad so for a little while he won't be so angry.

Last summer Fortune came upon a nest that had fallen out of a tree in their yard, with a baby robin in it. Dad put the little hunched-up bird in a cage he found on one of his jobs, lining it with newspaper and an old baby blanket, and he got up at all hours to feed it some kind of mush with an eyedropper a wildlife website recommended. But it died anyway. "There's nothing more we could've done," Dad said. But Fortune thought there was; they could've put its cage in a sunny window, found it tastier food—worms maybe, or what if they talked to it, encouraged it some. Dad said that was ridiculous. "People are losing their jobs, homes, bank accounts, a way of life they could *depend* on, and you want to encourage a dumb bird!" But he kept the cage out, as if another might come along. Fortune had noticed something in Dad's face when he fed it, a kind of concentration, something almost tender that might've been there before the rage got in and erased it.

She settles herself on the canvas seat, avoiding the dick-hole, lifts up her spyglasses hanging on a rope around her neck, and adjusts them just right to look into the window at the tied-up girl. She's a little hard to make out because it's a frosted window, but there's a clear part at the top of the glass, and Fortune has the best spyglasses, having once belonged to the Beatnik (he left them on his patio, where he'd been gazing at the river, and Fortune snuck onto the patio after he went inside and snagged them). She remembers hearing something on TV a while back, about some girl disappearing from a parking lot—could this be her? Will Dragonfly, secret-agent spy, be in the news for finding her? Maybe there's even a reward. She'll have to think about it, what the next step should be. Meanwhile, it's the biggest secret in the world, though a little boring since the tied-up girl does nothing but sit there all day on a mattress. Sometimes the man drifts by, but that's about it.

She imagines what it would be like to be tied-up and fed her meals three times a day, nothing to do but watch TV. They couldn't make you do chores if you were tied-up, no Grandma Edna's diaper pants. If they were agreeable people who tied you up, not criminals or *deviants* (another word she learned in her English class) like in the police shows, it would be a kind of *cherishing*, the way the man offers food to the tied-up girl, arranges the pillows behind her so she can see the TV better. He might be crazy, Fortune decides, but he seems nice enough.

Fortune thinks about tying herself up in her fort—she knows where Dad keeps the rope in his shop. She imagines looping it around the deer skull, and then her wrists—except how could she tie it if it's around her hands? Or maybe an ankle? Maybe the Beatnik could bring her food, strawberry smoothies and Oreos, her favorites, place pillows behind her back, tell her she's *cherished*. Oh Fortune, you're so cherished! The problem is if she tied it herself she could always break free, and even if she didn't, she knows no one would come feed her, bring her up a TV so she could watch her favorite shows, none of that. The Beatnik barely knows she exists—she's too good of a spy! Only Grandma Edna might miss her when she needed help with the diaper pants.

Anyway it's the spying that counts, since when Fortune's not doing it Mum says she's *Hyperactive* and speaks too *Loud*, and is always on the run. Except when she's spying, which she can do for a whole hour. Dragonfly the secret-agent spy, still as a held breath, eyes trained into the spyglasses, becomes like a statue, her own eyes the spyglasses, her voice frozen. Afterward she rolls down the hill where the dirt road is, into a field where the grass and weeds are taller than her, in a barrel she found on the other side of the woods, where one of the old IBM buildings used to be. Both ends of the barrel are rusted out, the metal rippled inside with some white powdery stuff that smells like ant-poison and makes her sneeze. Dad said IBM changed everyone's lives when it moved into the area and gave people jobs, then did it again when it left, firing them all.

"GE, ANSCO, Link Aviation, even a goddamn candy company," he said, "made BB Bats, off to Paducah, Kentucky. All of them gone," he said, "and not a one of them coming back."

Sometimes Fortune lies at the bottom of the hill in that barrel and thinks about things. She likes to imagine her sister's last hours here. Had she been planning her escape or did it happen at the spur of the moment, one of them crying out to the other over the roar of the engine: *Let's just go*! How they must've felt airborne for a moment, the motorcycle flying down Kamikaze Hill under a sky that color at the end of a glacier; like being in the lip of one of those ice-melt waves, a perfect aquamarine.

This Is a Success Story

There are over five hundred diseases that list headaches as a symptom, from hangovers to brain tumors to the bubonic plague. There's encephalitis, which could kill you or leave you with brain damage, or mucormycosis, caused by fungi in the soil, which will severely disfigure you and on top of that there's an eighty-percent chance it'll kill you too. If your face is flushed along with the headache you could have yellow fever. If your face is twitching you might have Parkinson's, which could eventually kill you, or Tourette's, which won't kill you but won't win you any friends either. I obsess over diseases the way some stalk celebrities, with a kind of appalled reverence. Ginger tells me she doesn't appreciate my input on her headache, that she suspects it's a result of too much time in the walk-in freezer where we work, and not enough in the arms of some hot-blooded, barrel-chested, *Homo erectus* (she likes the second word) male of the species, and that when all is said and done she'll probably get hit by a bus anyway.

Ginger's had over a hundred lovers and with all of them, she says, she tried to convince herself she really didn't want to see them, that they weren't worth seeing, but she'd wear herself down and go back for more every bloody time. "Abstinence may lead you to God," she said, "but in the end it's hunger that'll get you fed."

It's Freddy who's leading *me* to God, Frederick Jameson Heinz Jr., not the catsup Heinz, who I think were part of the John Birch Society, right-wing fanatics, but this might be close. I'm Freddy junior's art coach at the Community Center's After School Program for teens. He's the son of a revival preacher, what they're calling a prosperity preacher of the prosperity gospel, the ones who preach how to come to Jesus and make your fortune doing it. We're talking private airplanes, yachts, Harleys sent by anonymous supporters, vacations in Hawai'i, New Zealand, Costa Rica, Paris, designer handbags, Prada this and that, and this preacher, his dad, wears a pinkie ring plastered with emeralds and diamonds—someone is prospering all right. "God knows where the money is, and he knows how to get the money to you, praise Jesus!" the revivalists shout, and I'm ready to commit about the worst sin you can, around here anyway, which is to say the preacher's son, sixteen years old.

"I'm going to fry for this," I tell Ginger.

"Be like that Smart chick," she says. "Was it Pamela Smart? Goes to prison for having sex with one of her students, gets out and she's right back at it. Wasn't she the one that ended up having a kid with him?" Ginger stubs out her cigarette, stabbing it with the spiked black heel of her boot. We're on our break at the Bagel Palace, outside in the alley behind, rain flogging the tin roof of the shed we huddle under, drops whizzing over our heads.

"You're confusing your Jezebel educators," I tell her. "Pamela Smart's in prison for plotting the murder of her husband, which she persuaded her teenage lover to pull off. You're thinking of Mary Kay Letourneau, who did it with a twelve-year-old."

"Whatever, he was big for his age," Ginger sniffs. "Look at it this way, that she *could*, well hell, you got to give it to her." She shrugs and straightens her eyebrows with a licked finger. "They have those hard young bodies," Ginger sighs, "and they'll never be as handsome again."

My father told me about the handsomest man he knew, part Cherokee, his friend who helped him after my mother died, a generous man. Then Alzheimer's struck and the last time my father went to visit him, this handsome man had climbed up on a cabinet and was howling like a wolf. Just one month later he was gone.

After a careful study of diseases that can kill you I have come to believe that people have sex to stave off death. Death is in the driver's seat, the fear of it, mourning what it's taken, the embrace of it for some, its inevitability for the rest of us. Sex stalls things, the physical weave of two bodies, two lives, however long it lasts means for those minutes anyway death can't snuff you because you're part of someone else. And if it tries to, the old climactic heart attack, you'll live on in the other, particularly when he tries to have sex with anyone else.

While not up to Ginger's stats of a hundred lovers, I do have a history.

There was the baseball player, who was actually a minister, but he wore his Red Sox uniform good and tight around the butt the way they do, with those well-packed thighs, shoulders too. Should be a sin to build a minister with muscles like his. I figured this minister would rather have been a baseball player, which is why he and his almost-as-hot friend played dress-up in these uniforms, tossing a baseball back and forth on the wide, green lawn of the United Church of Christ. When he invited me inside the parsonage, the little house they kept their ministers in, I didn't have my diaphragm and worried about that, but as it turned out this muscular minister couldn't get it up and we didn't need the thing. Though he sure seemed to have a good time trying.

It started when I was in kindergarten and used to hum and click my tongue against the roof of my mouth during nap time, and when the teacher made me pull my pallet in the corner I'd open my legs so Dougie Dorfman, who always got in trouble too, could see my underpants. Pink, with smiley-face butterflies pale as pears. There was the cute mute who used to smoke dope on the rock wall that separated our yard from his, and one day he knocked on my door when my father was out; I'm in my bra and panties and I let him in. He placed his hand on my chest and pushed me down on the bed like toppling a tree. Didn't even slide my underpants off just twisted them to one side. Which is good time-economy, because he was coming to the sound of my Dad's Toyota Tacoma roaring up the driveway and he wriggled out the window, still buckling his pants right before the key clicked in the lock. The street kid with the waist-length dreads outside my dorm at art school, *townies* the rich kids called them, who banged out a rhythm on whatever he could get his hands on—garbage-can lids, old coffee cans, wailed on a mouth harp too, peering up at my window, that beguiling grin. When I invited him in I said, "Here, slide down the zipper so I can check out of this dress"; his hand lingering as I knew it would, the dip in my back, my hips, my butt, he who probably didn't own a second pair of pants to change into. Driving home with the rock-'n'-roll junkie and his car slides off the road into a Mill Valley stream. Instead of asking if I'm all right, him on top of me and both of us in the black freezing water, he goes, "My guitar! Where's my guitar!" But I showed him. I spent the night with the baby-faced cop who investigated the accident.

It wasn't always this much fun.

There's getting sandwiched between two greasers on a packed subway in the city, one thrusting one way the other behind. Another who will forever be faceless, the salty smell of him like raw shrimp, his breath hungering on my neck, his hand swimming around inside the waistband of my pants, pressing behind me in a crowded *malasada* line at the old Halawa Stadium those years after my mother was gone and my dad said why not try Honolulu for a while? This after we lived in Dallas, Las Vegas, LA, he just kept heading west. What could I do, eleven years old, but buy my *malasada* and Coke? The one in the Chiclet-yellow Corvette, who promised dinner but instead takes me to his house in Mānoa, breaks a popper under my nose and dives down on top of me on the kitchen floor; we never even made it to his bed. In a van at Sunset Beach, God was he all of thirteen? Sun like a dragon's breath and his hand, a little brown snake wriggling into the open window, stuck inside my bikini bottom, latched on like a leech. The Panther's paws squeezing my neck so hard the bruises looked like I'd survived a strangling and the dorm R.A. said *You have to tell* . . . his teeth at my throat, roaring me down into a cave so deep and black it would be another decade before I could begin to crawl out. Maybe the worst was Mick Knowlton, my surfer boyfriend, after we moved back to California, San Diego this time, his hurting sex that made me cry, and how he would comfort me when it was done. He liked to remind me that *his* father looked like Kirk Douglas, like this was supposed to make any difference at all. "Shhh," he'd take me in his arms, rock me against his suntan chest, "it's over now." As if this too is just another thing we are born to endure.

IF YOU HAVE blurred vision and a sudden, severe headache you might have a cerebral hemorrhage, which means you will probably bleed to death in your brain. Though you could be a hemophiliac and bleed to death from any orifice. Or maybe you have Stokes-Adams syndrome, which could stop your pulse due to a heart blockage—now there's a way *not* to bleed to death.

I used to have nightmares about my mother abandoning me, particularly the years when we lived in Hawai'i, a recurring one on Kailua Beach. At least I think it was my mother, a woman who looked like the photograph on my father's dresser, the one in the koa frame with her long black hair flying out, like a hard wind was blowing and she's just trying to hold on. In the dream it's stormy, pounding surf, its whipped, gray froth like a bubbled-over gravy and the churning clouds overhead. My mother and I sitting cross-legged on the sand at the water's edge, and suddenly a big wave swoops over us, tugging me out. I stretch my child-arm toward her, still close enough she could grab my hand and hold on, but she doesn't. Sits there as my mouth fills up with seawater and I am being dragged out into those deeper, darker places.

We lived in Kawela, a three-room cottage in the Norfolk pines. At night geckos chirped and the trade winds whispering through the open screens, and I pretended she was there too. Would she have made my clothes? Made us all manner of delectable food, instead of the nightly SpaghettiOs, my dad's signature dish? I imagined watching her get ready to go out, the tangy scent of her— my father would keep her well stocked in French perfumes. Her small, rounded shoulders in a sleeveless shift she made herself, her tiny waist in the fit of it, the matching heels. Then my father would go out and I'd feel a small terror that he wouldn't return and hunker down in his closet, inhaling the Old Spice fragrance of his shirts.

ON MY WEDDING night, room service at the Kahala Hilton sent up the customary champagne, and right beside it in a decorative crystal decanter the milk my new husband ordered for his pregnant wife and fetus. The next day we flew to where I live now, fourteen hours later and my history remade.

After viewing the *Bodies* exhibit in New York, with its jars of fetuses at various stages of development, Ginger tells me as we're trying to flag down a taxi, about the illegal abortion she had back in the sixties when they poked something metal up you to dislodge it, only she was a dancer in those days with tight musculature and nothing happens. So she goes home, and later that night she's doubled over in the bathroom, cramping, bleeding, sobbing, and she catches the twelve-week-old fetus as it slides out of her, cradling this curled up, petrified *almost* human the size of a peapod in the palm of her hand, and her mother, a former English major, calling from downstairs, "Everything *copasetic* up there?" For the rest of her life, Ginger tells me as we climb into the cab, she will have recurring nightmares about what happened next: flushing it down the toilet.

When I gave birth to Pet I hyperventilated and passed out. I had read somewhere that in 1940 hyperventilation was used to alter a woman's perception of pain during labor, forever after known as Lamaze, so I figured why bother with the classes? Scared the bejesus out of my OB, who when I explained about this later said, "Well sure, and once upon a time they punched you in the jaw to knock you out before surgery."

You can bleed to death from a childbirth hemorrhage, or a botched abortion for that matter.

FREDDY JR. SAID to come to the revival service because he has to be there, his parents said so, and maybe we could sneak out, he said, there's an old abandoned building next door and there's bats in it. His eyes shone, pupils small and black as peppercorns. He grinned but I wasn't sure at what, me or the bats? We haven't done anything yet, at least nothing I could be arrested for. A tentative kiss in the playground tunnel as we walked through the park behind the Community Center, and it was him yanking me in there, one of those frothy canvas things painted to look like something that flies. I thought maybe he'd smell like bubble gum or puberty sweat, but there was no scent, just the push of his chapped lips against mine, the tenderness of his tongue licking my palate. "Monty!" he whispered, blushing. I had told him to say my name, that moaning *Ms. Trent* while he kissed me didn't do much for the libido. Working with clay at the center it was Freddy's hands, sliding up and down the wheel's spinning, sloppy movement, attempting to shape something or other and I put mine over his and felt that sixteen-year-old fire. "You have great hands," I said, and he thought I meant his potential as a sculptor or someone who makes clay pots, which I thought showed a kind of maturity.

WHEN THE THOUSANDS of migrating birds soar through the night over New York, you can watch them from the Empire State Building's observation deck, eighty-six floors up. With the city lights illuminating them from below they look like little shooting stars. Peregrine falcons, once on the brink of extinction but who have now adapted to life on the skyscrapers, pick off a good hundred or so every season. This is a success story. They must think they've died and gone to heaven, the skies raining goodies, the ultimate piñata. They hover up in the clouds, waiting to swoop down on the migrants like bats on a mosquito. I read in a poem that bats can't fly *up*, as in they can't lift off; they have to swoop *down* to glide. Figuring poems aren't necessarily a source for facts I looked this up on the Internet and never found it. What I did find was a report from some classroom where the kids studied bats, and one little budding CEO proposed that the reason bats hang from their feet is because it's easier than hanging from their thumbs. What the poem was really about was the coroner's report for the poet's brother's death: *heroin, cocaine, marijuana, unresponsive....*

When my dad found my mother unconscious in their bed it was already too late, but he called 911 and told them she was unresponsive. Not cocaine or heroin, the old-fashioned way, her wrists sliced open with a razor. Probably he had to throw away the mattress and definitely the bedding, though I never asked and he never said. I was in the next room, three years old, and she put me to bed first, as I picture it, kissed me and tucked me in, told me she loved me. Sometimes I think I can still catch a whiff of her, a mingling of cinnamon and defeat. Maybe my father was supposed to come home before he did. Stopped for gas, groceries, traffic sluggish, a meeting that ended too late. Maybe if I had cried for her, the sound dragging her out of her perpetual sleep, back into her life as my mother . . .

The poem began with a bat and ended with one, *falling to glide; gliding to rise.*

HERE'S WHAT I know about bats. The deadly white-nose syndrome is a new disease and it's affecting bats throughout the Northeast. Thousands of them have died from New Hampshire to Virginia. A bat colony right here someplace in upstate New York has had a catastrophic number of deaths in young bats, this article said, which means not a lot of old bats down the line. They call them maternity colonies, where female bats gather under the roof of a barn or attic, maybe even Freddy's old building, where whatever heat there is rises to the ceiling—they like it hot—to bear and raise their pups. If they have this disease they get a white fungus on their muzzles, wings and tails, become emaciated, and die. The females give birth to just one baby and many of these babies have disappeared. It's been reported that mothers are abandoning their babies.

I read about stuff like this to avoid doing other things, such as my paintings. I've got enough talent, whatever that is, to train kids. Why would the world need one more mediocre painting that says nothing about diseased bats, disappearing pups, the things that are here then gone?

Of course there's also histoplasmosis, a fungal infection contracted by inhaling dirt or dust where the fungus has grown in soil enriched by bat guano. Or how about rabies, the majority of recent cases having been spread by infected bats? Viciousness, rage, excitability; after this comes paralysis then death.

What I'm afraid of is if I go to that revival Freddy senior will see it in me, the bad, and drag me down front to try and save me. I've been to one of these before, with my husband when we still thought there was a chance, and nothing excites them more than finding the worst person in there, waving their fleshy arms in the air like antennae, belting out their hymns while somebody leads you down under the lights in front, all blazing hot and airless, then Freddy senior will put his hand on your forehead and you fall back with the spirit, or because it's so stifling you're about to faint, and start ranting in tongues, the language of the saved. Then you're supposed to be healed, sins washed clean, good to go. Except with this one, the prosperity gospel, for the rest of your remaining days as a reborn prosperous Christian you're supposed to give all your money to their church, then pray for more. "God knows where the money is," Freddy's father was quoted in the newspaper, "and he knows how to get the money to you."

I ask Ginger to come with me but she says no, that so many Jesus freaks under one tent gives her the willies. She shimmies her head, her shoulders, shakes her head, her hair dyed the color of a mango. We're working our shift at the Bagel Palace, rubbing our gloved hands up and down the rumps of bologna, hunks of roast beef, slicing deli turkey, shredding the ham for the Palace's famous ham-and-egg bagel sandwich. We're the meat ladies. I come here after working at the center because part-time there doesn't give me near enough money to pay child support to my ex-husband, who does nothing all day while Pet is at kindergarten but lie around in what used to be my house too, toking cigarettes, chugging beer, eyeballing ESPN, you name it and it's not getting a job. But because I'm the bad seed who left our son alone one day while he napped, for a *dalliance with another man*, Jody's lawyer called it, I get to *pay the piper*—that was my husband's way of putting it. "You screwed the pooch, Monty!" Another of his witticisms. Jody boinked his skanks at night while Pet and I slept, which by rule of the court makes him the model parent.

THE TOWN I live in, Jody's home town, is on the Susquehanna, cited as one of America's most endangered rivers—we're talking animal carcasses, fertilizer run-off, industrial chemicals, and human waste, judging by the plastic tampon applicators whizzing by on the current. Eventually it empties into the Chesapeake, at a place ironically enough called *Havre de Grace*. On the night a man dove into all of this I slept, waking to what sounded like a train wreck, the howl of airboat engines battling flood stage currents, the sound that something inside me knew before the news told it, was death.

Last time I called my father he was trying to get my grandmother up. Home for him now is St. Louis, his mother's house. "Am I dead yet?" she asked. I pictured her hunched into a sitting position at the edge of her bed, her blunt shoulder blades, soft doughy skin of her back as he removed her wet nightgown, slipping a dry one over her head. On the days when she is unable to get up at all (and there are more and more of these) he changes the wet sheets right out from under her, sliding fresh ones on. "Am I dead?" I heard her ask again.

Here's another thing about bats: they fly at night around the bridge the man jumped from into the roiling river water below. They look like little black firecrackers shooting up into those bridge lights, then soaring down, winking out. Probably the lights attract insects, which attract the bats, but what attracted him?

How hopeless was he, the man who jumped? What is the line for this, where on one side of it we hold forth, soldier on; step over it we slit our wrists. Earlier in the week I started drinking again. Nothing earth-shaking, a vodka tonic in the late afternoon, a glass of wine with dinner and another before bed to help me sleep. I had mostly stopped when Pet was born so I'd have a clear head looking after him, but of late life in its razor-sharp clarity has become more bearable blunted. A partial list of things that make me miserable:

Squirrels huddled in the rain.

Rain.

Stop-Loss and the exhausted soldiers—kids, eighteen, nineteen, whose only hope for college, for a *life* was to sign up, sent back to war again and again.

Manhattanites who live in designer high-rises, shop Fifth Avenue for luxury goods, and in our little town half of Main Street's out of business, its black and empty storefronts.

Birds dropping like wet leaves onto the feeder in the dark fist of a spring that may as well be winter, for all its rain, rain, rain.

The chiming of my phone that day when before I picked it up life was one way—I had just returned from buying a steaming mug of Green Mountains coffee, chocolate milk and peanut butter crackers for Pet from the Quickstop, both of us settling in to watch *Animal Planet*, Pet's favorite—and after I hung up it was something else, the lawyer's call that my son would no longer be allowed to live with me. Child endangerment and my insatiable appetite, they called it. They weren't talking about food.

THE RAIN HAS finally stopped and the late afternoon sky is the color of dishwater when I get to the revival, figuring I can sneak in at the back of the tent, lift up one of the flaps and if Freddy is looking for me he'll see me, and if he's not, well, I'll consider it a sign. Maybe from Jesus himself, who knows? *Suffer the little children . . .* only I don't think he meant Freddy. Who I see right away as I slip inside and head up the bleacher stairs, two by two to the top. He's in the front row beside a jowly woman with pink hair. His back is to me and his head is down, and I can see the outline of those diamond-hard shoulders through his white shirt, that perfect triangular shape of a teenaged boy. My heart is beating too hard, my breath in my throat.

So the worst has already happened, my son living with Jody who sued for custody to punish me, locking me into a financial obligation that'll keep me rubbing bologna rumps and trying to convince yawning teens that art matters for the rest of my attractive years—by the time Pet's finished college I figure I'll be dried up. What's at stake? I think, listening to them belt out some hymn then another, hands pulsing upwards, and Freddy senior, who isn't too bad looking himself, though with the well-fed middle-aged man's gut bubbling over his belt, its giant silver buckle that I can see from here has a cross on it (I'm betting it's real silver), howling about the wages of sin and being saved from the bad we do in the name of the devil to do good in the name of Jesus (he pronounces it Jay-suss). The air inside the tent is stagnant, the dankness of our sodden spring compounded by however many sweaty bodies, arms waving madly. *Wages of sin,* I'm thinking, these prosperity gospels give that a whole new meaning. Maybe he's saying you can buy yourself out of the bad you've done, for a price and you're home free. What would it cost me, how many decades of beefy contributions in the offering plate to purchase back my soul after I lost it, snorting a line with the bouncer at the Positively State Street Bar then blowing him in the storage closet while my two-year-old napped in his crib, a mile away?

Freddy Jr. as if on cue twists his neck around, stares up at me and grins, makes a motion with a jerk of his heart-breakingly blond head toward the flap of the tent that leads out. He whispers something to the pink-haired woman who nods, then gets up, that lanky, jangly body with its adorable teenaged butt and moves toward the exit, with me lingering just long enough for him to step outside before I'm there too.

I asked my father once if it was because of me, a kind of prolonged postpartum depression, and he shook his head. "She was just a lost person," he said. "I thought I could save her."

BATS ARE WARM-BLOODED animals that bear their young live and nurse them, leaving them with the other babies while they fly off in search of food. Bats eat about six hundred mosquitoes an hour, one bat, six hundred biting, blood-sucking bugs. "Bats are good," Freddy tells me and I nod, though stare up with a little trepidation at the rafters where they hang like bunches of bananas, the building old and decayed and smelling of some sort of rot—just another structure that once housed some failed enterprise long since abandoned when hard times struck. Hard times have been going on here for Freddy's entire lifetime. "It's called *torpor*," Freddy explains with an impressive authority—what did I know about when I was sixteen beyond smoking pot and inviting some boy or another inside my pants. "When they rest their temperature drops," he tells me, "to whatever the temperature is around them."

Freddy's eyes are glowing in the sunset dark of the room, or what I imagine to be near sunset, who knows with the thatch of gray sky outside thick as a shag carpet. "Did you know," he says, "that during their mating season males will do it with a female just coming out of torpor where she's all sluggish, and when that's done they'll go after another female, even other males. They're freaky horny," he tells me, flashing that grin. "Huh," I grunt and grab his hand that's been nervously fiddling with the buttons on my shirt cuff as if opening these will expose something. I consider a strategic placement on my inner thigh but feel instead its smoothness, its newness. Slender long fingers, fully formed, not like Pet's that are encased in baby fat, the dimples where one day his knuckles will protrude, grow hairy, and then he'll become a man. How much of that growing up, I wonder, will I be there for? A weekend here and there, take him to a ball game like the non-custodial dads do, a hot dog then home to Jody and his skank of the week? Though maybe that's not entirely fair. After all it was my father who stayed with me, my dad who didn't give up.

The wreck of the building is drafty and I shiver, watching the bats start to stir, a wiggle of an oversized ear here, a sketchy wing there. Bats are not pretty animals. Freddy slips his arm around my waist, not with the sureness of a man, rather the boy trying to figure out what the next step should be. "Let's sit," I tell him, thinking I'll help him along, as we collapse onto the cold concrete floor. I run my fingers through his hair, his scalp warm and a little oily—amazing how teenage boys can feel hot even during these damp spring days, their inner furnace fueled by raging hormones. A memory of a night when we lived in Hawai'i, on Kawela beach with one of them, sneaking out after my dad was asleep, snuggling up with this hot-blooded boy in a sleeping bag on the sand, trade winds blowing the palms above us, rattling their fronds, the moon coating everything with a milky, stippled white. I barely knew him but let him do what he wanted; what did I have to lose then?

Freddy's hand has almost made it to my breast; I can feel his fingers trembling on my sternum. My heartbeat thrums and there's that familiar ache, that physical yearning, but something else too, more empty, a longing, but for what I'm just not sure. I take his hand in mine and kiss his fingers. "Do your parents do things with you?" I ask him.

He shrugs, "What do you mean?"

"I don't know, ball games?" I stare at him, his funny, distant look that won me over his first day at the Community Center. A look like he's with you, but not. Like maybe he has another, more essential life somewhere else.

"They're pretty busy," he says. "We have a lot of stuff though." I nod, remember Ginger telling me I should do the preacher instead of his son. "People think the Holy Spirit has commanded them to write checks to those guys," she said. "That's got to beat the Bagel Palace."

The bats are randomly flying about, a chaos of flapping wings above us, then gliding out through a hole in the wall near the ceiling, one after the other. "They're going to look for food," Freddy tells me. "It's sunset." He points to a weak orange light shining through a cracked window; some of the clouds must have finally cleared. I gaze at Freddy, his golden arm hairs in the pale light, the perfect line of his spine, his expensive haircut purchased by the grace of the prosperity gospel. "They'll find their food by echolocation," he says, "where they make these little noises, clicks and purrs, and bat mothers find their babies that way too, making sounds that the babies recognize. But they're not blind. People think bats are but they're not."

I have a sudden image of my father making clicking sounds to my grandmother as he brushes her hair, my grandmother who has macular degeneration and can no longer see. She was once an impeccably dressed woman, her cashmere jackets, Italian-leather pumps, the best bridge player in her neighborhood. A former librarian who taught my dad to treasure books, my dad who read to me every night for years, even after I no longer wanted him to he insisted on that half hour, the two of us. How must she feel now, or maybe she doesn't, can't think it, remember it long enough to know, that all of it is gone? The most intimate of one's grooming, using a toilet, is beyond her. When I visited them last year, in a glimmer of her former droll humor she said, "Not a problem, I just wet." She keeps losing weight, dissolving away. Is my father afraid of her dying? Or perhaps he's afraid of her not dying and losing more and more of her every day. Does he worry that one morning he'll wake up and the woman that was his mother will have disappeared?

I think about clueing Freddy in on the white-nose disease, about how a number of those bats he's watching fly into the night may not return. "Do you know, Freddy . . ." I picture myself saying to him, staring straight into his earnest eyes, still filled with something like hope. But why spoil it for him. Besides, maybe enough will survive and eventually become like the peregrine falcons, hanging out in the clouds, under the stars, hovering over a world filled with migrants, theirs for the taking. A success story.

Dog Days

The day begins like every other, an early sun through her kitchen window, gurgling of the coffee pot, its warm dark smell. If only she could've known this was it, right there, as good as it gets. Maybe then, when she stared at her husband's photo on the sideboard, she would've thought *yes, this is the day we move on*, taken the photo and placed it in the boxes of his things she had stuck in the attic. Someday, he would pick these up, then all traces of him would be gone.

Around this pummeled land, people have been losing jobs. Did she glance at the morning paper and see that her neighbor's house up the road had been foreclosed on, just the latest of this sort of thing? First the mills close, manufacturing dries up; then businesses go, Lockheed Martin loses contract after contract, and there are people who have to move away just to eat. Once upon a time, this was the cigar-making capital of America. Not a lot of that around here anymore, decent cigars or capital of anything. Sometimes they can't take their dogs when they move, new rental, no pets allowed. Sometimes they can't afford them anymore. Does the toddler get a meal or Spot? Sometimes they're just so beaten down by it all, they don't give a damn about the dog, the kids, themselves.

A middle-aged woman, hair the color of concrete when she neglected to dye it, which was often since her husband left, what's the point? He was the one who liked her to look a certain way, not that she ever hit upon the winning combination—makeup, hair, the Thighmaster; none of it was enough in the end.

So maybe a year or two, she cheated on her taxes, nothing too terrible—she never made enough money to really matter, a cashier at the Rite Aid. But those years when John tried to start his own business, Meg claimed the laptops they bought for their daughters as part of it.

She had a past no one would expect. The disco years, a kind of nighttime abandon, and Meg and her friends used to pick up men in bars and take them home. She gave all that up to wake next to John.

Two daughters and her greatest guilt, the thing that gnawed at her, was loving one better than the other. No one intends for this, but all else being equal, one was just easier to love, with her teacher husband and golden-haired child and every-other-week Sunday dinners with Meg, all of them together. The other was probably a lesbian. Not that Meg would hold this against her. But still. She's more brittle, her smile less easy, harder won. Doesn't call often, and when she does Meg can hear it, the hint of something sour, reproachful, the unspoken accusation always hovering between them, that Meg wasn't quite good enough. The older daughter. *The practice child* her own mother used to say. Like learning to play the piano—the concert is the second child.

Still no one would say she deserved it, this loneliness. And Meg tried. The Christmases where she made sure everything was even down to the last penny. If one got just a tad more, why Meg would take a pair of earrings out of that one's stocking and slip them into the other. She kept track of the things she bought the girls, and John, too, in a little notebook—the prices she paid, value to the receiver (if one of them requested a certain item that always counted more) versus resale value, a sort of Blue Book for gifts. If one of them had more to open, it was because her sister's were more expensive—and Meg would make sure they both understood this.

Fair she was, as fair as she knew to be. It was just that little stone in her heart, the secret she kept hidden like the pansies from a mostly forgotten boyfriend pressed between the pages of a rarely read book—one of them loved just a little more.

A few miles up the road from Meg's pristine place is an older house with a slumped, defeated-looking porch, and this is where the dog named King used to live. The alpha dog, appropriately named—canines, a noble creature, animals who eat and sleep and play and love and will be loyal to that which gives them love, and even when it doesn't—more than what most humans would put up with. It was Meg, after all, who told John to leave, bringing the scent of the other into their bed, and she decided enough was enough. He couldn't have his cake and eat it, too, as this would defy that essential fairness Meg needed to believe in. Clearly, she couldn't believe in her husband anymore.

King didn't get to decide these things. First the steel mill shut, but that was expected, then there was the camera equipment factory, until that closed too. King's man tried sales at the Home Depot, he knew about tools and what to do with them, but the economy slid down even more, and people stopped fixing up their houses or lost their houses altogether, and the man was let go. For a while, he drove the hour and a half to Corning for a factory job making CorningWare, but his truck broke, and when that was fixed the gas hit sky-high, and he started missing one day a week just to save on the cost of getting there. When his truck broke down again—first the distributor and then the transmission went, it was always something—they gave his job to someone who lived five minutes away. He started to drink a little, just to pass the time, then a little more. His wife got sick, they didn't have health insurance, and the chemo would cost more for six weeks than the man could collect from unemployment in ten years. She stopped cooking their food, and then there was no food, or not enough of the right kind of food, and the boy, their son, stayed away more and more, going to a friend's house where he could get a sandwich at least, a piece of meat, something other than a handful of chips and a bowl of Corn Pops.

On top of all this the dog. King was his wife's really, who had brought him home from Pet Mart one day. He would've never picked out an animal that big. Not those yappy little powder puffs pretending to be dogs, but one in between—one who wouldn't eat you out of house and home, and now there wasn't even enough people food. The dog was always begging for whatever the man brought to the couch, he's trying to relax, watch a game on TV and the damn beast underfoot or whining to be fed. Plus it stank. His wife couldn't bathe him anymore, so who the hell was going to step up to the plate and wash a dog the size of a goddamn bear?

One late afternoon when the boy finally came home, the man, who had been drinking all day, strapped the whimpering King to the railing, the porch with its sagging steps (why should the man do anything about them, the house is a rental and the landlord could give a shit, and besides if one of them fell through he could sue the fucker!), tied up so tightly with a rope the color of butterscotch that the whimpering became a howling, and that howling was driving the man crazy. Plus there wasn't a scrap of kibble in the house; how the hell was he supposed to keep feeding this damn beast, part Lab, part everything *huge*. The man shook his head, scratched his neck viciously, stared up at the clay-colored sky, and cursed.

Then he ordered the boy to take King to the river. At first, the boy tried to refuse, but the man whacked him between his shoulder blades, practically knocking him over, then threw a sharp smack across his face, snarling, "Take! That! Beast! To the river, now!" Told him to use a boulder, tie the rope around it. "Drowning's a mercy," the man said.

The boy led King deep into the woods, sniffling, rubbing his swollen cheek. His father didn't hit him much, but when he did it was without any awareness of flesh, flesh of my flesh, the father's own reborn in the son; he may as well be slamming his fist into a wall. Probably it was King tugging him along, eager for the walk, to be away from that house and the man. The boy untied the rope, slipped off his collar, and trying not to look at him, not to think of it, what had to be done, told the dog to go. Still loyal at this point, King would know better, he's supposed to stay with this boy, but then the boy starts pelting him with rocks, sticks, fallen tree branches, anything he can find, tears streaming down his face, hiccupping, coughing, "Go, Goddamnit, go!" King yelped a couple times, and the boy began beating him, something killed inside him every time he hit his dog, but he's scared if he doesn't and King follows him home, then maybe his father will drown them both. King squeals, cries, looks bewildered then finally, slowly, turns and takes off, deeper into the woods, his lopsided run, a pain in his hip from where the man kicked him, but in time this will go away. The pain in his heart though, what he can't articulate, can't understand, love gone bad, the betrayal of this—will not go away but will be usurped by that greater need for food. An empty belly versus an empty heart, the belly inevitably wins.

The rest came over the weeks, months, what is time in an abandoned dog's life, no longer leading it to the rhythm of the household, no longer a household. Some driven to the woods in cars and forced out, others left behind when their family moved away, a house abandoned, weeds clawing at the door stoop where one dozed listlessly in the unrelenting August sun when her people inside stopped opening the door. They all found King, or King found them. A social creature, pack animal, the dog is not meant to live alone.

Meg didn't have an opinion about dogs, never had one as a child—her mother claimed they were too messy—and John preferred cats, so the girls had cats. The ones her friends owned she petted politely, wishing fervently they wouldn't jump up on her. Occasionally she played fetch with her neighbor's dog, Suzy, who snuck into her yard sometimes, tail wagging back and forth like a tassel of corn, bearing a Frisbee or a tennis ball or stick of some sort. Wasn't that what you were supposed to do, throw it so the dog could claim it, then bring it back? "Suzy!" The neighbor called, and the dog (a golden retriever her neighbor told her, what did Meg know?) would go running home, and Meg's obligation was over. Suzy. She had read that pet owners these days were giving them human names, those who could afford to love pets this way, to make them part of their family. Meg's neighbor even arranged play dates for Suzy, and if she was good—which invariably she was, how much mischief could a doted-upon dog get into, Meg wondered, it wasn't like having daughters who came home after curfew, dated the wrong boys or didn't date boys at all—Suzy got to gnaw on the steak bones whenever they barbecued.

No fetch left in King and his pack, no play, and certainly no barbeque. Life was lived raw. If you bear something in your mouth it's to determine if it's edible, for the others to tear into after you've had yours; every stomach an ache, a howl, a chasm, something to be filled.

She loved, yes, but maybe not enough. The lesbian daughter, and to be honest the other's child with her golden curls (Goldilocks, her father called her) was pretty, sure, but not very smart, not even reading yet at almost seven years old and the father a teacher. She had told her daughter to set her sights higher; he wasn't even a high school teacher, who opts for seventh grade? Not that Meg had ever amounted to much, but at least she had the good sense to marry up, as her own mother called it, a Sears department store manager, something with promise. Twelve years later, when the branch closed, John tried to start his own retail business (sports equipment, pretty ridiculous in retrospect—it wasn't like John was any kind of an athlete; he watched sports on TV and figured everyone else around here did, too, which was the problem—they'd rather watch than participate). When this didn't work he was hired at a bank. The business degree, and he looked sharp in a suit. Meg could've gone back to school, had thought about it sometimes, but the girls had needs, and John made enough; they weren't rich by any means but they got by. Her money from Rite Aid was for treats, extras for the girls, ballet lessons, soccer team, summer camp, a wedding. Even after he moved out John still paid the bills, *blood money* Meg called it when she griped to her friends. The turn of her mouth, bit of a leer, the bitter taste that snuck down her throat when she imagined it, John with someone else.

The women who made the discovery were Jehovah's Witnesses, the one leading the other, first time witnessing, spreading the Good News and truly uncomfortable, the August afternoon so stifling you could see it, heat hanging in the valley like fallout. Lorna in her plain, black skirt, mid-calf length, the white tucked-in blouse Judy insisted needed to be buttoned at the neck, and nylons. Who wears nylons anymore? She's just a girl, eighteen and a little cranky. Her parents made her do this, after they caught her *tipsy*, their word for the giggly, mushy way she felt sneaking home after a glass of plum wine and some puffs off a marijuana pipe with her new friend Jasmine, who called the pipe a *bowl*. This was the condition for staying in their house, for not being shunned. Where else would she go? It's not like there were any jobs around here, or apartments she could afford. She wasn't a bad girl. She believed in God and the 144,000 anointed who will live with him in heaven. She just didn't want to do it, was all, knock on the doors and listen to Judy over and over try to convince the belligerent people who stuck their scowling faces out, that here was the answer, in *The Watchtower* magazine—if you just let us in we will talk about how *you* can be one of the saved. Lorna wanted them to do it, prayed for it, let them in so she could cool off, even for just a minute. Maybe they'd offer them a glass of water? Or a Coke! Lord, what she wouldn't have done for an ice-cold Coke, hot as it was. Forget the Coke-Zero stuff; she'd take hers with full-on sugar, thank you very much. Many of the houses were poor looking, shingles missing, in need of paint, siding hanging. What could they get from *The Watchtower*, no promise that things would get better, not now anyway. Salvation doesn't come with a job. From some of the houses dogs growled and barked at them, and these they left alone.

Cicadas and crickets hummed from the trees and swatches of weeds at the side of the road, wasps and all manner of buzzing, whirring things the size of little helicopters dive-bombed their heads; they were chewed on by gnats, a horsefly bit Lorna's neck and she scraped bits of cobweb off her face from having walked through one on the overgrown path from the last house, batting at her hair in case the spider was in it.

"Good grief!" Lorna wailed. "It's like these bugs know it's August and next month they'll die, so get all they can in now."

Judy shrugged. "Everything dies," she said. "It's a matter of who is saved." The August air blazed with heat.

Lorna scratched her leg, those sticky, sweltering nylons, and imagined herself in the river, the place she secretly went to swim at night sometimes, an inlet where things were calmer, the currents swirled further out and when the moon lit a path in the water she would take off her clothes and float in it, dreaming of her future—she hadn't figured out where yet, didn't know enough about other places really—but it would be as far away from here as she could get. Was it worth it, the pipe and that plum wine? Lorna shook her head, her needle-thin hair the color of bone and parted in the middle, framing her peevish face. The wine came from Japan, Jasmine had said, pink as a cat's tongue and too sweet, like guzzling cough syrup. The marijuana made Lorna cough.

They might've knocked on King's former door, the porch steps so profoundly sloped Judy would hesitate a moment before walking on them. But this is what it means to be faithful to one's calling, and she would've taken the reluctant Lorna's sweating hand and headed up. You cannot pick and choose your flock.

By then King's former man would be drunk, the middle of the afternoon and he's had it with everything. He'd taken his wife to the County Hospital's emergency room yet again, since that's the only place they'll treat her without insurance. This time he just left her there; what's the point in waiting? They won't see her for another six hours at least. They stuck her in a room, put her on oxygen since the cancer's gotten so bad in her lungs she wheezes and chokes every time she takes a breath. She can't talk, and he can't smoke in there, what's the use?

Once upon a time he wasn't the man he is now. Filled with as much hope as the next guy for a future that never materialized, but for a while he could still see it, glimmering like an iridescent bubble, floating just out of his reach. Not happiness exactly, he wouldn't be so presumptuous, but something like contentment, bills paid, food in the fridge, everybody feeling OK. He played with Transformers as a child, kissed a girl for the first time when he was fifteen, made passable grades until he dropped out—school wasn't really his thing; had a job in the afternoons sweeping out the neighborhood Quickstop, mopping the floors, stocking the shelves; went steady with Trish Walters then married her; it was the right thing to do, when she got pregnant. Things just finally got to him, the way they add up, no more jobs, the truck that won't start when you need it to, Trish's cancer, no insurance, the sullen boy who gazed at him with such goddamn reproach, and the neighbors with their humongous flat-screen HD TV—seems like if one's got to suffer they all should, and they shouldn't be flaunting it, the TV, the new SUV, which no doubt they bought into a shitload of debt to own. Once in a while he thinks of the dog. Trish asked him and he told her it just disappeared. Sometimes there are moments of regret—he can feel it in his gut, curdling. Once he even threw up. The doorbell, along with everything else is broken, so if the women made it up the steps they'd knock, and if King were here he would've barked and growled and scared the bejesus out of them, and they'd be out of his hair. As it is he'll have to get up off the couch where he'd sprawled in a stupor from the heat, and tell them to fuck off—he has no use for what they're selling.

The boy too, might've been there. He's lived in terror that King would show up one day, forgetting what was done to him, thinking it could still be his home. Then his father straps them both to a boulder and rolls them into the river. He has nightmares about this. He can't look at his father anymore without seeing that potential for cruelty. And with his mother probably dying, who will he have to love him? Sometimes in his nightmares King comes home to him emaciated, ribs sticking out like piano keys, even dead once and he woke up sobbing, knowing it's his fault. He never hit anything before hitting that dog. He's not a boy who hits things; rather he's one who is hit, his shoulders small and shaped like a girl's and his shag of black hair that his mother used to cut; now she can't trust herself with scissors, never knowing when the racking cough that sends tremors through her whole body will strike. He's learned to lay low, and he does have some friends—none of them at their school are from families doing well enough that they can afford to humiliate others who are not.

He needn't have worried. King won't be coming back.

When the women moved on, down the dusty road, cicadas chattering from the trees on either side, something shiny caught Lorna's eye. A watch, delicate gold links and a rectangular face with Roman numerals, the clasp hanging open like a yawn. She picked it up, and holding it next to her ear she could hear its ticking, the kind of old-fashioned watch that needed to be wound. The time was correct, 2:24. A little farther, through the Queen Anne's lace by the roadside, she noticed how the thorny blackberry bushes and tangles of weeds were bent over and flattened, forming a trail of sorts leading into a clearing. Judy tried to hold Lorna back, clawing at her arm. "Dear Christ!" she whispered, slapping her hand over her mouth as Lorna stared into the tar-colored eyes of a huge black dog, with as many as a dozen or more behind him, crouched over what looked like a hoodie, cerise pink with glitter on the sleeves. The dog, baring its teeth let out a low, throaty growl, warning Lorna not to come any closer.

By late afternoon, the town's animal-control officer along with the police department and the Humane Society had corralled the dogs, tested them for rabies, secured them in crates at the County Animal Shelter, where an effort would be made to "rehabilitate" them—but given their feral condition, they might prove unrehabilitable and would then have to be euthanized, a spokesperson from the shelter warned. The hoodie was tagged, then sent off to the forensic lab, where it would be identified as having belonged to the girl who vanished from the former IBM parking lot. Strands of her hair were embedded in the sweatshirt's hood, but other DNA swabs were inconclusive: no body fluids, human prints, bloodstains or evidence of foul play, the report would state, though noting a multitude of canine teeth marks. Inappropriate chewing is common in untrained dogs, the shelter spokesperson said; if they were someone's pets they would've had toys or a bone. The police scoured the area, yellow-taped the surrounding properties, but found no trace of the girl or indication she had ever been there.

Later that night in the basement bedroom of her parents' home, Lorna would take her mother's sewing shears and shred the black skirt, the white blouse, knotting her stockings around the tattered strips of clothing—those disgusting nylons still stinking of her damp swollen feet and the heat of the afternoon—dangling all of it along with the roadside watch, from a hook in her ceiling like a noose.

Perhaps, when Meg walked out that morning, it was with just a bit of hope. Fastened the watch around her wrist, squeezing the clasp—it had fallen off before and she would hate to lose it (John gave it to her, first Christmas together and it still worked), her wrist that was as thin and light as when he married her. *Sparrow*, John used to call her, his little sparrow. An hour before she was due at Rite Aid meant an hour that belonged to her. The morning wasn't hot yet, the smell of the heat to come in the air, but the air still good, breathable, twittering of birds, the crickets, a fine August day. As she strolled along the unpaved road, maybe she was thinking of ways to spend her paycheck; the golden-haired child's birthday was coming up, what would she like? What could Meg give her granddaughter that might, somehow, make a difference?

Erosion

2008

Marty the shoes guy assures me he likes it rough. "So hit me!" I demand, straddling him on a table in the Kmart stock room stacked with boxes of New Balance athletic shoes, size baby all the way up to a gargantuan 14 E, Bigfoot on steroids. A tower of boxes slides to the floor. I've just slammed three shots of Jose Cuervo from a bottle Marty hid behind some desert boots, and apparently I'll have to prove I'm serious. So I do it, haul off and slug his begging-for-a-shave chin and for a moment he looks surprised—I'd like to think because I've got a good arm, trained as it was from having to defend my autistic cousin when we were kids. Marty's face the color of a condom flushes a splotchy, lipsticky red. Then he punches me back in the cheek, *kapow* and we're off, me popping him in the mouth, his hands squeezing my neck until I'm coughing, gagging, and it progresses from there, him ripping my shirt off, which I told him he could do, the buttons I said (I can sew those back on) not the fabric. We're in retail for chrissake and nobody's buying these days, and I don't have the kind of bank account that says sure, go ahead and trash a silk blouse for fifteen minutes of break-time fun. "I wanna tear the whore's clothes off!" he slurs, like this is supposed to be seductive, chomping down on my earlobe. We're playacting, Marty calling me his whore and he's my dog; not exactly Shakespeare but what can you expect after two more shots of gold and no script?

Later at home after surveying the damage in the bathroom mirror, spaghetti-sauce-colored cheek, bite marks on my ear, the collar of finger-shaped bruises around my neck, a confetti of black-and-blue and yellowy-green marks up and down my arms, I tell Jake I had a bike accident to explain it all, the bruises, torn shirt, the post-Tequila despair. And he buys it, or anyway doesn't question me. Decent of him, since we don't own bikes, which meant I had to invent another story to support the original: that I borrowed a bike from a coworker. Tequila does this, fuzzying my brain so I can't even contrive a logical lie. We're not the biking type, Jake and me; they're skinny as popsicles, their holier-than-thou attitudes taking up half the road even after the town goes and chalks in a special little lane just for them. Plus I look a horror in spandex. Spandex demands no hips and I've got childbearing ones, wasted on me since it seems I will never have a child.

That's what I was thinking when Marty invited me to have sex with him on our break. Better for you than candy bars or a smoke, he winked, like I was some kind of a health-nut and this the deal breaker. We're the late shift, Tuesday night, deadest of the week, nobody around. Made a mental calculation of the time of the month ovulation-wise, figured if Marty got me pregnant then I'd know for certain it was Jake's fault. Cuervo-fueled thinking but there it was.

"You do realize they have medical procedures for this kind of thing?" Kandi, our coworker sniffed, rolling her eyes when I told her my plan, asking her to keep a watch out. "They'd probably do a blood test, Nora, and your husband whacks off in a Dixie-cup." But she was in favor of it anyway, said women should be free as men to have meaningless hookups they'd regret in the morning.

But let's get down to the nitty gritty. When Marty hit me I liked it. Even more than I liked hitting him. I liked hitting him because he's an idiot who deserves for someone to pop him every time he opens his mouth, but *getting* hit, the sting of another's flesh against mine, there's something personal in it. Take last week when I stapled my finger accidentally to a scowling lady's receipt for her bullets-sized push-up bra. Blood sluicing all over hell and creation, I paged Kandi in *Women's Sportswear* to key up the register for a duplicate copy, but secretly I was into it, the slickness of that blood coupled with the sting of metal in fingertip flesh. It's concrete. A change in the physicality of things when you can't change anything else.

I've got what you could call a retail history. Sold shoes at Payless, linens at Sears, home goods at Kohl's, cosmetics at Bradlees right before they went bankrupt, stock girl at JCPenney, accessories at Walmart, cheap jewelry, and prior to this Kmart lingerie gig I was a floater at the Dollar Store, where Julie the manager catches me lurking among the analgesics, stuffing a bottle of ibuprofen into my jacket. I had a headache that wouldn't quit and figured I was owed the pain killers, since being there as "service" to the whiners and bitchers who slunk in looking for the ultimate cheap laundry soap, and why if it says *Dollar* Store does Tide sell for $5.99? caused the throbbing in the first place. I was invited to leave on a permanent basis but not before I pilfered a jar of cocktail peanuts, popping off the plastic lid, yanking back the foil and snaking a handful into my mouth.

After my mom left it was cherries, not the fresh kind, but maraschinos, the dye-covered ones that reportedly cause cancer, and I'd pinch a jar from Giant where I bagged groceries, slip it into my backpack and on the bus home grab a front seat all to myself, twist open the lid and love would happen on my tongue, down my throat, my teeth stained red with the cancerous evidence. When my autistic cousin was with me I'd give him half, but mostly he liked olives, sticking them on his fingers so it looked like he had fat black fingernails, and on days when the bus stopped at the after-school program for the special kids, I'd make sure to lift him a can of these too.

Once a languid size two, extra-long "associate" I worked with at Kohl's told me how when she stood really still people thought she was a mannequin. She liked to startle them, she said, by blinking. She liked to just stand there and inhale the crisp scent of new clothing. Not me. I'm all about food, the greasier smelling the better. Anyway, they don't make mannequins squat and sullen. "You're smart enough," my dad told me, when I bitched about the serial store jobs during one of our weekly phone calls, "but you have no gumption. Gumption gets the good work," he said. What I wanted was a baby.

SNAPSHOT: 2007, THE *last year when the silence between Jake and me wasn't loaded with blame: Whose fault is it? Whose problem is it? Whose body is failing? That year the little, yellow house we rented for a week every June on Hunting Island, South Carolina, still looked out over a big-enough beach, summer in the air and everyone's lives still whole. Jake and me in the futon bed on the screened-in porch, our last good sex, ocean rocking outside, and it wasn't about baby-making, what became a clocked and calendar-relegated duty. It was love.*

    I watched this show on *NOVA* once where some scientist said that bodies in space keep moving away from each other, and that for unknown reasons the pace of this has been accelerating. Dark energy is thought to cause this, he said, though scientists don't know exactly what that is, this force that pulls things away from each other faster and faster.

2009

THERE'S A MOMENT when the glob of sun on the horizon seems like it could go either way, rise into daylight or cut its losses and bail, the way it hangs like a question mark just above the sea. Her house glows in the weird light, the sun glimmering into the plate-glass window where I've seen her peer out, white hair knotted on the top of her head, the windowsill filled with shells and ceramic sculptures of gulls stuck on driftwood stands. Lottie Stein. A Jewish name, my mom would've pointed out, the chosen ones, she'd always add. I never got that. A bevy of travails from the Bible on throughout the rest of recorded history. If this was what being *chosen* meant, I'd vote for slipping under the radar. Apparently my mom never felt chosen, not even by my dad who married her when she got pregnant with my sister, and so she chose to leave us.

At one point Lottie Stein's house was painted an egg-yolk gold, Jake told me, to emulate the sun he figured. Jake's like that, proposing theory as fact, as if saying it makes it so. Like how he justifies his job: Transition Man, he calls himself, for IBM. I've started feeling like the enemy just being married to him, even though all he really did was not get fired. So now he's doing the firing, out-sourcing the work to places like India and the Philippines where they pay the workers eight bucks a day. "Somebody has to survive," Jake said. "Besides," he said, "it's what makes it possible for us to come here." Hunting Island, where Jake used to summer as a child, *a barrier island with such extreme erosion accelerated by global warming and pollution that scientists have determined it will disappear in 120 years.* I got that straight off a pamphlet from the State Park headquarters. They built groins along their state beaches to hold on to at least some of the sand, but where the houses are the people are on their own. Jake is the only guy I know whose childhood involved using the noun *summer* as a verb, an action, a way of life. "Don't worry, we'll always land on our feet," Jake told me, after I lost the Dollar Store job. He was blessed with good ones, feet that never had to climb a hill every morning, watching for a mother to come back. "Just because you're looking for her doesn't mean you'll find her," my father warned. Jake was born into a family that argued about which movie to go to on "Family Day."

Lottie Stein. Wasn't Lot some biblical character, the one whose wife was turned into a pillar of salt just for being curious and looking back? "She's got staying power," Jake said. Her house surrounded by the ocean at high tide, waves lashing the pylons as they come roaring in and she's inside. I think Jake would like to rescue Lottie, those storms in the fall with the big waves, like the hurricane that stalled off the coast and fifteen foot waves smashed the island for three days wiping out the little yellow house we used to rent; all that was left was its deck and the webbed chair I put on it to lounge in the sun, a cold one in the cup holder, watching the dolphins cruise by. Soon the deck will go too and the only sign that a home was there will be its septic system, a concrete block in the sand.

Lottie Stein has been on Hunting Island since Jake started coming as a child, same old woman refusing to leave. He wants to sail in like a hero when the waves bring down her house and bear Lottie to dry land, since even her own son couldn't get her to move, attaching a retractable ladder that could be hauled up during high tide then let down again during low so she could go out and get food. She's got a generator for her lights and a portable compost potty—*the comforts of home*, the realtor we rent from told us.

Jake is always trying to save something, right down to the ants on the drain board, rescuing the ones that fall into the dishwater by dropping in the dishcloth like a lifeboat so they can crawl on it, attracted by their tiny struggle, that something smaller than the half moon on his pinky fingernail could want life this badly, hoisting their segmented little heads above the water like miniature buoys. The *positive spin*, he calls his way of looking at the world; the way he still pretends any month it could happen, our child, despite the hysterical pregnancy, our doctor labeled it in a whispered conversation to Jake, but I heard all right, my uterus a balloon, nothing in it but air. Every monthly bleed a small death.

Snapshot: 2009, another *house wiped out in a storm surge, only a blue canvas chair and a Formica table remain. Somebody sat at that table, vase of peonies on it or a bowl of fruit, the newspaper, a cup of morning coffee. House next to it gone, four pylons poking up in the sand, smattering of wires, a broken pipe, the fleshy leg of a doll.*

Each time we come back here the sea has taken more: sheds, porches, sinks, toilets, bathtubs, recliners, coffee tables, sofas, bunk beds, linen chests, kitchenettes, whole houses, ransacked. We come in June, the minute school is over and the girl I work with at the Bon Ton, my job this year, can cover for me. She's one of the lucky ones; most of the high schoolers waste their summers, or spend their summers wasted, since mostly these days there are no jobs. Jake knows about this. At first "downsized" from IBM he hit the road selling semiconductors out of the trunk of his Chevy Cavalier. "We'll get by," he said, and we did. Then they invite him back, the Transition Man. One of the people he fired was that poor woman whose daughter a couple months later disappears from their deserted parking lot. Kidnapped, I think, they don't just walk away having a mother who loves them, that's something, isn't it? The boy she was with said she just *uppedandgone* from the empty lot. Mid-afternoon, that parking lot should've been full.

Neither of us felt like shopping today and so we are stuck with the remnants of the refrigerator, partly ours, the rest from a history of renters. First I tear into the pretzels and when these are done I plunder the tortilla chips. After a while it's not enough to have them plain despite the salty tang, a salsa is in order and of course there's no fresh tomatoes so forget the homemade—a jar of almost empty Verde *hot*! it warns but it'll do if I mix it with a little catsup, have to hold the bottle down and squeeze it with pliers to get the humidity-gelled goop at the bottom out. When this is gone I tackle the Smart Balance, because Jake accused me of buying two of them—"Two!" he said—like why do we even need one? Slather it on the chips and if they break just stuff them in my mouth by the handfuls, after which whatever isn't nailed down in the fridge with the rest of our bottle of Chardonnay. "Nothing for me, thanks," Jake says, shooting me his injured look.

Later we'll pretend, as we have every evening since arriving, that I am going to look for some other kind of work on Craigslist, my hours at the Bon-Ton slashed almost to the point of no return. "You have two years toward a college degree," Jake said, "so go for something besides retail." That's an example of positive spin. I say

I *dropped out* after two years of college, though neither description guarantees a job. And since there's no Wi-Fi on the island this involves driving to the Beaufort library, stuffed to the gills, having to leave my jeans unbuttoned. Last week before school was officially out for the summer, Anna Drew, one of the remedial girls the Bon-Ton hires at minimum wage, poked her dyed tomato-red head into the squirrel hole of a break room where I sat at the lunch table sobbing. She studied me while I tried to snuffle it up, cough into a handkerchief, pretend, I don't know, allergies?

"You get splotches on your neck when you cry," she observed. "My mom does too. Is that an older woman's thing?"

"Who said I was crying?" I snapped. And then in an uncharacteristic display of honesty (I'm sure it would be described that way but I mean really, she's an eleventh grader, she'll forget in two minutes since it's not about her, and anyway it's not even true): "Fine, OK, I'm thinking about leaving my husband," I told her. What is truth anyway? Do I tell her I'm empty and dried-up as the Mojave, so even though I don't know for sure why I cry, this is *probably* why I cry? That it's Jake who should leave me, get with someone who can fulfill her evolutionary role and bear him Jake junior?

"You could blog it," she shrugged, didn't even miss a beat. "There's this website that lets you post the minute to minute of personal tragedies, and if you get enough hits they might even pay you."

"I'm going to go cull the racks," I told her, which is retail-speak for ferreting through the racks of size-segregated clothing searching for anything that's been put back in the wrong category, a Medium masquerading in the Smalls, heaven forbid. Or worse, a Petite hanging out with the Big Girls, the ones with Xs on their tags.

Instead of a job search I waddle down to the beach. The misshapen moon looks like a glob of moisturizer through a spray of clouds, the tide low and the night dark enough where I can walk out in front of Lottie's house and stare into her window without her seeing me. What could I say anyway that would make a potential employer consider me over the neverending parade of Anna Drews waiting in the wings, younger, more malleable, fruitful? I'm the coral reefs dying, the hole in the ozone, pollution, drought, the planet's bad news.

Removing my spyglasses from their case I attempt to peer inside, a bit daunting, involving tiptoes and a stork's balance. Since erosion has ferreted away so much sand, Lottie's one-story home is now a second story with the inner workings exposed, twisted pipes, dangling wires, clumps of insulation, like having your organs turned inside out, the pylons holding it up are the bones. Towering a foot over me that extra-long "associate" I worked with, destined for a life imitating mannequins, might have managed this easier.

Battered by waves the sand is swept into the St. Helena current and deposited across the sound on the rich people's beaches of Fripp Island, where they vote to do nothing about the erosion on Hunting since it's improving their coast. Because of this there are mutations on the island, years of inbreeding, a shrinking of what land the animals had to share. An Australian-looking creature was spotted lounging in the dirt road accessible only by golf cart now, the asphalt washed away by the sea, chunks of it peppering the sand, sludge where once there were sedans. The thing just sat there, humpbacked and kangaroo-like with teeth. A black raccoon, the park ranger called it, a cover-up Jake thinks. *Black raccoons, an albino one, mangy deer that walk right up for a handout, skinny as rats. Pelicans cruising long beaked as pterodactyls, black shadows of their wings as they patrol the coast, kamikaze dives into the sea. In the end the ocean will win and everything is perishable except honey.* I learned that from Jake. Although honeybees are also bailing. "Colony collapse disorder," he said, "most likely caused by the pesticides folks use to have weed-free lawns."

Last night curling up together in bed (he reaches for me but we don't do *it* anymore, *it* became too much about defeat), Jake speculated if humans finally cause their own extinction and only birds and insects are left, would birds evolve into dinosaurs again and eventually people? Or would it stop right there, the birds and the bugs, wiser this time around, knowing the planet was doomed if we took over again.

"So much for the positive spin," I whispered, as he drifted off to sleep. Still, I can't imagine waking up next to anyone but Jake. What does sex mean in the long haul? I want a more practiced intimacy, like the older couple Jake and I saw in a hospital elevator after visiting Jake's brother, who was recovering from a car accident. He was pushing her in a wheelchair and she was haggard looking but sort of beautiful too, a kind of dignity in the way she sat, shoulder blades snake-thin but straight. She probably just had chemo; he kept handing her that pink kidney-shaped vomit-bowl hospitals use. She'd do this unapologetically, handing the bowl back to her husband who emptied its contents into a bigger container. Then they'd do it again, like some strange dance, his eyes locked into hers, waiting for her cue.

I watch Lottie through her window and I see she isn't afraid. Photos of her family line the wall behind where she sits, knitting maybe? Why do we always picture old ladies knitting? What if she's reading—*Moby Dick*, Jake might think it, the right fit for this. The black raccoon curled up in a tree in her yard, the mangy young buck she feeds apples to, broccoli from her own stash, food brought up the ladder at low tide, cooked later with the ocean surging around her house. Maybe this evening the mangy one brought along his pregnant friend, a doe about to have her fawn, and Lottie slips back into the kitchen for another apple.

Waves rising, roaring, thrashing, chewing up the sand then spitting it out into the St. Helena current, bearing the contents from gutted houses hunched in the moonlight like ghosts: dishes from one, linens, a bed frame, chairs and tables off decks that held court over a golden beach, refrigerators, microwaves, coolers, sunscreen, mosquito repellant, hoses where once there were gardens, all making their way to the St. Helena Sound, every tide going higher as the ice caps melt, the sea warms, polar bears disappear, or maybe one washes up on

this island someday, little bump in the ocean, returned to its state
when no people lived on it and they came from the mainland to kill
its animals, Hunting Island. Would they take him out too, this last
polar bear?

I see her, white hair glowing in the moonlight, floating out with
the current the way a leaf does, like how I used to imagine my bed
would, sailing away, first alone, then with Jake, then alone again,
or maybe with Jake. Maybe we'll make it to the Heaven of the Lost,
where the missing go, like the girl who disappeared from the parking
lot, and our babies who might've been, tiny eggs like perfect bubbles,
untouched, unbroken, their DNA uncharted, their histories clean.

Jam the buckle from the spyglasses case into the palm of my
hand; in the morning there will be a heart-shaped wound.

2010

JAKE AND I hike up a hill in our neighborhood to watch some meteor
shower he read about, but the sky just keeps getting brighter and
one by one the stars wink out. I figured it was something celestial
but Jake says no, it's the damn halogen lights they shine on the
high-school football field, illuminating the night. I snuggle closer
to him, stare up like there's something to see. Think about having
sex with him, just for the hell of it, ask him to rough me up a little,
or maybe I could hit him to get us started. But that's not who Jake
is and it's not who we are together. "I like the ocean better anyway,"
I tell Jake. "The sky can be kind of empty."

During my junior year of high school my dad sent me to live
with my sister in Portland, Maine, an ocean city, said there'd be
more opportunities for me there—my mother would not be coming
back, and me climbing that hill to look for her just reminded him
of what he'd lost. I knew after a week of doing it I would not see her
blueberry-colored Honda round the curve below on its approach,
but somehow felt if I stopped pretending it was possible, the thing

that was breaking apart in my dad would shatter, so I kept climbing that hill. I stole my mom's jewelry before I left, what she didn't pack and take with her. Probably he would've given it to me if I asked. Split half of it with Lauren; to my knowledge neither of us has ever worn it.

Lauren had a new baby and a friend with a withered arm, who also had a new baby, plus a toddler. I wanted to know what happened to her arm and my sister frowned. "You don't ask things like that, Nora, but probably her mother took thalidomide for morning sickness when she was pregnant. It mutated their babies' limbs," she said. Her friend's baby came down with meningitis and she asked Lauren to take care of the older child so she could stay in the hospital with the sick one. Lauren said of course, but then she's terrified to let the little girl come near her baby for fear she might have it too. One night the child cried and cried and Lauren shut her own bedroom door, her and her husband and their baby inside, so I went to the little girl and held her, her hot little body against mine; I hugged her and whispered things to her and when she finally fell asleep I curled up beside her.

SNAPSHOT: HUNTING, 2010—THIS *house was once on the other side of the road, but when all those other houses washed away it became beachfront, a taxable yard flowing down to the sand. Then the road cracks apart in a raging storm and it's 180 degrees of oceanfront, yard gone and in its place lashed together trees and sandbags.*

On April 20 the Deepwater Horizon explodes, killing eleven workers and creating the worst oil spill in United States history. Pictures of the dying marshes, poisoned sea life, green and blue herons slathered in oil, dolphins smothered, breathing it in through their blowholes, drives me to tears; seeing those quivering, tar-slicked pelicans I want to do serious damage to the people responsible for this. But, who am I kidding. I seem to only know how to damage myself. Maybe my dad was right about me lacking *gumption.*

I do it all the time now, pins in my extremities, razors working the soft flesh at my hips, Jake's lighter tanning the tender parts of my underarms. He started smoking again; where's the positive spin in this? He had stopped when we read that smoking affects a man's sperm count, but then we found out the problem wasn't him. He can control it, he says, a quarter pack a day. The sad thing about this is he will.

Struck up a conversation with a clown at a rest stop off Route 81, one of those needful whims. I was headed to South Carolina. He was on his way to a kid's birthday and drunk as a skunk at his fate, he said, having to make a living as some brat's entertainment. After he left in his VW with a mechanical clown head on the roof I imagined what it would be like if he stayed. A tryst in the woods behind the bathrooms? Would he have tried to make *me* laugh? Something about having a nose light up, snorting *honk honk* as he goes down on you . . . And thinking about this did make me laugh, hysteria more like it, I couldn't stop and it was knifing my sides, straddling my chest, my eyes going all teary as I imagined the clown gazing amorously at me, his eyes with their spikes of fire-engine-red-painted lashes. *Hit me, hit me, hit me.*

Jobless now, except for the envelopes I address at home, stuffing them with flyers for the self-employed consultant up the street so she can do more essential things, like figure out who owes her what, I slipped away early to Hunting this year, before Jake, to what will be the last time in this house, the last time *for* the house, the ocean crashing up against the barrier wall of dead palmetto palms they bulldozed into a pile and lashed together with cables, along with the 10,000 sandbags to hold the water back, high tide hammering at the door you used to walk out of. A door to nowhere now, minus the steps that led down to the yard, minus the yard. The hurricane season starts soon and they predict one of the worst ever. I take the serrated knife the owner of the house left to chop vegetables for the ravenous deer, work it into the flesh above my left knee, a ragged, messy wound (note to self: must use paring knife next time!), twisting the roll of paper towels into a tourniquet around it so the blood doesn't stain the linoleum floor. Imagine jars of honey in an empty pantry, what's left when the sea takes everything else.

Sizzle of the waves over sandbags. Buzz of cicadas in the almost-dead redbud, what's left of the yard, a grassy nub surrounded by sand. Spanish moss hangs from this tree, a prickly-pear cactus in the salt-water-killed pine in front of it. The house next door is empty now, the front porch washed away, just a door leading down into dirt, kids toys, buckets, a plastic rake. The battered shells of the rest of the houses all in a row like tombstones; when the wind blows, a ceiling fan on a screened-in porch spins lazily, as if it's got somebody left inside to cool.

At low tide I walk on the sand to where a bunch of clams washed up like they beached themselves. I think of whales doing this when something isn't right, and I think how the sea here must be poisoned, the remains of all those houses, septics, household chemicals, all manner of plastics that will never biodegrade, yet it looks so perfect on the surface, shining and untroubled. Who can tell what damage lurks? I dig out a shell from where it was mostly buried under the sand, a whelk, salmon colored and smooth as metal on the inside. The animal lived out its life and left this, the proof.

Later, after strolling down the remains of the dirt road I yank out a tick burrowing into my ankle, imagine in three days the bulls-eye rash of Lyme disease, aches and chills, wanting only to sleep, waves battering against the bedroom wall the way they must've before Lottie's house finally broke in half. Less than a month ago, the realtor said when she handed me the key to our rental. They had a last Mother's Day celebration in it, the son, daughter, their families, and then they brought Lottie to one of their own homes. Days later, not even a storm, just a full-moon tide, pylons weakened from repeated thrashings of the waves, it cracks in half, the front toppling into the sea. You can still see Lottie's white quilt, the realtor said, on the part remaining, hanging like a flag of surrender.

For the rest of the week I feed the deer that come in a herd to chew on the small bit of grass remaining in the yard. Put out a big pail of fresh water and they drink it dry every night, after munching on the apples, lettuce, even sauerkraut, when I have nothing left to give them.

Jake calls me from home. "You'll never guess what happened," he says. "A sinkhole opened up in our driveway! It's huge, almost swallowed the Chevy. Went to bed and we have a driveway, wake up to a hole." He tells me the contractor he brought over to evaluate it just shrugged. "What do you expect?" the contractor said. "Your house is close to the Susquehanna. There's only a thin layer of soil here and under it's sand. Always shifting," he told Jake, "wants to find its way back to the river."

Maybe there's something in us all, I think, that makes us return to the water. "Come down here," I plead. "Never mind the sinkhole."

It's just that I don't want to be the person who fantasizes a love affair with a clown so heartsick at his own life he can't face it sober. I want to be the old couple in the hospital elevator, with someone who loves me when I'm throwing up. We'll spend our days like we always do, walking the beach, when there is one at low tide, commenting on the skeletal remains of the houses, his memories of summers spent in them. And then Jake and I will go home, where he'll continue to work for a business that isn't even there anymore. In 120 years the ocean will swallow what's left of Hunting Island, Lottie's half of a house with its quilt hanging like a flag—but not surrender, she held on, after all. Over the week I'll take more snapshots and maybe these too will disappear; if no one is there to witness did any of it exist? Maybe the pelicans, if they aren't wiped out from the oil spill, will still dive-bomb the ocean for fish. With any luck, there will be fish.

I have an image that comes to me sometimes, a memory I think, or did I dream it? Our family at a beach somewhere, maybe the New Jersey shore where sometimes we'd drive for the day, the water a more steely color than it is off Hunting, colder, but still the Atlantic, its hidden depths. My mom is with us and she's holding me in the ocean, teaching me to float, her strong hands clutching the small of my back as she stretches me out, her head with its pale hair cut short and spiky like a boy's, looming over me. I'm scared and keep trying to grab her shoulders. "No Nora," she says. "Hold out your arms like you're flying and let the water bear you. Watch," she says. "I'll show you." And she lets go.

Finding the Body

When he's high and in his dreams it's Troy who finds the body. Let's say he's with his best friend Shane. Sometimes he is and sometimes he isn't but when he is they're walking along the banks of the river, the path down by the swamp (Shane insists it's a pond but Troy thinks *swamp* is the accurate word and whose dream is it anyway?), all overgrown and snarly with reeds and cattails and the red-wing blackbirds swaying from them, their shrill whistles. They've been smoking pot cut with crystal, and this is where they like to hang when they're tweaking because no one much goes down there so it feels like a secret, a good one.

Maybe it's her foot they see first—no make that him, Troy sees it first—small because she's only twelve but still the arched shape of the almost young woman, that age between childhood and arrived. She won't arrive though. Shane's going, "Holy shit, dude! Holy, *holy* shit!" Troy wants to keep it quiet, for just a little while—something they have that the rest of the world doesn't.

The way it really went? A couple of duck hunters found her body among the reeds, the cattails, pond scum green as an inchworm, like even the river didn't want her and shoved her into this little tributary, with its bullfrogs and peepers and the occasional lily in the darker, deeper parts; but where she is it's shallow, drying up in the late summer sun so it's mostly mud she's on. Instead of cleaning her up first (which Troy would have done out of respect for chrissake, she's a fricken dead child!), they called the police and she was rolled into a body bag and ambulanced to the coroner, who said her body was too badly decomposed for any positive ID. They knew she was twelve from her teeth and bones, but that's about it. They couldn't even tell for sure how she died. No evidence of foul play, the police said.

The news called her body a *corpse*, which is that much more removed from human life, like it's a *thing*, not a dead child. But it was clear that a child had been in trouble. You don't just drift up in a swamp, surrounded by croaking frogs and covered in pond scum when you're twelve. What got to Troy is how nobody claimed her. No one seemed to be missing a child. It's like she just appeared in the world, already dead.

TROY'S TASK EVERY morning is to slide on his grandpa's socks and shoes, his grandpa beached in his chair, the reclining one he spends the day in after Grandma plunks him there then goes to work. He already has his jacket on and a tie—this gets to Troy, why for chrissake the tie!—and the dress shoes with the thin gray man-socks complete the charade. His grandpa used to be a systems engineer for BAE then had his stroke and collects pretty decent disability, Troy figures. He can barely move a muscle without help, his wife guiding him, tiny shuffling steps, his plank of a body leaned up against her like it's an ironing board being dragged across the room, and when he talks (which is almost never) it sounds like he's underwater. She dresses him every day in the getup he wore for thirty years, then parks him in his chair and waves goodbye, her silver-streaked hair in an Olive Oyl knot at the back of her head, bobbing in the window as she climbs into her Prius. That kills Troy. What kind of a life is this? "He has his dignity," Grandma said.

Troy's grandmother is a history professor at SUNY, and her face is mostly nose-down in some book nobody else would read, or an article she's writing that nobody will read. "The past teaches us how to live in the present," she told Troy, but he doesn't buy it. He's much more in dread of what will happen the next day or the day after that. With his grandmother always reading or writing and his grandfather sitting and staring, it's a pretty quiet house in the quiet part of town where things aren't falling apart, where bad things aren't supposed to happen and if they do you slap a fresh coat of paint over them, the yards all fussily landscaped, houses renovated to look like *new* old houses, their occupants mostly older, quiet people like his grandparents. Troy jams in his earbuds and plays tunes on his iPod not to hear it—all that quiet.

It's like he was dumped here, his parents *guilt-traveling*, his grandma called it, all over the globe because of the accident that crippled a young woman. Troy was in the back, his mother in the passenger seat up front. His father swerved to avoid a deer that appeared out of nowhere in front of their car, slamming into a biker in the bike lane. After the court determined his father was blameless, the slick of rain, fog, making it difficult to see the young woman on her bike (plus it was dusk, a dangerous time for biking in the first place—*a tragic accident*, his lawyer said), Troy's parents took off and haven't been back, almost two years now.

Except it wasn't a deer. Troy saw it, and he's pretty sure his father didn't despite what his father told the court, because his parents had been arguing, and Troy's father took his eyes off the road for a moment to look at his mother. That's when it loomed in the headlights, big as a fricken tree and bipedal, Troy swears—bigger than a bear but at least that hairy, a wolfman? A yeti?

They were arguing over King Tut, which would've been inane in anyone else's life, but Troy's father is an archaeologist who thinks he knows everything, and his mother's a field researcher who knows she does. When they have their fights about these ancient things no one gives a crap about Troy just plugs in his earbuds, which was what he'd been about to do before he saw that creature, then the crunch of metal under the Jetta's tires.

"They're frittering away your college fund, calling it *cutting-edge research*," his grandmother scoffed. "More like *cutting* their obligations and responsibilities." Troy just rolled his eyes. He's not exactly college material. For starters there's his dyslexia (which his grandmother says is no excuse, spouting her litany of famous dyslexics who made historical contributions, starting with Einstein and working down). It's like his brain takes everything in on one lobe then has to translate it to another, the one that was supposed to get it in the first place. Like trying to read off a mirror. If that's not bad enough he hasn't been able to concentrate on a damn thing since they found the body, then just a few months later his father's accident, then the girl he was hanging with goes and fricken vanishes off the face of the earth! Periodically you get your Columbines, your Bundys, machine-gun-toting mall shooters, shoe bombers, 9/11 for chrissake. People just go off. Or maybe they're born off. Some might not even *be* people, in the human sense. They walk and talk and look human enough, but something's missing, a hole where their conscience should be, the *moral center* his humanities teacher called it. Where do you get one of those? Maybe it's a mechanical part but in some the battery is dead.

Can they blame Troy for the drugs? He didn't slam at least, no needles, and only snorted when he craved some sense of well-being, to check out for a while from his own noisy head, that lovely brain numbness. When he smoked he was mindful not to do it straight, cutting the glass with weed so he wouldn't get too addicted or anything, but now that they've taken away even this he's been feeling gnarly and nervous and prone to doing even crazier-ass things than he would've done enjoying the occasional snort.

The thing with Loulie made the papers, TV news, the Internet, you name it and Troy's mug was on it, his shaggy hair plastered against his forehead, his little eyes black as a beetle's. He looked like a deviant and of course his grandmother *had* to tell his parents he'd been pulled in for questioning, which means they'll probably never come back for him. (No, he didn't see anyone, didn't see another car—that was the whole point of going to the old lot, so no one would be around. Loulie kneed him in the balls—OK, he was getting a little heavy on her, he'll admit this, but by the time he looked up again she had bolted from his Corolla and that's the last he saw of her. No, he didn't hear a thing—well *maybe* the crunch of tires on gravel but when he stepped out of his car there was nothing.)

Troy confessed to the drugs when he realized he was a *person of interest,* that what they suspected was worse. ("You were the last to see that girl!" the snarly-faced detective who interrogated him kept repeating, but I mean really what's he going to do, kidnap her and hide her in his closet, or do her in then call the police and *alert* them to her being missing, for chrissake?). Since Troy didn't have anything on him and his car and his room, which they tossed, were clean (he'd snatched her pink hoodie out of his Corolla the moment he figured there might be a problem, chucking it into the woods), he was put on probation—"We'll be watching," the police said. "You won't like Juvenile Detention," his grandmother said, then took him out there one day, a three-hour drive, his grandpa packed into the backseat of the Prius like it's some kind of joy ride. He'd never seen razor-wire fences except on TV, and a group of boys slaved over the grounds, mowing and haying a wasted field. "You best keep your nose clean," his grandmother said.

Now that it's summer he'd like nothing more than to hang with Shane, smoke, maybe snort a little—he wouldn't sell it, that was small-time, peanuts man, mostly because it gave him a rep at the school—*Troy-boy!*—and helped him buy gas for the Corolla. With the price of fuel these days you need a job, but there's no jobs or he'd be going to work. Anything to distract him from thinking about things, like how nobody even mentions her anymore. It's as though she never existed, an anonymous, twelve-year-old dead girl.

THE STALKING STARTED on a dare, eights months ago. "I dare you!" Shane said. Troy felt a little uncomfortable about it, something didn't seem quite right or fair, but what the hell else was there in his life these days? Plus he had her book, a secret not even Shane knew about. Troy's father had ordered him to stay put in the backseat until the ambulance left, but when he noticed it lying in the street near her flung backpack, he cracked open the car door and nabbed it while his parents talked to the police. For just a moment, a split second, he worried she might have seen him do it—she was on the stretcher and probably passed out, but a sudden glittering about her mostly indecipherable face in the darkness made Troy wonder if she had briefly opened her eyes. *The Collected Plays of Samuel Beckett*, difficult enough to read with his dyslexia, what he could make out was like slogging through jello. Still, having something of hers made things feel more personal, like she was in his life even though she didn't know it. Maybe he could justify tracking her down with a plan to return her book at some point, stick it in her mailbox or something. "You have to come too," he told Shane.

Late fall and a clarity in the air such that when they peeked into the window a beam of sunlight was on her and the wheelchair lit up all silvery like she was sitting atop some altar, but the thing that got them was her hair, long and white as the moon. "Holy shit, dude!" Shane whispered. "Why does she have white hair? That happen from the accident too? Why would someone's hair turn white when they're paralyzed, like the blood stops flowing to it or something?"

"She's only paralyzed from the waist down, a paraplegic," Troy said, as though this would explain it. He thought she was beautiful, and it kind of turned him on, staring at her when she didn't know it, the intimacy of this.

"She's pretty hot for a crippled chick," Shane said.

Troy came back a few more times alone, always with her book in his jacket pocket and always he left without putting it in her mailbox. Then he stopped bringing the book. Once he even stalked her in the Giant market, she's zooming the aisles in one of those motorized carts they make for handicapped people, Troy tagging at a safe distance, plucking random stuff off of shelves that he'd later have to scrap. Each time he was struck by how pretty she is—not just the hair but her face too, like some wild cat, a panther or a cheetah, animated and alert. The girls in his high school all manufacture the same kinds of expressions, mostly of put-upon boredom. More and more Troy felt something else, too, gazing at her, something achy and foreign and a little sad. Sometimes she had an aid helping her, another young woman dull as bread, despite having working legs. Mostly she was alone, wheeling herself about in her single-level house and Troy felt there was something irrevocable here—how it was his dad who did it, put her in that chair—that because of this Troy had a connection to her, but was afraid if she ever met him she would hate him.

THEN ONE SMOLDERING July day it happens. Wiping sweat off his forehead onto his jeans with his moist, sticky hands, Troy inches up behind the juniper bush under her window (he knows it's juniper because his grandmother likes to identify plants not tend them, she'll tell you, she's no gardener) and is about to peek in when something hits him on his lower back; not a punch exactly, but hard enough to make him jump. He gets his snarly face on and turns around slowly, heart thumping. It's not like he's anyplace he should be.

She's in her chair, on the concrete path, a fistful of some kind of walnut-sized, prickly fruit, which she lobs at him again, the whole bunch this time, pummeling his neck, chest and arms. "Jesus!" he yelps.

"I know you," she says.

Troy shuffles his sneakers in the dirt, nods. "I'm sorry," he mumbles. There's tightness in his chest, like a python got in there and wrapped itself around his ribcage. He wonders if she'll call the police, figures he should've thought about this before; why is he such a screw-up sometimes!

"Oh so you're here for forgiveness, is it? There's a Catholic church down the street. I don't do redemption. Did you think just because I'm in a wheelchair I would? Like it makes me a saint or something?"

The wheels of her chair flash in the sun like quicksilver; Troy almost wants to shield his eyes. He's aware of the hiss of traffic off Route 17, a constant whine like a bad soundtrack. He frowns. "I don't know what you mean."

"Yeah, sure, like you don't believe blind people have extraordinary hearing too, huh? Give it up for the *super*disabled! Sorry to disappoint, but I'm just a gal in a wheelchair who can't use her fuckin' legs, kiddo, they hang like cooked noodles. No confession prospects here."

Troy's cheeks flame. "Sorry!" he says again. He hears the rumble of an approaching train, its whistle. It occurs to him her house sits in the crotch of things built for speed and the quick exit, a highway, train tracks, and here she is.

"What, for making like you're the Dark Knight or something? I've seen you watching me. I decided to let it play itself out a while, see what happens. Call it entertainment without the cable bill. You're not exactly CIA material. You're the one that girl who disappeared was with. I remember your face from the news. Guess I should be terrified, huh? But you seem pretty incompetent for a killer or a rapist, no offense, plus what do I have left for you to nail, my arms?"

Troy lets his breath out in a whoosh—he hadn't realized he'd been holding it in. He thought she must have recognized him as his father's son, but this is about Loulie. He sticks out his chin a little, steps from behind the bushes closer to her. "It wasn't my fault," he says.

She nods. "Yup, just like I thought, you're here for redemption. Do I look like some priest? I was a theatre grad student when this happened to me. How many people you think are hot to see Lady Macbeth in a wheelchair? I guess you know where the front door is given the number of times you've checked out my digs—may as well open it for me. You get to use the ramp like you're a *special* person."

He follows her inside like he's being pulled, expecting any minute she'll wheel around and order him to leave. He's not sure what to do for her—should he offer to push the chair? He's hammered by her good looks this close to her, but the whole thing feels awkward as hell. Confusing too, like she's accusing him of something, but what he feels guilty about, she hasn't a clue. She's got a chip on her shoulder, that's for sure, though he supposed he would too in her shoes. Does she even wear shoes? When she turns around facing him he stares down where her feet rest on the padded footrest. Ankle high leather boots, cool ones too—he's seen that brand.

"Right," she says, following his gaze. "They're mostly for decoration. What sucks is sometimes I imagine I can still feel my toes inside them, but the good thing is I'll get bored with them before I ever wear them out. Plus, since my feet can't feel heat I can wear them in July, what a windfall, huh? Sit!" she commands, pointing at a chair opposite from where she's parked herself. It's overstuffed, or maybe under-stuffed, as Troy sinks down into the grainy seat cushion giving her the height advantage, which is weird, he thinks; he has to look up to meet her eyes.

"I'd offer you a beverage but I'm not one for company these days. Since the accident I've freed myself of any obligation to be socially graceful. And let's be straight, you're a stalker not a guest."

Troy nods, even though he's not exactly sure what he's affirming.

"You know about it, I assume, the accident?"

His face burns and he stares at his own feet. What should he say here?

"Just figured if you've been checking me out you must, or is it that the wheelchair thing turns you on? You a freak like that?"

He shakes his head. "You're really pretty?" he offers, his voice faint. She'll think him a pussy but he's feeling kind of sick, sitting in her tidy living room, surrounded by her stuff arranged on shelves that have clearly been lowered to accommodate her new stature, books—lots of these, and Troy briefly fantasizes breaking in one night and depositing *Beckett* on her bookshelf; she can't ever know he has it or she'll recognize who he is—knickknacks, even seashells, and he's aware of how she won't be strolling on some beach picking these up anymore. The person his father crippled and she doesn't even know. *Lois*, he remembers her name, even though his family mostly refers to her as "the young woman from the accident."

She nods. "I *am* really pretty, and guess what else? I used to have great legs! No kidding, the kind you'd flaunt in skinny jeans, mini skirts, shorts, a bikini, whatever the season called for. I don't do seasons now. Just ice, I have to watch it wheeling on the ice. If I fall I can't get up. So for me there's ice, then everything else."

"Do you like summer?" Troy asks, his ears reddening—what a stupid thing to say when she just said she didn't do seasons. "I mean because it's hot," he stammers, his cheeks flaring with spots now like the pinpoints of matches. "You know, because there's no ice?" he adds—may as well make a complete idiot of himself.

She stares at him, her pale-blue eyes, like water he thinks, like he could swim in them. "How old are you anyway? You're still a kid, aren't you? I seem to remember those articles about the missing girl said you were both at the high school. You're pretty young to be a stalker. Is that a career track these days? Entry level as a stalker, promoted to flasher? You going to show up in a trench coat next time?"

Troy knots and unknots his fists. Why the hell did he ever take that dare, anyway! He should've never told Shane about the accident; there are some things better kept to yourself. His parents managed to keep it out of the news, so *he* goes and blabs. His nerves are just so jangly, like somebody hotwired his brain. Give him a hit, a job, what's he supposed to do with himself all day, sit around and watch Grandpa turn to stone? It's as if his grandfather's become a monument to his former life, all dressed up like he still has anywhere to go, and it just makes Troy so damn sad. She's got a mouth on her, this Lois, but he can't refute any of it. Well? she says.

"I'm almost eighteen," he tells her, which isn't exactly true—he just turned seventeen. Some birthday too, his grandma schlepping a cake home from the market after work, and Troy gets to feed it to his grandpa, shoveling pieces of it into his mouth snapping open and shut like a fish. "He likes it!" his grandmother announced. "Don't you, Vernon? You always did love coconut cake," she cooed. Like Troy wasn't even in the room, birthday or not, and never mind that Troy's favorite cake is chocolate.

She leans forward, closer to him. He can smell a cloying but not unpleasant ripeness about her, maybe from that fruit she pitched at him. "So, do you blame yourself?"

Troy frowns, his breath quickens. "What do you mean?"

"For her disappearance, you were the last one with her, right? Paper said you were doing drugs. I don't get that. I spend my days trying to feel something again and you druggies get wasted to feel nothing at all."

He shakes his head. "I don't even know what happened to her and that's the honest truth. One minute she was there, the next she's gone." Troy stares out the window, the same one he had peered through on the other side. He doesn't know what to say when people bring up Loulie. Are they blaming him? Probably. She was a nice girl, he knows that, the kind of "nice" that if he had a sister, or a girl for a best friend instead of Shane, maybe he would've felt bad trying to get her tweaking so he could hook up. OK, this wasn't honorable under *any* circumstances but maybe if he knew more nice girls, *really* knew them, he'd think about them more in an honorable way. Take this girl, Lois, who's more like a woman—she's at least twenty-five—he feels really bad that because of his parents' fight over King Tut she's paralyzed, and weirder than that he thinks if she'd let him Troy would try to protect her; he'd make it so nothing else could hurt her, if he could. "I wish to Christ I wasn't the last person to see Loulie!" Troy says.

"I'll bet you do," she nods, "but you are. Can't change that any more than me rising up and walking across this room. I'd as likely walk on water. So if you're not here for forgiveness, then what are you here for? You don't look the theatre type. You want me? That why you've been checking me out? That's it, huh, you've got the wheelchair fetish thing going on. Well you're too young."

"I'm almost eighteen!" Troy says again, though he's not exactly sure what he's defending here. Still, he doesn't like her thinking him such a kid.

She grins. "*Almost* doesn't make the cut, kiddo. Why would *I* want you anyway? Turns out 'abled' guys are overrated. When I hookup again it'll be with someone like me. I mean, look at you! Everything works, I assume, and yet here you are. So OK, maybe I'll let you ogle but you can't touch. Wheel me to the bedroom. I guess I don't need to tell you where it is."

Troy's heart is drumming like a drum circle's in there, a mixture of excitement and dread, clutching the black plastic handles of her wheelchair. He should maybe walk out now while he can, and yet he can't; it's like the chair's a magnet and he's stuck on. There's a ragged cobweb in the corner of the hall ceiling and Troy thinks how she won't be able to reach up and swipe at it. He supposes she can use a broom, something with an extra-long handle. She's had to reconfigure her entire world, he realizes, while his parents *research* somewhere in Africa. A sudden ache like he's been socked in the gut, the taste of metal in his mouth.

It's hot in her bedroom, a pole fan spinning and a fat black fly crawling on the window-screen above her bed. He parks her chair on the bare, wood floor between the bed and the door, worrying that if he puts it too close to the bed she'll figure he's expecting something. She motions him to stand in front of her, starts to slide up her tank top then grins. "Ha! Got you! Did you really think I would show you my breasts? What, I'm some sort of pervert, making it with a kid? Too bad, because they're stunning. But I'll bet it's my legs you really want to see, how the withering has progressed; they do that, you know, when there's no hope of using them for what they were intended. They just curl up and go dormant. So let's not spoil the anticipation, let's have you do the work."

He blinks, "What? Me?"

"Yes of course you, why should I do any of it? I get to see them every bloody day for the rest of my life. You have to lift me out of the chair and put me on the bed. Then you slide down my jeans, just like a real date, huh? This is purely clinical though, no unnecessary touching or tenderness allowed."

His hands are sweaty and he hopes she doesn't feel their wetness as he slowly reaches around her, fumbling under her arms. For a moment he's distracted by a bird outside her window, so weirdly brilliant in the mid-afternoon light Troy imagines it's a phantom bird, not quite real, like it's some colorful being *imitating* a bird. It takes sudden flight, soaring from the electric wires over her street and Troy wishes he could do this too, escape. Would she be offended if he told her he *doesn't* want to see her legs? It's not that he wouldn't under other circumstances, and yeah he gets it, stalking her made it feel like a bit of a freak-show, but he didn't mean that, did he? Honest to god Troy doesn't know why he does half the things he does! He's the family fuckup, that's for sure, the first one who won't even get the dream of college. He'll live and die in this dying place.

"Christ!" she snaps. "Am I a toddler now? Don't lift me under my arms. Scoop me up, one of your arms under my knees, the other behind my back. Pretend we were just married and you're carrying me over the threshold, would you hold your wife like she's two years old?"

Troy is afraid he'll stumble, stagger a bit but luckily she isn't too heavy. He thought it might hurt her feelings if he wheeled the chair beside the bed, like he was *expecting* her to be heavy, like he thinks she's fat or something, but now he has to take actual steps with her in his arms. He's about to place her on the bed, one step at a time he thinks—then she tells him to stop right there and look her in her eyes.

"Are you kidding?" he yelps, trying to catch a breath. OK, for a crippled chick, as Shane called it, after a few minutes in his arms she's not exactly a lightweight. He should've taken the gym membership his grandmother offered after the police tossed his room. "Muscles or methamphetamine!" she chirped, kind of snarky he thought.

"Did you do it? Look me in the eyes now. What really happened? A girl doesn't just up and disappear."

Troy drops her on the bed, the mattress bouncing a little under her sudden trajectory. "Jesus but she did!" he roars. "They do! For chrissake, I thought you of all people would understand! Don't you get it? Doesn't anyone? One minute things are the way you think they'll be for the rest of your life then the next it's all caved in on you. They do disappear, bad things happen, they turn up dead, nobody misses them, nobody cares and it's like they were never even in this world!"

He's appalled to find actual tears running down his cheeks, but once they've started it's like he's broken the seal, a waterfall unleashed and he can't seem to shut it off. He has a sudden vision of the supposed deer his father swerved to avoid hitting, hairy and fat as a billboard in the headlights of their car, that terrible crunch of the bike under its wheels, her scream—didn't he hear it? he thought he must have as her legs went under—then that silence, the car stopped, the thing bounding across the road swallowed up into the darkness on the other side. For all they know the accident that took out the bottom half of her may have saved her from worse! Troy's even wondered, though he'd never say it to anyone as they'd label him delusional on *top* of the dyslexia (Shane, the one person he told said he must've been smoking, man, a little hit before getting in the car with the parents?), if that *thing* out there is what happened to Loulie. Whatever happened to her he knows it can't be any good, and for the rest of his life that's who he'll be, the last person who saw her, and what was he doing to bear this weight? Trying to score!

Lois smiles at him, teeth the white of her hair, radiant in a dusty stream of afternoon light from the window over her head. She pats the bed beside her. "Sit," she says. "It's OK. You did come here for forgiveness, didn't you? I thought so, and I didn't think I could but maybe I can. We'll see. Here," she says, after Troy hunkers down beside her, still sobbing, his thin shoulders hunched into himself. "No hands-on," she tells him, lifting her tank top. "And shut your eyes. I have my limits."

He nods, swipes his hand under his nose, sniffles.

"Good," she says. "This is about your salvation, after all."

She strokes his neck then guides his head down against her chest, her arms around him drawing him in. Troy hears the rhythmic beating of Lois's heart, the in and out of her breath, as steady as anything he's ever listened to.

The Man Who Jumped

All night and into the morning and throughout the lengthening spring afternoon, the roar of the rescue boats, airboats blown across the swollen Susquehanna, swarming like black flies, searching for the man who jumped. I slept uneasily, fitfully, waking at one point to what sounded like a tornado, the howl of engines battling near flood-stage currents. Ruth sleeping still as a rock beside me through all of it, and when she finally wakes she tells me she's going back on antidepressants. "I can't bear it anymore," she says.

"Bear what?" I ask.

She frowns, shakes her head, her exasperated shrug. "Try this," she says. "How can we call ourselves lesbians if we don't make love?"

I study her, her long, sleep-tussled hair the rouge-black color of currants, imagine snaking my fingers through it, twirling them up in it like vines. "Do we call ourselves that?" I ask.

"I share a bed with you, Janis. We have to call it something."

I think about the man who jumped. News junkie that I am, I had checked the news at regular intervals for facts, stats, photos, the what and why, but the news had nothing. Only that he stopped his car in the middle of the Four Corners Bridge around 9:30 P.M., got out and without hesitation, witnesses said, climbed onto the concrete railing, perched there for just a moment like some night bird, like he belonged, opened his arms and plunged. He was a blond, somebody said, or maybe he had white hair. It glowed in the lights from the bridge.

Later, as the boats continue their trolling back and forth and walkers poke about in the mud, the reeds, the banks of the river below us, I wonder what it was *he* could no longer bear? *Just this week the Chinook salmon suddenly vanished from the northwest. Frogs, salamanders, amphibians in an extinction disaster the world hasn't seen since the dinosaurs, with three thousand more species expected to disappear in our lifetime. The Western states have become a killing field, open season on wolves, baby buffalo. And cattle, it turns out, are a significant contribution to greenhouse gasses with their farting and belching. Will we start offing them too now, the ones we don't target for our barbeques, our Happy Meals? In one week a typhoon in Myanmar followed by an earthquake in China and two hundred thousand people eradicated, over five million homeless.*

Maybe his own house went victim to the real-estate crisis, the mortgage disaster. A wife leaves him, a daughter grows up, abandoning the house that is (now?) no longer theirs. Who sleeps in their bed and what can he name it when the bed no longer has a bedroom? Recently I read that with so many houses foreclosed on people are living in those steel storage containers they rent to store their stuff, slide open the door and a bed's set up, breakfast table, a lamp, just like home. When they can't afford to pay for even that anymore their belongings are auctioned off by the container full. This week the price of fuel at the gas pumps hit four dollars a gallon and nobody, not even the president, pretends that the economy isn't in a recession.

So I do it. Reach out and stroke Ruth's hair that is as velvety and sure as the undersides of leaves.

DAY TWO AND no "victim" as they politely refer to the jumper, they've called in forest rangers, more police boats, two helicopters. A rescue worker said he thought he heard a cry for help, saw a blond head for a moment—the way the light shone, he said—"But let's face it," a blogger on the newspaper website writes, "nothing out there anymore that could call for help." Ruth stands at the aluminum sink chopping a 10 mg Lexapro into quarters, then fragmenting these into eighths. "Just a tad," she says, "to take the edge off. I think such bleak thoughts," she says.

"Can a pill stop your thoughts?" I ask. A sudden image of the fandango-pink hoodie on the evening news last month, found by a pack of stray dogs, belonging to a missing girl. Nobody claimed to know anything about it, but a person who lived in the vicinity speculated that somehow the whole thing smacked of drugs. "See?" Ruth had said. "You can't really disappear. People will make up your life whether you have one or not."

Now Ruth shrugs, smiles—but sadly, I'm thinking. "Pills can stop anything," she says.

HE CROUCHES ON *the concrete railing and the night dissolves around him to mere flickers, gleamings of nickel-colored lights reflected in the surging river below. He can't take much time to contemplate what he's about to do, what with having to park on the two-lane bridge and the cars all piling up behind honking. (The survivor of a jump off the Golden Gate, interviewed in "The Bridge," said people saw him standing there on the water side of the railing and nobody tried to stop him. The last straw was when a German tourist asked him to take her picture.) Just do it, he thinks, slip like a fish out of this world and into the next, brown water cold as a fish's heart (did you know it still pulses for a while, this quivering little organ, even after the fish has been caught, clubbed and sliced open? Life wanting to live). The moon's reflection in the rolling current ripples like a cloud, and maybe he imagines for the second or two he's airborne that he's not really jumping into a river, rather it's the sky he soars to in a burst of glory, extinguished like a shooting star.*

HELICOPTERS HOVER BELOW the canopy, perusing the river as it becomes calmer now, the fill of it easing down, the rains having stopped and no more snow melt from the mountains. We learn on the third day he was a young man, younger than her own son, Ruth says, if she had a son, if she had at least done that. Although, she tells me, if it *had* been her son now captive in the river, perhaps trapped under a tree branch, or even someone's refrigerator, refuse from the floods, from the things people do to get free of their waste, well how would a mother live with that? "No," she shakes her head, chopping up the Lexapro on the cutting board like it's cocaine, licking her finger then driving it down into the powdery mess. "It's better not to have children," she says. "They'd only remind you of the ways you failed them." I think about the age of the jumper, barely an adult, too young to have become so certain that nothing can change.

The first time my marriage failed I fled to San Francisco and took up with a cocaine dealer who drove a silver BMW and saw me only at night, late, my apartment. In the morning, after a quick peck on the cheek he'd take off, leaving the sweet steamy scent of his shower, from soaping off any traces of me, and a finely-chopped and ready-to-snort line of blow wrapped neatly in paper. Payment. Services rendered.

A neighbor who knows the jumper's family got the inside-scoop, she tells us, says it was an argument, maybe even a suicide pact but the girl chickened out. The young man, his girlfriend. They'd been drinking, *funneling*, she whispered—what they do, these kids, to get the alcohol from point A, the bottle, to Point B, the bloodstream, as fast as possible—dumping the stuff into a funnel stuck down the throat. She said she heard how some even do it in an enema, gin, whiskey, whathaveyou. If you squirt it up *there*, if they make you take a breath test you pass, she said. The young man parked his car on the bridge and told his girlfriend: *You're not going to like what I'm about to do.*

Later, a mid-afternoon nap, Ruth with her spring allergies snoring gently beside me to the rhythm of the airboats whining up and down the river, I close my eyes and follow the path through the woods, down the hill to where the red-winged blackbirds sway upon the shallow shore reeds, and I dive—the river in the afternoon sun shining darkly, down to the junk-strewn bottom, the silt, the rocks, the sunken things, cars, houses, a city block, lampposts, neon signs, a barn, a horse, hoses, plumbing fixtures, metal cans, a pizza oven, plastic this and plastic that, and miles of toxic chemicals spewed from dry cleaners, filling stations, post-industrial waste suctioned into the river through rusted pipes, where the fish bellied-up even before the two recent floods-worth of more and more things that do not belong (*the Three Mile Island Nuclear Reactor is on an island in the Susquehanna, river like a blood vessel, bearing what it's given until it bursts?*) to where he waits for me, he and the rest of them over the years, the ones who gave up. "I'm sorry," I tell them, "but I can't save you.

FROM ALL OVER the region they come, a pilgrimage to ground zero, where their boats are launched—volunteer firefighters, EMTs, Elks Lodge, Shriners, Truckers For Jesus, folks from the Department of Fisheries, anybody remotely having to do with river anything, trawling it for his body. With flood-stage receded and the currents calmer, they're using sonar to try to locate him. He has a name and a family, a history, a place in the world he left. An aunt quoted in the newspaper called his "A useless death. No reason for it," she said.

We're standing at the kitchen sink staring out at the river, a shroud of fog hovering over it, and Ruth asks if I could love her a little. "It's not like I'm mentally ill," she tells me, palming the bottle of antidepressants. "It could be I'm just a little emotionally . . . compromised," she says, her sharp eyes, the pupils black and round as olives, now scouring my face. *Independent woman seeks female companionship, share water-view home; light housekeeping a plus,* her Craigslist ad had said.

Ruth dumps another Lexapro onto the counter, little chopping motions with the paring knife and again I'm reminded of cocaine, chopping it, rolling up a dollar bill and snorting it way up to where it smarted and burned and your teeth, your tongue, the roof of your mouth felt tangy and switched on, and later stuffing cotton balls up your nostrils to staunch the bleeding from all that snorting, cocaine, cocaine, more and more. Once after my creative-writing class, back when I was a student, when I thought I was still headed toward a journalism career—*Journalist Janis*, pictured myself jetting all over the world, Geneva, Beijing, Rio de Janeiro, wherever news broke I would be there to hunt, expose, and document its truth for posterity—another student seduced me with it, after I had defended his story, insisting to the others that the *writer* wasn't a misogynist, even though his character was; that the writer wasn't his character. A couple of lines and some painfully rough sex, my head slamming down on his concrete floor, I knew this wasn't true. Everything I touched in those days went wrong somehow.

Journalist Janis, a byline for the pseudoscience column I inherited in the local rag, *Our Magical Universe!* Factoids about the natural world for people with no working knowledge of astronomy, biology, chemistry, physics, or anything theoretical, until it was pulled along with the print version of the newspaper. I stroke Ruth's sharp little face, the perfect shell shapes of her cheekbones.

AND STILL THEY search. When do they tell the family *we're sorry, but . . .* When is one corpse no longer worth it? *Sixty-nine thousand bodies buried under the rubble of their former lives after the earthquake in China. Seventy-eight thousand dead in Myanmar.* In Chicago a cougar is discovered wandering through a neighborhood, hanging out behind a school playground like the pervs do. No registering this one though. Bang! And the crippled wolf out West, Hoppy they named him; blasted him too. From the bedroom window I watch a blue jay light upon the feeder, then soar up in a flash of indigo and disappear into the white pine. Once we saw a little gray bird hunched under the mountain-laurel bush beside the feeder, glassy eyed and shivering, and we noticed he had no tail. "What's a bird without its tail?" I asked Ruth. "Grounded," she said.

Every day spring pops out a little more, more green on the trees, chickadees chattering their mating songs. *During the 1990s famine in North Korea you couldn't hear any birds because all of them had been caught and devoured.* PBS called it a massive human tragedy, and it was, of course, though I couldn't help but think it: what could it be worth to wake up in a world without the impassioned song of the scarlet cardinal and some horny finch warbling his aria?

Ruth on the bed curls into herself like a snail. Helicopters darting about the tree line, gigantic mechanical crickets, circling round and round over the river, drifting, dipping, cruising like sharks.

Hawai'i, 1958, Billy Weaver, a winsome lad from a prominent O'ahu family was attacked by a shark and 690 sharks were slain to avenge his death, some so rare they had never been seen before in Hawaiian waters. A list from just one of President Roosevelt's safaris to Africa, 512 animals shot from his train. King George V was said to have killed a tiger and a bear with the right and left barrels of his rifle simultaneously. He was one of eight guns that brought down 2,190 game between 9 A.M. and 4 P.M., and one day he shot single-handedly a thousand birds for the sport of it. During the reign of Titus, nine thousand animals were killed at the games honoring the completion of the Coliseum in AD 80, and eleven thousand were slaughtered to celebrate one military victory a few years later.

Now the big mammals are disappearing, at different rates but all of them on the clock: great apes, elephants, polar bears, the large cats, wolves, giraffes, the massive and intelligent animals of the sea. Some that can be captured are locked up in zoos, barred environs that at their best try to mimic the land they were stolen from, but in miniature, of course, like crawling into a painting of a landscape and trying to live there.

ON THE SEVENTH day it is quiet, only the low rumble of the expressway, like thunder from a distant storm. "I wonder if they found it?" Ruth says, referring to the body as *it*. I don't tell her the truth, that they finally gave up, let the river claim its own. She refuses to get out of bed today, and later I will go to the empty lots near our house (a developer's dream, before the housing bubble popped, home to woodchucks and rabbits) and pick wildflowers, arranging them in a vase on the table beside her where maybe their fragrance will remind her of something, who knows, a good day.

Yesterday in the lots I came upon a yearling turned loose by her mother, the does ready to give birth to the next round. She didn't know yet to be afraid. She watched me, those unblinking eyes, all the while her jaw was working something, back and forth, up and down, like chewing gum. Fur taut, her graceful neck, tawny and right. Come November, December, the killing season, she'll be fully grown and a target, but in the meantime there are green things to munch on, and that good hard sunshine on her back. I think about those zoo animals, pacing, eating, sleeping, their hours defined by these things that prove they are not gone yet, their patient, ponderous, futile wait to go home.

Spring keeps filling out the forest, hiding the river below. Soon we will not be able to see it at all but for the occasional watery glint, back lit by a setting sun, glowing through the trees when the wind moves their branches just so, and only for that moment.

I'm Just Here until I'm Gone

I took the job at the prison because nobody else would and we needed the money desperate, the kids on free lunch. "Like we're retard poor," snarled the oldest. Said he's embarrassed to eat in the cafeteria, but I doubt he's the only one. This region would scream rust-belt if there were still enough decent factory jobs; there's rust though, downtowns with abandoned buildings like the aftermath of an apocalypse. One town has Lockheed Martin where your job comes and goes on the political mood swings (PMS I call it) of Congress—will we or won't we build a new presidential helicopter. Who gets stroked, who gets soaked? Most of the region's your basic poor as a bag of bones.

Marcus says the lunch sucks and he's all, "Why can't you just make us a peanut-butter sandwich?" I'm of the mind that since it's a free *hot* lunch it's got to be more nutritious than SHOP 'n SAVE brand peanut butter, and anyway, damnit, you don't turn your nose up at *free*! their dad out of work yet again. Of course the inmates were all for it, a *woman* helping them get their GEDs, and most of them have been pretty sweet to me in the ways of captive guys— freshly combed, shaved, polite like I'm the virgin or some such saintly untouchable come to bless their days, though god only knows what they do with my image at night in their cots, the shower, don't want to go there.

What I'm saying is they appreciate me coming inside and helping them, so I let things ride. Didn't tell them how terrified I was that first day, how the guard made me take down my hair, all done up professional in a French twist: "Bobby pins," he scowled, *sharp metal objects?* His wooly-bear brow shot up, as in *duh!* Then he escorted me through five metal gates that buzzed us in then banged shut, like it would take an earthquake to crack them open again. My heart hammered inside my chest, and the only thing that kept me going was the thought of those two faces, my sullen teen and sweetie-pie the nine-year-old, sucking down their government-issued food. "Like they owe us a living," Marcus whined, picked that one up from his dad who believes anyone with two legs and a set of lungs owes him something.

Six months I'm doing this and the first three fly by like time does when you've got a job shaping your days. I'm feeling OK about it, working with these guys who never finished school, dropped out or kicked out, got in trouble or just quit going because no one at home gave a shit either way. You get a bit of the holier-than-thou over it, as in *I'll kick my teenager's butt if he ever stops going to school and he knows it.* But then this sonofabitch joins the group, the slickest most manipulative bastard you'll never want to know. Shot his fiancée and then his fiancée's father, haven't a clue what he might've done to the mother who got to witness that carnage, tied up on her couch. The guy's got a hole where his soul should be, you can see its absence in his eyes—pale blue wolf-eyes, only a wolf does what he does to feed his pack; this guy works alone, his eyes like some iced-over lake, trapped underneath you'd just keep going down.

He joins the group not for his GED, but get this: he's been assigned by the prison education director to be my *assistant*—the ED's all bragging because the guy has a *bachelor's* degree from some top-of-the-third-tier school, like his presence gives the joint some class. Says I teach the lesson plans, then our *educated* psychopath will drift around to make sure they're doing them right.

This soulless man, whose name is Trey, starts his game immediately, brushing his hand against mine when I put down my papers, stalking my ass when he's behind me—I can feel his eyes there, the kind of perv who when you talk to him face-to-face fixes his gaze on your mouth then slowly travels down. By the time he hits your crotch you've been undressed, skinned, and splayed for the butcher.

Then come the notes. Slips them into my book bag when I'm not looking—they don't let you carry your purse into prison so instead I've got this zippered canvas number, my nine-year-old's before he graduated to a backpack, red and cute like him with crayon marks and magic marker drawings on the inside. I carry my notebook, lesson plans, and the GED text in it, and now Trey's *poems*, gross rhyming ditties, Hallmark goes dirty: *Red are your lips, green your eyes, thinking about this, makes my manhood rise.* It gets worse. What he's going to do with me when he gets out—two generations of scenarios: the first *with* me, then we get *to* me. I can see myself teaching the GED difference: *with* is a preposition, I'd write on the chalkboard, you do it *with* someone else; to is the *to* verb, transitive or some shit like that (will have to bone up on this myself), *to* me, *to* you, I will do it *to you*… like blowing his fiancée's head off by sticking a .357 down her throat. He did it *to* her.

There's something about working in a room full of men, maximum security so all of them did something fairly extreme to get in here, most because of drugs—dealing them, robbing to pay for them, one day in the throes of addiction murdering for them. You feel their want, what's left after the shakes, the sickness, and not much else to fill that ravenous hole: anger, regret, but some hope too, that maybe by doing this, getting their GED, when they're out they'll have a job, a new start, be the person they may have dreamed they'd be before the drugs. History and our prison system doesn't bear this out. They'll be broken by the time they're released, shattered when nobody will hire them, nobody wants them, not even their families a lot of the time, but for now the fantasy keeps them going. And it keeps me going too, collecting this piss-ant paycheck, thinking for once maybe I'm doing a job worthwhile, contributing something, not just a waste of a fine body like my ex seems to think, since he's not getting any of it anymore.

Trey is killing all of this. Makes me feel like I got to shower when I get out of there, his eyes like dirty hands moving up and down me, and his notes, his *poems*. Not even zipping my bag stops them—he slips them in the pockets of my coat slung over a chair, once in the boots I slid off because they were wet. I should tell the prison ED. But I'm scared. There's threat in Trey's eyes, damage and danger. He's got me locked into some frozen place I can't seem to move out of, like those layers of ice in his eyes, trapped underneath like a leaf. You see its outlines. It's not going anywhere.

Today he sidles up to me, rain slamming so hard against the barred windows and the lathe whining from the workshop below, I almost think I didn't hear him; but maybe I did. "Your ass looks ripe in those slacks," he says, or I think he says. I try to focus on slacks. Who says *slacks*? How old is this guy and where's he from—not my people, not the other guys who mostly come from deadbeat dads, mother's a drunk, welfare if they're lucky, kitchen-turned-meth-lab if they're not, the projects, trailers, some falling-apart house on its way to condemned, no place where there's *slacks* in the closet. Don't think I'm pulling the bleeding-heart card here. They talk about this stuff in their personal narratives, which is how I know, the five-paragraph essay I'm supposed to teach them. Can you imagine telling some dude with head-to-toe tats, writing about his mom's hookup burning him with a cigarette, how he's got to introduce this in his thesis sentence, then a conclusion in the fifth paragraph that sums it all up? Now remember, the three middle paragraphs are your body, and each one has a topic sentence that supports your thesis: *My stepdad got wasted one night and autographed his initials on my back with his cigarette.*

No wonder they're turning to Jesus, my guys who come to me for English and basic math ("The calculator is your friend," I tell them, never much of a numbers-prodigy myself). Convenient, as the class itself is in the chapel under the watch of a life-sized crucified Jesus, hung from a big plaster cross on the wall behind the *mantel*, they call it, your basic podium a politician might use. Here's the kicker: in the shelf under the podium there's a little box full of mini Jesus figures, three-inches high, a good baker's dozen of them, brown eyes, blue eyes, brown skin, white, all with carved plastic beards and robes. Like action-figure Jesus—does the chaplain take them out for the guys to play with if they've been good? I could ask them, but I don't want to risk this kind of a discussion. I might believe or maybe not, haven't figured this out, and what about Jewish inmates, Muslims or Buddhists, or even New Age types who worship wizards, save your soul through colon cleanses and yoga? I just can't see how a little plastic Jesus is going to help any of these folks, about as down with fate as anyone I've met.

Trey's not coming to Jesus, and if I were Jesus I'd feel pretty pissed nailed to a cross for someone like this. I keep his notes in a manila envelope tucked inside my underwear drawer, my own words on the outside: *If I disappear, read these!* A scarlet arrow (Toto, my sweetie-pie son's a Magic Marker freak) points inside. I imagine how it might happen: Trey breaks out one night and shows up at my door. Or he's out on parole, which isn't likely, not even rational, the guy's got forty years, but it's not a life sentence, though after forty damn years may as well. I can't see my way through forty years of being here, teaching men to pass a test they believe will make a difference.

He's started creeping into my dreams like an intruder, like he's jimmied the lock on my brain, crawled in through an effing window. The dream won't be about the prison, won't even be in upstate, someplace far away with sunshine and beaches and silky waves lapping the shore, then suddenly I'm in a wasted building, the color drained out and he's there too, trailing me from room to room, my heart kicking in my chest, trying to find the exit.

I invite the ex back into bed. One night at a time, I tell him. We still live together because we're poor as dirt with him not working, so we can't afford two places, though he's the kind of husband gets you so mad sometimes you *wish* he'd go deadbeat. He hangs in, sleeping on the couch where he can watch late night porn-TV (he thinks I don't know) and drink himself stupid.

"No touching," I tell him. "Like I want to," he says, but he does. There's still something in his eyes when he looks at me, even though when I look at him what I see is the drink, him not holding onto a job because he gets bored, or he doesn't like how the boss treats him, or everybody else is an asshole and he thinks that gives him license to quit, or he decides some other place is the promised land, another city, state, a place that's never where we are. I know if I tell him about the notes he'll be at the prison ready to bust in and kick Trey's ass—which is a funny thought, my wiry-tough ex thinking he's man enough to rage through five metal gates that clang shut and lock him in—he'd freak at the first. Takes grit to do that, a kind of mental stamina that has nothing to do with biceps, trapped in with the rest of them. I like my guys, but the best part of every day is reversing those gates, sailing through the last that pours you out into what's left of the day, shutting tight and impenetrable behind you. That's when I can breathe again, and there's even pleasure in the mindless shit, shopping for dinner, having to pay for it with my effing credit card, the only one that still works because my bank account's zero-balance until payday, chauffeuring the boys about like a carpool mom, how normal it is.

It wasn't always like this. A March snowfall blowing ghosts through the pines in the back yard of our rental, and I'm sucking down a cup of ginger tea, feeling the way you get sometimes when it's gray and cold and you're thinking how there used to be that hint of a brighter life, an assumed path to a place you'd want to end up. Never knew exactly what or where that would be, only that I'd want it. Got a BA after all, or they wouldn't have hired me for even this plum, GED coach, and I wouldn't use words like *assumed*. I didn't come from *assumed*; it either was or it wasn't. So how did I derail? The bar jobs were supposed to be temporary, a blip on that shining path. There was the night I drank too much after my cocktailing shift at Reilly's, then came home and burned my bedroom down, placing my jeans on the radiator so they'd dry faster while I had a bath, because I forgot to take them out of the washer before I went to work. I'm a long-legged gal so the dryer with its shrinkage threat wasn't happening.

It was this brilliant act that led to the ex, *Pretty Paulie*, they called him, a bouncer at my neighborhood pub. After incinerating your jeans, your bed, the drapes over the windows becoming two blank spaces in the glass like eyes gone blind, what do you need? Why more drinks of course!

Four martinis, straight up, and all the while in between checking IDs, kicking folks out, Paul's telling me how green my eyes are: "No *great*! You have great green eyes," he says, upping the stakes, and that no chick's been able to hold her drink like him until now. (Should've known that was the tip-off, run run fast as you can . . .) I just kept remembering that fire.

"*Damn*," I said, "flames licking those drapes—almost obscene," I told him, "my smoldering bed, I'm flying back and forth from the bathroom to the bedroom hauling buckets of bathwater, hurling them in. Like dumping pins in a room full of knives," I said, shaking my head.

He kissed my hand like it was his to do that, each finger got a warm pair of lips. "Poor Gracie," he said. "What about the fire department?"

"A flock, a herd, no an *invasion*, all in black like an army of ants. Raced up the stairs, swept me out of their way!" I told him, flinging my arm across the bar for emphasis, knocking over my glass.

After his shift was over and we'd closed down the bar, Paul drove me back to his flat, passing the Eighth Avenue rubble that used to be my life. "If it weren't for those wet jeans," I sighed.

"Lesson here, don't ever dry your jeans on a radiator," he said, his hand squeezing my knee, slides up my thigh, the hand not steering his Chevy. A fog rolled thick off the ocean, blooming over Golden Gate Park, obscuring its boundaries, like something you could get lost in. My dad once told me about the mosquito men, how they used to drive their trucks through the neighborhoods of the Jersey suburb where he grew up, humid summer evenings, spraying their toxins in a thick, sweet fog. The kids would all run after it, losing themselves and each other in it. What did they know then about DDT?

"I'm going to be an English teacher," I told Paul. "Maybe even a professor—all of this is temporary."

"Me too," he said. "I'm just here until I'm gone."

WHEN MY MOM was a kid she saw a man electrocuted by lightning. "*Struck* by it," she said, "*lit up*"—the way the shock snaked through him, pitched him to the ground, jerked him about for a second or two then he was still. Years later, dragged down into a depression not even psych-ward electric shock could reach (how terrified she must've been when they strapped her down, the bolt blowing through her, remembering the man's body twitching on the ground), she caught MRSA in the hospital and jumped ship, leaving me with two pieces of advice: Don't go outside in a thunderstorm, and don't marry a man who won't stay in one place. My father met her on the east coast, moved her to the west and she never got home again. 'When I die," she said, "face my casket east."

The ex and I hooked up in San Francisco where I was the happiest I figured I'd ever be, the fog, the hills, the bay, two gorgeous bridges to everywhere I thought I'd ever want to go, the way the city shone in a certain light like some glistening god, over the Golden Gate into its heart, young and wild, the way I still felt. Then we moved to Austin because the ex thought he'd like to be a cowboy, and failing that there was always music—he could play a mean guitar, Austin was known for its music scene. Turned out he was still afraid of horses, one bit him as a child, and there weren't a lot of them roaming downtown Austin anyway. There were a lot of guitar players though, a dime a dozen. So Maryland, crabbing, even gave me the T-shirt that claimed it: *Maryland's for Crabs.* Marcus was born there, conceived one sultry July night, the ex fresh home from netting crabs, all skin-hot and that skunky low-tide smell. Talk about your pheromone rush. My diaphragm sat lonely in its bright blue case next to a package of unopened condoms.

On to Maine where he figured lobsters were just bigger, tastier crabs with a lot more money at stake. He hadn't a clue how territorial those lobster-dudes were, tenth-generation Mainers with saltwater in their veins. Slunk home one night minus the used skiff I bought him with the last of my cocktailing tips, his traps trashed, two black eyes and a limp that culminated in pity sex and Toby. (Toto we call him after Dorothy's little dog—the kid has a thing for *The Wizard of Oz.* But I draw the line at Kansas! I told the ex after he's all *hmmm*, maybe he could be a storm chaser.)

Then upstate New York. He's an *awesome* mechanic, knows his way around things that make other things run; he'll set his sights on helicopter maintenance, Lockheed Martin, maybe even learn to fly one of them! My whole knowledge of upstate was the Adirondacks, waterfalls and wildlife, a beer commercial, not these lost little towns along the river like runs in a stretched-out stocking, signs of used-to-be everywhere. Except for the prison. The prison's big business, hiring guards and desk personnel, cafeteria workers, grounds upkeep, what they don't make the inmates do; folks are happy to have it sitting high on a hill in their community, watching over them. You could almost imagine them inviting the convicts (they call them that) to dinner some time—a town potluck—convict-appreciation night!

The ex couldn't get security clearance at Lockheed Martin, quit his guy-who-changes-your-oil job at Midas then Quick-'N'-Lube, because he thought his coworkers were dissing him, or someone was cheating him, or his boss was an ass—pick a scenario—the usual drill. Too antisocial for a greeter at Walmart, and we've hit the end of my line. With both kids in school I said no way to anywhere else, so he moved onto the couch and we agreed we were over, shook hands on it, even though we didn't have the means to make it real. "Call it a separation," I said, though what's separating us is a fist-thin wall between the bedroom and the living room.

I'M NOT SURE what made me do it, steal the plastic Jesus. For one thing there's a bunch of them in the box now—I swear they've been cloned, so it's not like they'll miss one—is it still stealing if no one knows it's gone? The lesson plan is on *paragraphing*, a term I remember from English 101 at State, so why not bring it back? It's not like I'll use it anywhere else at this point. I'm at the podium yacking about paragraphing, citing some examples after drawing a diagram on the chalkboard, how each sentence supports the topic sentence. Trey's staring at my breasts the entire time. After a while they feel so dirty I want to suck them back into whatever body cavity they grew from, but given that impossibility the other option's making Trey disappear; that's when I discreetly reach under the podium into the box, slide my hand around a Jesus, drop it in my bag. Don't even know what color it is, whether its one of the blue eyed or brown, dark plastic or light. They won't check my bag going out, though they do coming in—who's going to rob a prison? Most everything is chained down anyway, and they ration everything else: one pencil, one pen, one piece of chalk—one Jesus.

"Gracie!" Darrel waves his hand, a question about supporting sentences. "Oooh oooh I know," goes Blake, chin scruff bobbing—he was a moderately successful drug dealer until he *accidentally* ploughed a man over in his truck on a drop. With all of the guys, whatever they did to get in here was "accidental," or it wasn't their fault, though the more papers they write for me the more ready they seem to admit to some culpability. Maybe they've realized I'm correcting *how* they say it, not what they say. Who am I to judge? I just snaked Jesus.

I reach into my bag on the shelf, wrap my fingers around it, its hard, cool feel. Answer Darrel's question, acknowledge Blake's effort, but my voice cracks, getting more upset by the minute at Trey. Effing belligerent, I'm thinking, the way he's leering at my breasts, an act of war. He'd probably get off if I hauled my ass out there and slapped him, the manipulative freak. For some reason I think of the dove in the prison parking lot after I left yesterday, standing sentry over what must've been its dead mate, hit by one of the cars. When I got here today it was gone—someone had swept up the dead one and its mate was left, with what? I peer out a barred window facing a swatch of gray sky, all you can see from here. "OK," I say, suddenly afraid I might cry, "time for me to go."

THAT NIGHT I put mini-Jesus on my night table, the boys in the next room fighting over who watches what on TV—Toto wants his *Wizard of Oz* DVD and Marcus snarls, "How about you fly the *eff* over the rainbow!" Toto wails, the ex is somewhere else. Crawl into bed in my sweats and my *Maryland's-for-Crabs* T-shirt, and stare at the little Jesus. Reach into my bag on the bed beside me, pull out Trey's latest penned porn and place it at Jesus's plastic feet (one of the blue-eyed ones, robe the color of cream gone bad). Folded up it looks innocent, the origami version of itself, a deviant with paper wings. Turn off the light, close my eyes and dream of the dove, the dead one, placed at Trey's feet like he's a plastic icon and this, my offering.

The next morning is a drizzly one, the eternal gray of a river valley, the way it traps the clouds, looming like wings of a giant bird of prey hovering over your head. I yell at the ex, crashed out on the couch—he's supposed to be the one who gets the boys off to school. Marcus decides he's vegan today. He narrows his eyes, tells me the eggs I scrambled were chicken fetuses, tosses his into the trash. Toto has to change his shirt from dribbling strawberry jam all up and down its front, so forget the bus, it's come and gone. "Gracie," the ex says, yawning and scratching his butt after I finally drag him off the damn couch, to drive the boys to school. He doesn't finish his sentence.

I pack my bag for work, the GED text, an anthology of contemporary poetry to share with the guys—there's a couple they particularly like by a prison poet—and that's when I get the start of an idea, just a glimmer at this point, not fully thought out, an impulse we'll call it, staring at Trey's note at the feet of Jesus. I'm going to do something about this and the intent buzzes through me like electricity, like getting *struck* by it; here's me writhing on the ground, twitching with some spirit whose name I don't know yet, but whatever it is I have a feeling Jesus won't like it. "You'll have to stay here," I tell him, snatching up the note, sticking it inside my bag. I open the bedroom curtains so there's natural light for him, however gray the day.

Two hours later I mosey down one side of the chapel checking the guys' homework, a grammar exercise on articles and conjunctions, boring as shit, make Trey check the other side, pews divided by an aisle so he can't sidle up behind me. There's ten in the group, but I have to shift them around each time because none of them want to work with Trey. I get it. There's a prison hierarchy over who you deal with and who you don't, and the ED messed this up by making Trey, a prison pariah, my assistant. I'm with the guys on this but since the ED's my boss, I have my own hierarchy to get down with. And I'm becoming more and more unhappy about it.

"OK!" I chirp, imitating that cheerful mom voice, syrupy-sweet, its own kind of manipulative, "today we're going to critique some poetry." I stand up at the podium and read some selections from the anthology; we agree they're good, especially the prison poet's. "OK!" I say again. I've got that electrocution buzz shuddering up and down my spine, like Jimmy Page singeing his guitar, or maybe Jim Morrison, *Light My Fire*, that slow, fierce burn, a smoldering bed burn, a burn that takes out your apartment, derails your life.

The burn of endings. I reach into my bag on the shelf under the podium for Trey's note, hand shaking, clutch it in my fist.

"Vocab word of the day, *anonymous*, can anyone tell me what it means?" I don't wait for them to answer. If I hesitate even a moment I might lose my resolve. *Resolve*, another word for another day. "There's two kinds of anonymous," I tell them. "For example, let's say you read a really old poem from *anonymous*, before there was publishing a poem, before Random House, way before Kindles, so how would he print his name? Or, you get the kind of *anonymous* that means the poet—I use that word generously," I say, avoiding Trey's eyes, "knows his poem is so bad, such trivial, cliché crap he wouldn't (or he shouldn't!)" I hiss, "*want* to own up to it."

I walk to the chalkboard, my back to them so I don't have to see Trey's face, and start writing what it says on his note, replacing all the four-letter words with *dot dot dot*, I tell the guys (in case the ED strolls in, his wire-rimmed glasses pushed down on his nose, his face all red and puffing). "Check out this line," I say. "*I want to f . . . you*; wow how original," I say. "*I want to lick your . . .*" My face is flaming but they can't see it. I remind them of Shakespeare's sonnet, *Shall I compare thee to a Summer's day?* "Remember when we read that? Now compare Anonymous' backwash," I tell them, "so *banal*—another vocabulary word, means boring, stupid, worthless crap."

The guys are roaring, whooping and hooting, and when I finally turn around Trey's face is the color of a radish, white at the tips of his ears and chin, red everywhere else. I wonder if the others have figured it out and are plotting cell-block revenge scenarios for later tonight; or maybe they're just laughing because, god knows, there's not usually a whole lot to laugh about in this place.

"Who's the audience for this—dot dot dot *poem*," I say, because we've talked about writing for an audience.

"Some poor chica?" Darrel guesses and they howl.

"Right," I say, my heart banging in my chest, my breath squeezing in and out like a python's wrapped around my lungs. "But here's the thing"! My voice is loud now too, and shrill, soaring out of my mouth like the shriek of a hawk. "No *chica* who reads anything this bad would dream of getting with ANONYMOUS, in fact nobody wants anything to do with Anonymous, he's so *banal,* his life so meaningless he'll drift through the world like a teeny-tiny speck of dust and no one will ever notice or care."

It was like a cold wind blew through. Everyone goes quiet. I close the anthology, its covers snap together like a slammed door. "Well . . ." I start, clear my throat, blink down at the closed book in my hands like I'm wondering what it's doing there. "So much for poetry," I say. I feel a strange kind of hollow inside. Trey sits in a pew by himself, head down, worrying his hand over his shirtsleeve like he's trying to smooth its wrinkles out. Then he rises without looking at me or anyone else and walks from the room. Standing at the podium watching him leave I feel the eyes of the crucified Jesus behind me, the one hanging from the cross on the wall, and whether they are blue or brown, hardly matters. They are the eyes of fate.

MIDDLE OF THE night, everyone asleep but me and plastic Jesus, whose eyes can't close for even a moment, nod out and let the world fall away. The ex, who read tonight instead of switching on the TV, is sprawled on the couch, book face down on his chest. I stand over him before turning off the light. His face is still pretty, downy blond stubble like he's a toddler or a duck; there's weight on him though, our years since leaving the West. He sighs, his hand on top of the book twitches. Like a delinquent kid, I think, sometimes it's easier to love him when he's asleep. From far away a train whistles, cars swish by on the highway, east to west, coming, going.

"There isn't a happy ending to this thing, is there?" I ask Jesus, back in my room, he's in his place on the night table. No redemption here. I knew it in the way Trey walked out of the room, head down, shoulders tight, more bull than defeat. I can *say* I won, beat him at his own little shit-game, outwitted and defeated he'll ask the ED to give him a new assignment, laundry maybe? Or maybe in another scenario he'll want to get even, up his game and then I do…what? I'm not that kind of hero and this isn't that kind of story. There was something in his eyes when I read aloud from the anthology, when I dared to peek, an appreciation for the right word maybe, a moment of truth. For just a second our souls may have met over a Billy Collins-poem moment, but let's get real: Trey will be back, small and wrecked as the rest of us, scared he's even *smaller* than the rest of us, and he'll need someone to pay. This is where the hero runs.

In the morning I call the prison ED. "I'm sorry, but I can't come in anymore," I tell him. He asks me why and I have to think quick "Because we're moving," I say, something permanent enough so the guys won't think I'm another person giving up on them. But once those words are out I know it's true. It's what the ex has been waiting for, waiting for me. Soon as school's done, one month and we'll be packed. I can see it now—Ohio was the last place the ex mentioned, he has a cousin in Columbus.

"The test ground for everything Middle America!" he told me, like this is something to be proud of. He could manage a Wendy's— corporate headquarters. Head up north to Lake Erie, fish for those zebra mussels wiping out the ones that belong, or protect Lake Michigan from the invasive Asian carp.

"What about my job?" I asked him.

"There's prisons everywhere, Gracie, job security, good as a nurse!" He's quick like that.

I can see us now, passing through Pennsylvania all green and cool, our windows rolled down because it's finally spring and we're leaving the gray behind. Toto's singing *Somewhere over the rainbow.*

"Not Kansas," I remind the ex. "I draw the line at Kansas."

"Can we blow away in Ohio?" Toto asks.

"We're blowing this town!" the ex says, his grin that got me our first night together, four martinis and here we are.

After Ohio, who knows? And there will be *after* Ohio, let's face it. Flipping Wendy's burgers, the post-pubescent boss won't like him or he can't work for a boss whose pubes are barely in. Could he harvest corn in Nebraska? Or up to Minneapolis where there's some giant mall ("Retail!" he'll chirp), where folks travel in tunnels like tunnel rats to get out of the cold. Protecting wolves in Wyoming; Hoover Dam might need a water man; in Las Vegas he could deal cards; vineyards in the northwest; and why not bypass California this time, fly straight to Hawai'i, with a volcano so productive it's building new land, five hundred acres since 1983, *Pretty Paulie*, realtor for the future! Marcus nodding to his iPod, heavy metal howling in his ears, the ex slides his hand on my knee. "We're still separated," I'll remind him, it has to be said, and he'll point out this time there's only a gearshift between us. Warm air pours into the windows the further west we ride, peepers singing from a pond somewhere, and Jesus on the dashboard, all of us already gone.

Wild Things—II

MIGRANTS

Where I am, I don't know, I'll never know, in the silence you don't
know, you must go on, I can't go on, I'll go on.
—Samuel Beckett, *The Unnamable*

Loulie peeks out at the old woman from between her knees, her
legs scrunched up between her arms, her wrists tethered with
the rope, chain and padlock, perched on the mattress hour after
hour until her butt goes numb. The man thinks she's a ghost, but
Loulie's about decided she's just an odd old woman with a humpback,
a limp and a mask on that *looks* like a face, has all the right features
and symmetry, but no face would be that frozen, no animation in
it whatsoever. He calls her his mother the ghost, has conversations
where he does both speaking parts, which makes Loulie wonder if
the old woman speaks at all. If she does, perhaps that means she
listens, and maybe when the man isn't home Loulie could appeal
to her, beg her to set her free. Loulie had pretty much given up, but
now the old woman is around more; in fact, it seems like she may
live here too, maybe in that back room Loulie's never seen—"No
reason to take you in there," the man had said when he was showing
her around the trailer like she was a guest here. Because Loulie
won't speak and the old woman doesn't seem to either, it's a strange

household with the man, the halting way he talks like he might be a little retarded or something, speaking for them all.

Though sometimes Loulie wonders, does she even remember how? One day when the man wasn't around Loulie opened her mouth just to try it out, a scream—she'd long since realized the trailer is too far away from anyone who might hear her—but just to give it a whirl, as her mom would say, and . . . nothing; it was like her voice was encased in ice, a glacial hardness that stuck in her throat and then the taste of bile when nothing came out.

She wishes she could stand up, just that, of her own free will, instead of only during her programmed bathroom breaks, a pee-on-demand sort of schedule that Loulie has taken to because she has no choice. Stand and stretch out her legs, her spine, which feel like they're permanently bent now, like a shell, the humped ones the man displays on a shelf opposite her mattress, monuments whereas the rest of the room is a scatter of stuff: clothes tossed into a box in one corner; random dishes—clean though, she'd have to admit the man keeps the things they eat off of clean; a few books on the floor, Audubon guidebooks, insects, birds (he seems to like animals, does he imagine *she* is one, tied up, fed, led to perform her bodily functions like a dog?); some ancient *National Geographic* magazines; a makeshift desk with a panel of wood balanced upon concrete blocks, an old iMac on top; posters on the walls of nothing special, like the man just plucked them from a Hallmark store, laminated generic photographs, somebody's idea of what people like—a squirrel on a birdbath, purple flowers in a field, a beach with footprints in the sand. This is Loulie's world now.

Then, just like that she feels it, her blood, and with it the physical sense she gets of her mom, like they are connected by more than chromosomal materials, her flesh, her mother's—*Annalee, Annalee, Annalee.* They used to get their periods together after Loulie first started hers in math class one day, thirteen years old and it made her weep, hunched over the toilet in the Lincoln Middle School Girls' bathroom as if blood flowing out of her meant some kind of loss. That night Annalee made Loulie spaghetti, her favorite. "You're a woman now," her mom said proudly, like she had played some sort of essential role in it. Well, maybe she had, she was there anyway, in their little, gray house that was clean and kept up; Annalee and Loulie would make a game of it on Saturdays, challenge each other to a race, vacuuming, dusting, toilet scrubbed, sinks, kitchen floor mopped, and whoever finished first got to pick out what they'd watch on television that night while the other ordered takeout, whatever the winner wanted, Chinese? Pizza?

It was a small life but a good fit and tears sting Loulie's eyes, willing them not to fall, concentrate on the blood, she tells herself, what will she do about it? It stopped after he took her, the stress she figured, or maybe the food he fed her—what she managed to eat of it, which wasn't much in the beginning. How long now? Weeks? Months? Years, even? No, not years because Loulie had devised a calendar of sorts, pulling splinters from the rotting wood off the window ledge into a pile on the floor under the molding and counting them; the problem being it's only an accurate record of the days since Loulie started doing this, defined by the light and then the dark, the slant of the setting sun coming through the window above her was the cue to pick the splinter. But Loulie didn't know how many had passed before this timekeeping, whether she's even still fifteen years old. She might've had her birthday and will never know it, that she made it through another year. Annalee would've baked her a pan of fudge brownies, packing sixteen candles into one of them, flame like a tiny torch. Sweet sixteen.

Maybe her blood will rush out of her, fill the small room until they drown. The man told her he couldn't swim. Matter of fact, like this is just the way it is. Mostly he doesn't talk to her at all but when he does, it's to confess something like this.

The man slides his key into the padlock, unchains Loulie, motioning her to follow. Loulie imagines for a moment running, but the man would catch her like he has every time she's bolted; she doesn't know if he's really fast or she's slowed that much, slumped upon the mattress day after day. Loulie shivers, blinks back her tears.

In the bathroom she soaks a washcloth in cold water then slides down her pants, the ones the man gave her to wear after her jeans were trashed from the oil in his shed, the time she tried to hide there. They're khaki and the stain is obvious, shaped like a toddler's hand, a smear of it like the kid had been finger painting and smacked its little hand against them.

When she emerges she sees the old woman lingering near the mattress. "He'll get you something to fix you up," the old woman says jerking her head at the stain. Her voice is like rust scraped off metal, and what startles all three of them when the rope is back around her wrists, the chain, click of the padlock, is that Loulie starts to laugh, a waterfall of it and she doesn't know what she's laughing at, nothing is at all funny, but gazing at the odd little ghost-woman, a kitchen witch who as it turns out does speak, she can't seem to stop. The other side of this is tears; Loulie knows because it's happened to her mom, laughing so hard then in almost the same breath, crying.

"What's wrong with her?" The man stammers, his face the color of a tomato.

"Release her arms and tether her ankle instead," the old woman instructs. "She can't get away so long as you have the key." She talks! Loulie thinks, and still can't stop laughing. The man sticks his chin out, scowls. The old woman shakes a knotted finger at him. "Never you mind," she says. "You don't make some concessions she'll go mad! You hear her? Madness!"

Loulie laughs until her throat burns, won't look him in the eyes as he appraises her like she's on display. "OK," he says, "OK, OK. Maybe you'd like to look out the window?" he asks her, politely, as if this has been his idea from the start. Then he unlocks her wrists, securing the chain around her left ankle, sliding the mattress with her on it in the opposite direction so it's sticking out from the wall and she's on the other end. Loulie can see daylight, the afternoon sun slunk low behind a tree whose branches from this angle she can make out even through the frosted glass. She blinks at the light, the sun in an actual tree outside, its lines waving delicately in the foggy panel, like an abstract painting, she thinks, someone's idea of a tree. She feels dazed, that sunstroke feeling when the afternoon is hot and you step into it for a moment from the cool dark of inside. She stops laughing as easily as it started, rubbing her wrists, her hands together, enjoying the simple pleasure of this, putting one's hands together then pulling them apart.

SINCE IT'S BECOME pretty clear Loulie won't get to have a life of her own she spends her days imagining her mom's life, because here's something else: if Annalee had made different choices, the way she told Loulie about making the *right* choices, in her own life—if Annalee had done that probably she would never have come here at all, with its promise of a good life for her and her child, a wholesome and satisfying one now gone to rack and ruin, Annalee said, what with IBM pulling out and before that Endicott-Johnson Shoes, which according to her mom might've been the last decent company in America, building nice little boxy houses for their employees, EJ houses they called them, medical care, retirement, a way of life that makes you proud living it, a product you felt good about making, "a job with dignity," her mom said. The abandoned factory sits amid broken glass and brambles, busted-out windows, a hulk of a building now home to bats and spiders and wasps nesting in the eaves. Twenty-one hundred laid off from Lockheed Martin, 274,000 private sector jobs lost in 2009, forty-three thousand factories moved to China in the last six years. How does Loulie know these numbers? Well it's easy, she's thinking like her mom now who after she lost her own job quoted these statistics; maybe she *is* her mom, because where else would Annalee want to be but with her daughter, right? Even if she believed her daughter was a bad girl who ran away with a drug dealer?

Oh, but here is a thought: if her mom had never moved from Longview, maybe Loulie would never have existed. If that were the case she wouldn't be tied up on this dirty old mattress, fed three meals a day with an evening snack if she wants it, five bathroom visits—first thing in the morning, noon, mid-afternoon, early evening and right before sleep—a shower twice a week, the murmur of the TV never turned off like it's a generator, something essential to running the trailer, and of course the perpetual drone from the highway near enough for Loulie to know it never stops, with its cars full of people going everywhere but here, and the freight trains that whistle by six times a day, twice in the morning (she knows it's morning by the slope of the light pouring into the window, its color whiter, cleaner than the yellow afternoon), a little past noon, late afternoon and eight o'clock in the evening (the man once said, that's the eight o'clock freight), then the last late at night, its mournful wail like everything else, passing her by—all of this is background now. Maybe her life is just background. Maybe she should've said yes to Troy-boy so she'd have her own memory at least, Troy-boy pushing her down, but *tenderly*, on the back seat that would smell of Fritos (what they'd snacked on driving from the school, Loulie's last food as a free person), and the splif cut with meth, *ice,* the gray smoke curling around them and ever so gently he'd slip off her jeans, her panties, and she'd have the image now of something inside her, something that made her *her*, Louise-Annalee Cross, *Loulie*, with a heart, breasts, stomach, legs and the opening between them, flesh. Somebody. Her best friend Josie said it hurt the first time but even that would've been OK, because if you feel pain, you're alive.

Annalee's own mother lingered, Loulie's grandmother, half alive and half not alive, the one time they visited in her Longview home and she was curled up like twine in a bed that looked like a mahogany sleigh. "Been like this for months," Annalee's brother's wife said, belligerent since it was she who had to take care of her, what with her husband at work and the father-in-law dead and Annalee gallivanting about on the east coast. She slept 23 hours a day and the one hour when she was awake she didn't care who Annalee was, who Loulie was—*your granddaughter, Mom*! A heart still beating, skin still warmed by the blood still flowing underneath, but retreated to some world in her head where she spoke to people the rest of them couldn't see. "I want my Mommy!" her grandmother whimpered, staring blankly at Loulie perched on the edge of the bed where Annalee told her to sit, one leg bent and ready to spring.

"That was the worst," Annalee said on the plane back, "your own mother alive but out of reach." Loulie, who had felt like an intruder in her mom's former home, stared out the window, the crops below in strange circles like they'd been stamped there, the backbone of distant mountains, flying out of what seemed to have been unending clouds in the northwest, headed home.

But Loulie does have a memory that's hers alone! She scratches her ankle viciously, she's taken to doing this, digging in over the bone where the skin is thin, where the rope is tied, and she makes it bleed, just a little—doesn't want the man having to tend to it, put a bandage on, touching her. Sitting on the edge of her grandmother's bed, her grandmother whose name was Ann, noticing one small, smooth and perfectly shaped foot that had snuck out of the covers, just one. Such a young-looking foot on an old and ill person, and Loulie had badly wanted to touch that foot, rub it for her—wouldn't that have felt nice? But she didn't, her grandmother didn't even know who she was. "It's the dementia," Annalee said. "It's gone and erased her. The last straw," her mom said.

Though she'd said it was the last straw when just a few weeks earlier she had discovered on some website that her name, Annalee, was way too similar to a Manga character named *Annlee*, bought by an American artist from a Japanese Manga agency, who made her "available" for other artists to work with. Bored, she had googled her own name and came up with this almost-match—*did you mean Annlee?* The thing about *Annlee*, besides her shadowy-haired beauty, is that she's an empty vessel, a shell, a ghost with giant, soulless holes for eyes and no inner life, to be filled with another's story—*any* story!—depending on the whim of the artist. So given that bit of info, maybe her own erasure is about complete, Annalee told Loulie, with even the "a" from her name snubbed out. And the irony of it, her mom said, is her name really *is* Ann Lee, but separated, your basic paper-factory-worker name from Grandma Ann and Auntie Lee, her mother's dead sister. Auntie Lee died from *cancer*, which in Longview back then was whispered, like some cancer-god might hear you say it and strike you with it too. Annalee shoved the two names together when she was eighteen and could get away with it, using the "a" to help it flow better. In those days, Annalee said, everything was about the flow.

Maybe the last straw was the article her mom read in the *New York Times Magazine,* then insisted Loulie read it too. It was about Annalee's former employer, how they've been hard at work on a new machine that plays *Jeopardy*: Watson, the super-computer. IBM put a lot of resources into this one, the article said, maybe money it saved from Annalee's own job and the jobs of hundreds of others when they downsized and outsourced. "It displayed a remarkable facility with cultural trivia," said the article about Watson. "He plays to win," lamented one of the whipped contestants. The computer scientist who created Watson said if he didn't do it another scientist might, "and then bang, you are irrelevant!" he said.

So *that's* it, her mom is irrelevant. Claimed to be a systems analyst but really she was just data entry. Anyone could do it. Anyone *is* doing it. Irrelevant.

Certainly it wasn't the disappearance of her daughter. Annalee must've deserved that, after all, unsettled and undisciplined, used to sleep with anyone she liked—she told Loulie all about it—tracking them down like a hunt of some sort, in the bars, on the beach, under her dorm window, the street kid whistling at her and she lowers the strap on her purple jumpsuit, motions him up, for god's sake! How could her mom expect just having a job you dressed up for might've made the difference?

Perhaps one day the little gray house's front door is padlocked when her mom comes home: *no rent, no roof,* says the landlord's note. Their electric would've been turned off weeks before and the summer burning down, not even a fan, so who the hell needs it, Annalee would think, hurling one of her shoes through that broken window in the bathroom the landlord never bothered to fix.

Maybe the last straw hasn't even happened, maybe it'll just keep getting worse. Loulie jams her forehead against her knees, bone on bone, rocks herself then *bang,* bone on bone again until she sees it: her mom walking the floodwall, one side the Susquehanna, brown and turbid, the other waving grasses and weeds, blue and yellow wildflowers with their assortments of bees and other buzzing, flying things. One foot in front of the other, eyes on her feet, do not look down the bank at the swampy area where someone found the badly decomposed body of a twelve-year-old girl. Loulie remembers watching this news with her mom, Annalee shaking her head in that remote sort of disbelief—the horrible things that happen to other people.... No! Loulie up and left, that's it, what her mom would think, and since the landlord padlocked the house so Annalee's essentially homeless, it's not like she's got anything more to lose.

Maybe it really was her mom's fault, stories about the wild-child days, each tale ending with a danger and a moral, telling her daughter as a cautionary thing and the damn kid takes it as permission, a culture where things were not as they seemed and Loulie couldn't recognize the truth in them, hanging out with that drug-dealer boy. Crystal meth, another girl gone missing, the police would've shrugged.

Loulie watches an umbrella spider (she calls him that, his thread-thin shape like spines in a sheath of plastic) dangling from the stained ceiling above her mattress, a ladybug ambling blindly toward it from the other direction. Who will she root for? The spider has been there the longest—eighteen days according to Loulie's splinter-calendar, so it has squatter rights, she supposes. But Loulie loves ladybugs, harbingers of winter, how they'd come into the little gray house every fall in droves and cluster in its corners, then one day they'd disappear. Occasionally she'd find one, sluggishly crawling on a window ledge or the bathroom floor when the weather outside turned unforgiving.

But wait! Competition today, Loulie's spider spies another that has come out of nowhere, it seems, or out of Loulie's vision anyway, into its territory. Her spider scrambles toward this intruder, then suddenly drops down on its web and snags, not the ladybug Loulie is relieved to see, but a fly. The other spider retreats, no fight today, and no ladybug for dessert, as she flares her spotted wings and flies away.

ON AN EARLY morning walk last week Jones had a wonderful thing happen, the best thing that's happened to him in a long time. He was on the path that leads around the field, the field maybe half a mile from his place, where a farmhouse stood with its clay-red barn, acres of what used to be crops overgrown now since the farmer bankrupted some years back and the bank couldn't sell it—who could afford a farm out here during these hard times? Though Jones liked to fantasize about it, growing his own food for the girl and his mother the ghost, and what they didn't need he could sell, make money for all the other expenses, electric for the trailer, propane and whatnot. But if he could grow their food, maybe get some cows and chickens, have eggs and fresh milk—he couldn't see himself slaughtering anything. It all seemed a little overwhelming though, as first he'd have to buy the land back from the bank, with the falling-apart barn still on it (a *termite palace*, his mother would call it). The house burnt down maybe a year or two ago, around the same time, give or take, that his mother's had so Jones figured the meth chefs had found their way in there too. Season of burnings, a rash of them, houses, trailers, trucks, overgrown yards where there'd been some sort of shed—the meth cookers were scouting out new digs as fast as they destroyed them.

But it made for a good place to walk, the field now filled with wildflowers and long grasses and paths through them where the rows for the crops must've been. He was strolling on a path, and all of a sudden from the rim of the woods beyond, two little fawns came running toward him, twin fawns, bumping into each other in their haste to get to him, those spindly legs all akimbo and when they reached him they started rubbing their soft little heads against his pant-legs and Jones realized they must not see too good and thought he was their mother. That is until he reached down to pet them and they smelled the human on his hand, made that *huff* sound deer make warning each other of danger and bolted. It was a good thing God or whatehaveyou did that, Jones figured, made the smell of a person an instinct to run, because Jones can't think of anything in this world more threatening. The moment before they took off Jones touched one of their cold noses and had known for just a moment some sort of infinite trust they were placing in him, the trust of the weaker for the stronger, that the stronger would not hurt them, and he decided it was a sign, to take the Paro for the girl. He'd been considering that, weighing it against what he knew to be true: that stealing is wrong.

The Paro is the next cutest thing Jones has seen, second to those fawns. There's a couple of them in the nursing home he sweeps out every Saturday, washes the floors, windows, things the regular janitor doesn't have time to do and since the regular janitor is Todd, who used to work with him at the Giant and managed the trailer park Jones lived in for a while, he's hired Jones as a subcontractor of sorts, Todd calls him—pays Jones so he can stay home that day, watch sports on TV and stick it to his wife, Todd said. Jones likes the sound of that, *subcontractor*, like he's doing something official. Todd told him not to tell Unemployment though or they'd cut his benefits, even if its just one day a week of pay. "That's how the government works," Todd said. "It's all or nothing. You want to be on the *all* end of things," he said.

The nursing home is called Willow Bend and it's state run so it doesn't have much, but some do-gooder donated a couple of the Paros to comfort the patients who have dementia, Todd told Jones. It looks like a baby seal, all white and furry with big black eyes and long eyelashes that blink when you pet it, makes trilling sounds and paddles its flippers, responds to your voice when you talk to it. It's a robot, Todd said, and it makes folks who've got nobody, who don't even know who they are anymore think something loves them. And when the battery runs down in two hours, the folks just think it's gone to sleep and they curl up beside it. Todd shook his head, like maybe he thought the people who slept peacefully beside the Paro had been duped, but Jones thought it sounded kind of nice. He'd seen the wild look on some of their faces, how they didn't even know where they were anymore, and the empty look others had like none of it matters, and what Jones was thinking was that maybe one of those Paros would help the girl, who also has this look, when she looks at him at all. His mother the ghost said she might be going crazy and he better consider letting her go. "Think catch and release," his mother said. "You just take her far away from here, like the Endless Mountains and release her there. When they find her they won't know where she's been, and she won't have a clue neither." But all Jones could think about was the bad people who might find her, ones like the boy she was with in the car who would make her do things and Jones couldn't allow that to happen. How could he live with himself if he did?

Did *he* steal the girl? Jones asked himself this, and the answer was clear: no, he did not. He rescued her. Maybe he could bring one of those Paros home for the girl.

But how to do that? Clearly if he asked to borrow one they wouldn't let him, who was Jones? Just a guy who helps Todd on Saturdays. And Todd said robots aren't cheap, that these are probably worth a chunk. Most folks slave their lives away, or they lose their jobs then slowly die, and if they get dementia their minds go mush and they wink out. "No damn robot takes the edge off that," Todd said.

Still, fawns don't come running toward humans thinking they can trust them, so it must've been a sign, Jones reminds himself. Perhaps if he has a good reason to take the Paro, to help the girl, then that negates the bad that is stealing. Maybe it makes it less of a steal and more just borrowing it, even though they wouldn't know who was borrowing it, and when the girl got better he could bring it back to them, he *would* bring it back. He'll sleep on it for a few nights, Jones decides, what his mother used to say when he needed to sort something out. "Just sleep on it," she said.

He gazes at the girl now; he guesses she's asleep. Since he tied her ankle instead of her wrists she's taken to lying on her back and staring out the window. It's frosted but there's the strip at the top that's clear, and one night when he thought she was most definitely asleep he lay quietly down beside her, careful not to touch her, his head on the pillow next to hers, so close he could smell his own shampoo's minty scent, the shampoo he'd given her to use for her showers and he imagined what it would be like, knowing her this way, the scent of her hair, sleeping beside her every night. He didn't close his eyes though as he was afraid he really would fall asleep and when she woke she'd panic thinking he'd done something to her. So instead he looked out the window. It was dark and he could make out a couple stars, little pricks of light through the clear part of the glass, just that. But it seemed like it could be enough.

LOULIE IS DREAMING of the barn owl her mom found at the side of the road, Loulie a little girl, watching as Annalee gently picked it up, wrapping it in her own sweater which she had taken off, despite the chill in the air. It had been hit by a car and in real life Annalee cared for it only until the people from the Wildlife Center came and took it away a couple hours later, but in the dream her mom cares for it for days, maybe weeks, until the broken wings heal and Annalee says it's time to set it free. So they do, into a line of trees Loulie doesn't recognize, and as it flies up toward the highest branch suddenly a murder of crows zoom out of the trees, the air raw with their screeches, black shadows of their wings and they mob the owl, swooping down upon it as it falls to the ground. Annalee racing toward it with Loulie screaming at her to stop, the birds lifting off the owl, hovering over her mom.

JONES IS A little irritated at his mother the ghost. Supposedly she died in that fire; the coroner gave him back some human remains, so charred from the explosion a court had to pronounce them hers. Jones was suspicious. They could've been hers along with the other meth cookers, since nobody claimed to even know those two let alone mourn their loss, but he buried them under that oak where she used to sit sometimes, daydreaming, she'd tell him, of Sam Shepherd. Jones glued a picture of Sam Shepherd snipped from *People* magazine onto the urn, and if the other meth cookers were in there too, who knew what they dreamt about, or if they dreamt at all.

But now she's back again and just as bossy, yammering about what Jones should do for the girl. He needs to help her, she insists, so why does she think the girl is here in the first place? "I saved her!" he tells his mother the ghost, and she says that's all well and good but the girl is going nuts, and insanity is no saving grace, as if he didn't know. He moved the mattress at his mother's request, put the rope and chain around the girl's ankle instead of her wrists; recently he even replaced the frosted glass with a regular pane (just a couple small nicks in it—he picked it up at the salvage yard), and now the girl stares out that window all the time, changing her position so her head is opposite and she's gazing out, or right under it and she's peering up. Either way she refuses to look at him.

Now his mother the ghost wants him to take her out for a walk. "What is she, a dog?" he asks his mother the ghost.

"That girl needs fresh air," his mother says. She's sitting at the Formica table glaring at him, or he assumes she's glaring, as the expression on her face doesn't change or even move, and it doesn't much look like her face to begin with. But her posture, the steely pose of her spine, the darts of her shoulders, even the growl of her voice speaks to his mother's former glare.

He remembers his walks with her, years before she was his mother the ghost, before she would've had anything to do with people who cook crystal methamphetamine, letting him lead her out into the darkness after she came home from work at the Night-Owl, watching fireflies like sparks on the long grass in their yard, which they left uncut as a haven for the flying, crawling, buzzing things he loved. Eventually she'd get sick of it and tell him he had to mow, which he did, his throat raw, nose running, snuffling it all up, thinking how he's killing them—the beetles with their shiny green carapaces, columns of ants, things that jump and wing across the grass, cicadas, moths, even butterflies—he imagined all those beautiful little creatures churned up like colorful bits of confetti in the mower.

So maybe he could do it, take the girl out, particularly now since there's nobody in the field, just the old barn caving back into the land. He could blindfold her and put duct tape over her mouth, not that anyone would hear her but just in case (it's for her own good). Or they could go in the other direction to the old stone church. Jones can't remember when it closed its doors, what was left of the congregation moved to the bigger Lutheran church in town. When he was twelve, old enough where his mother took the late shift at the Night-Owl and didn't worry about leaving him, Jones would eat whatever he could find, canned corn, a bologna sandwich, and later when the night wore down to the ticking of the furnace and he was afraid of the quiet he'd go outside where it wasn't the silence of walls, but a whole night full of living things, crickets, owls hooting, things rustling in the bushes, wild things and Jones was not afraid. He'd climb up on the roof of the old church and gaze out at the night, the river a dark slash on the horizon. *Roof Lutheran* his mother called him when she discovered what he'd been doing, "About the closest we'll come to religion," she said. He hasn't been to the church in a while. It had been for sale, but who's going to buy a church, especially now when half the houses around it seemed to have been abandoned, or just plain falling apart because the folks who own them have no jobs.

Maybe he could bring the girl outside instead of giving her the Paro, because Willow Bend had started locking them up when they weren't with a patient, and when they were Jones didn't have the heart to take them away.

SHE REMEMBERS HER mom giving her a model of a cardinal to assemble and paint—Loulie was eight-years old, a rainy, dreary Sunday and Annalee says here's something we can do. But it's the royal *we*, as her mom used to describe the *we* who means *you*, and Loulie sat at the dining room table, which wasn't technically a dining room table since the little, gray house didn't have a dining room, but her mom called it that, mahogany and scratched—she kept a paisley shawl over it. Annalee covered everything with old newspapers and gave Loulie a paint set in a tin tray that had all the primary colors plus a row of pastels, and a cup of water to wash the brushes in. "You like birds," her mom said, handing her the pieces and the directions for snapping them together. Loulie spent hours on that model bird, trying to make it right, painting it scarlet with a black mask around its eyes, beak and throat, just like the instructions called for. When she was done she showed it to Annalee who cocked her head, not unlike a bird herself. "It's fine," she said. "Looks just like it does in real life. But why didn't you try to create something new? A purple striped cardinal, or an orange and neon pink one. That's what we have imaginations for."

The roar of the highway, always the roar of that highway—close enough to hear it but never see it and the people inside the cars can't ever see her. Loulie's peered out the window in the bathroom when he takes her for her shower, facing toward that sound, a rush of it going forward and another in the other direction, cars going east, west, but looking out that window all she sees are the woods. One of the times she tried to escape she glanced around to get her bearings, to see which direction would be best, and she realized how isolated it was, this trailer, sitting on land outside of town like so many of them do, surrounded by woods, hunkered down inside a valley, a hollow between those endless hills and what links them is the highway threading through.

From her mattress Loulie studies the trailer floor. She starts with the squares of linoleum the mattress is on and works out from there, each patch and what it contains, its own little world. The one closest to her left ankle, for instance, has a lightning-shaped crack in the yellowing surface, what lightning might look like if you were drawing it coming out of the sky. But the sky in this world is tainted. It's not blue, not white, not a nighttime darkness, this dingy yellow that might be beige, the color of sand? Of vomit? It's the wrong color for a sky even if one did use their imagination. Let's say you're an artist, would you paint your sky the color of throw-up?

Loulie imagines following these squares if she were an ant; to move across them would be like moving through town, each one offering something, schools, a gym, maybe even a park of some sort. The next town over has grit in it, which might be crumbs from Loulie's lunch when the man picked up her plate. He had given her a peanut-butter sandwich and Loulie used to like peanut butter, in fact sometimes there'd be little else in the cupboards when Annalee had an especially long week at work and didn't have time to market, so Loulie would ferret out the jar, pop in a spoon and dig. But things have lost their taste, or the tastes of the foods he gives her blend into each other, canceling each other out so that sometimes it's like she's not even eating food. Today she spit the sandwich out because she had this horrible sensation that it was plastic or rubber or something inedible, and what was worse she couldn't remember what these might feel like either, on her tongue, down her throat.

"It's peanut butter," the man told her, as if she had asked. Did she? She can't recall if her thoughts are sometime spoken, or whether she has lost the ability to speak entirely and talks only in her head. But then why would the man say that? Perhaps he can hear her thoughts? Maybe that's what he's doing right now, sprawled on that couch studying her like she's the TV, pretending to watch the TV which is on at its usual drone, like insects buzzing around your ears—it doesn't bother her as it's the highway she listens to, everything moving that becomes the past, flowing away from her.

More and more Loulie's been thinking about Troy-boy, her last connection to her former life, the last person she was with. She wonders whether he's got a new girlfriend, someone who will let him do what he wants. Maybe Miriam Hopewell, that skanky girl he sold meth to sometimes. Loulie should've let him. She should've let Troy-boy strip off her jeans, her panties, and just kept doing those drugs, smoking that meth, she can see it now, the smoke curling over their heads, inhale, exhale, inhale; it could make it so she wouldn't feel a thing.

JONES IS THINKING about insects. He likes their ordered world, and sometimes when things feel especially out of control in his he thinks of theirs instead. Their world is so much fuller, so much busier than what humans think of as their own world. The sky, for instance, what humans look at as being essentially empty, a wide space over their heads that allows rain or snow to fall on them or wind to blow, something to fly airplanes through to get from one place to another, is actually filled with insects. There are ladybugs at six thousand feet above our heads, gnats at seven thousand feet and a spider was discovered at fifteen thousand feet in its web, drifting on a current of air. Theirs is a simpler world than ours, Jones thinks, because they don't have memories. They just live every minute like it's the first. And they don't have to judge others, or know what is right or wrong and act on it. They just are. Jones envies that lightness. It's a weight to try and do what is right, or to try keep others from doing wrong.

As a child Jones used to collect caterpillars, stuck them in tall glasses with foil on top, then watched them spin their cocoons and turn into butterflies. Then he'd let them go. But a man his mother brought home one night peeled the foil off Jones' glasses, dumped his caterpillars onto the kitchen counter, and laughed as they crawled around, his mother shrieking, pretending to be afraid. After that he stopped collecting them. Now Jones stares at the girl who is staring at the floor. She reminds him of a caterpillar, the humpbacked way she sits into herself on the mattress. She could become a butterfly and then he'd let her go, if she had wings and could fly up into the sky where it's safe.

MAYBE IT'S ANNALEE'S birthday today. Loulie remembers it was in August, and she thinks it must be August, the way the light is in the window, hard and long, a dusty, burdened red when the sun is going down. And it's hot, so hot and breathless in the trailer Loulie sometimes imagines taking her clothes off, stretched out on the mattress in her bra and panties like it's a bathing suit, like it's nothing. Annalee would. Her mom talked about getting old but everywhere they went men stared at her. What's fifty? Loulie probably won't even make it to seventeen.

Maybe she meets up with some friends who take her out to celebrate, sing to her over a cake, angel food, her mom's favorite. Make a wish, a tan brunette says, and maybe her mom tells them she has nothing to wish for, even though, as Loulie imagines, she's living out of the Plymouth since the landlord padlocked the little grey house. But they wouldn't know this. And her daughter is gone, which she wouldn't tell them either. It's a celebration, after all. And there's Annalee's pride; she wouldn't want them to pity her. That much, Loulie knows, is real.

What if they take her to a club, let's say, the kind where the girls dance around poles—when her mom was a wild child she used to go there, she told Loulie, and it's a fiftieth birthday after all. Aren't you supposed to do something a little crazy? At first she'd been skeptical, watching the girls, the way that pole twirled would hardly feel stable at all. But they were good, her mom had told Loulie. Some had been real dancers; you could see it in their muscles, a kind of muscle memory for the dance. Maybe Annalee watches them twirl on the pole while the muscles do their thing, like the carousel poles in the park she used to take her daughter to, those green summer days. Would she remember how when the music began, little Loulie clutched at the horses rising up and down on the poles, her knuckles white as paste, as if falling from one would be the worst thing? Neither of them had a clue then what the worst thing was. Not even Annalee almost getting smothered in a van back when she used to hitchhike was worse than this. Hah, what do you know! Loulie's one-upped her mom, after all.

"They don't think about the clothes they take off," her mom told her, "just that their body looks good." And even if it doesn't, the skin mottled in places, a little too much of it, it doesn't matter. It's a willingness to get naked that turns guys on (Troy-boy said that)—not how you look naked, just that you are.

As the birthday girl watches the women strut up to the center of the stage, shimmy out of their breakaway clothes, careful not to step on them in the jeweled stilettos, perhaps she is reminded of the little plastic heels she once gave her daughter, with straps around the ankles. And how she'd let Loulie dress up in Annalee's own clothes, her grapefruit-pink lipstick, clip-on earrings, dragging about the little grey house in this get-up like it was her inheritance— the *Annlee* smile, a cavern, an emptiness.

Jones is finally doing it, what his mother the ghost has been nagging him about: taking the girl for a walk in the field, if for no other reason than to get away from his mother who's permanent as a light fixture now, one you can't switch off, telling him what to do about the girl who at last started talking, maybe so she could defend herself from what his mother deems best. "I won't go outside with him in the dark!" the girl declared last night. She addresses the room like Jones isn't in it, but she's at least speaking.

The thing is, he saw something special a few days ago and then he saw it again yesterday, a new bird! He's never seen a bird like this, its wings green and pale yellow like pound cake, its head and throat a burnished gold, a white chest. The closest he could find to it on the Internet was a picture of a tropical finch, *palila*, one of the Hawaiian honeycreeper birds. The website said it's critically endangered. But what would it be doing six thousand miles away, feeding at Jones's feeder? Nervously, its shimmery little head popping about, glitter of its black eyes like slivers of glass, peering all around as if he knows he's the only one and therefore a target of some sort. According to the article, this bird could soon be extinct. It needs the *māmane* tree for sustenance, in a forest on the slopes of Mauna Kea, but these are also disappearing due to forest destruction and a prolonged drought. Which means it might soon be the last bird of its kind in the world, or else some sort of mutation and the beginning of a new species! Jones would like to figure out a way to keep it safe, but first he has to find out where it stays when it isn't at the feeder, a nest of some sort? Jones thinks this must be a sign.

No one ever comes to the field but him, so even though it's daylight nobody will see them. Still he insisted she be blindfolded; not sure why since no one seeing them means she won't see anybody, but it seemed a prudent idea and so he tied a red, checkered dish towel around her head, her wrists bound, and is now leading the girl into the field, clutching her arm, careful so she doesn't trip on anything, the uneven ground, tangles of tree roots. It's a hot afternoon, humid after the rainstorm last night and all manner of buzzing things are dive-bombing their heads and the girl shrieks, batting her tied-up hands at a horsefly that bit her neck. "Get me out of this thing!" she yells.

"Do you mean the blindfold?" Jones asks.

"Duh!" she says, and Jones smiles—it's the first actual conversation they've had, him saying something, then her responding, and him responding to her, then she's talking again—since he brought her to the trailer and she begged him to let her go. When she ran and he had to tie her up they had another conversation, but this was him talking to her, patiently explaining how it was for her own good.

"I'll take it off soon," Jones says. "I want to show you something but we're not there yet." He leads her deeper into the field, where there isn't a path, where they're having to part long grass, dodge creeping vines that hook around their knees and at one point the girl falls into him and for a moment he feels her body against his, her sweaty arm, her breast. His breath quickens and she must've heard the change in it as suddenly she stands still as rock. "I won't take another step until you take this thing off my eyes!" And then, in almost the same breath—but quietly, her voice a whisper and wobbling such that Jones wonders if he heard her at all—she says, "You ever kiss a girl?"

Jones blushes, ignores the question (was it really a question?). "Come on," he says, "we're almost there. I promise you'll like it," he adds.

"Take off this blindfold! I want to see what I'm stepping on. I won't go another inch, I told you."

"You should be grateful to be out of the trailer," he mutters, but he does it, unties the dishrag and her grey-green eyes stare into his. He expects her to look away, she never looks him in the eyes, but instead she inhales a shaky breath and steps closer to him. To avoid thinking about how close she is he loosens the tie around one of her wrists, frees the hand, then binds her other wrist to his. He hopes she appreciates this. She's trembling all over, the rope going taut with her tremors; like a high wire he thinks, like something very tiny could walk on it, crossing the space between them.

"Well? You didn't answer me. Have you? Kissed a girl?" She's watching him, her pupils large, her eyes seeming to lose focus, darting about, quick and gray as guppies, peering at things on all sides then back to his face. "I'm just asking if you have, that's all," she says, her voice squeaking high then cutting out.

"I know where a fox den is," he tells her, again ignoring the question. "It's under that big maple in the middle of the field. I saw a fox there." He's thinking this sounds a little stupid and wishes his mother the ghost hadn't suggested it; show her something *special*, she said. What does she think he is, a tour guide? Jones assumed foxes would be special enough, they are for him, but now the girl's unbuttoning the top button on her shirt with her free hand, and she grabs his free hand, placing it against the flesh over her heart; he can feel it beating, erratic little pulses like something wounded. "I'm a *person!*" she whispers, sun shimmering down, the warmth of her, everything glowing as he yanks away, then the shock of the rope around his wrist snapping him back.

Loulie forces herself to look at him, crinkling her eyes, sun like a blade. "Don't you get it?" she says, starting to cry, her lower lip quivering. "Please hear me! I know you think you were saving me, you've said that over and over, but it's not what you think. You say *no*, but maybe you don't mean it. Or maybe you do. It's not a clean-cut thing. It's a lot messier than that. You can't save a person from something they don't even know if they want or not. Haven't you ever felt that? Where someone wants you and you're not sure if you want them, but maybe you do? Who made you God anyway? Who said it's your job to save me, even if you could?"

Jones thinks about this; could be his mother the ghost was right about the girl going crazy—she isn't making a lot of sense. Then again, should he be listening to his mother the ghost? His mother believes she's been resurrected from the meth-cooking explosion, set back down again for some purpose she can't figure out. "I ain't no Jesus," she told Jones when finally he asked how it was she's here, out of the ashes he buried under the oak, said a few words over, then brought his trailer to her land, collecting the small amount from her life insurance to hook it up. "They wouldn't pay a thing for me being alive," she told Jones, "and what's more would probably put me in jail. I ain't no Jesus," she said again. "I'm back but with scars all over."

The girl looks at Jones with drenched eyes, chewing on her lip. "Don't you want to see the den?" he asks her. "Also there's this bird that's started coming around, a brand new bird, or one that belongs six thousand miles away. Could be a migrant but I've never seen its species here. He just appeared one day, no others like him. Maybe we'll see him."

"Answer me!" she squeals, her voice shrill, slapping a gnat off her cheek. "Haven't you ever wanted someone who wanted you, then got confused about if you do or not?"

Jones lowers his head. "Nobody would want me," he says.

Loulie collapses on the ground, dragging Jones down with her. "I just want my mom, that's all *I* want!" she sobs.

He puts his hand tentatively on her shoulder. The shirt is still unbuttoned and he can see the rounded tops of her breasts. "It's OK," he says. He had felt the need to say something; she'd been talking to him, after all, like he's a real person. Jones kneels in front of her and carefully, hand shaking, secures her top button. "Do you like butterflies?" he asks. "I know where there's monarchs. Edge of the field in the milkweed. Where they migrate their habitat's disappearing. And pesticides kill what they eat. In ten years maybe no more monarch butterflies."

Loulie peers up at Jones, his brow crumpled like he's feeling it too, the wreckage. She remembers again her grandmother lying helpless in that sleigh bed, and afterwards the plane ride with her mom. "She just hangs on," Annalee said. "She's not alive, but she's not *not* alive. We keep her like that so we don't have to face the empty bed." But we weren't keeping her, Loulie thinks; we were flying home. She wondered why her grandmother didn't do it, just fly away.

Gazing out the plane's window at those snow-struck mountains, Loulie had imagined the valleys below them, fields and plains, rivers, highways, sprawling cities, their skyscrapers like beacons. The world she would be part of someday, adventures she'd have, people she would meet that were still only outlines of possibility, like ghosts. But not dead ones, the ones who hadn't come alive yet in her life. Even Jones had been somewhere below her as Loulie flew into her future.

Her gaze is steady now, staring at Jones right in the eyes. "I believe you about that bird," she says, "the one you saw that shouldn't be here." She inhales a full breath, exhales. Jones presses his hand against his face, sliding it over the smooth pane of his forehead, scratchy-rough of his cheeks, hard knob of his nose, his mouth. He thinks about that bird. Why did it come here? Did the wind blow him here, a hurricane or a tropical storm? How will he survive their frozen winters? Or is this a new bird that no one but Jones has seen? Jones recalls a show on *NOVA*. He had it on to amuse the girl, but he got caught up when they said something about how most paleontologists regard birds as the last surviving dinosaur, the only ones to come out of the mass extinction and continue on. Maybe the bird is gaining strength at his feeder, storing up energy from the seed Jones puts there and soon he'll be strong enough to fly away. Soon he'll find his way home.

Jones stares into the waning afternoon toward a thatch of woods. Loulie follows his gaze, but she's thinking about the fox, maybe even the same one Jones saw or from the same pack. Do foxes live in packs or is that wolves? Jones would probably know. It was a different season, different year, the snow on the ground a salty, grainy white making it look more like a beach or a desert, someplace that was not here. She and her mom staring out from the little gray house and they saw it standing in the winter-dried weeds at the edge of their yard, the same wheat shade as the late afternoon so that it seemed to merge with the dying light, tan stalks the same height as its tan and gray neck, tan ears poking out of tassels that had already grown, turned green and were on the other side of things. The way it blended in made Loulie wonder if she was seeing a fox at all, its alert face, ears cocked listening for whatever was out there. Then it was gone, slipping into the woods beyond.

Suicide Birds

When Teeny blew out her daddy's sliding glass door with Todd's AR-15 assault rifle she determined the lord was sending her a message: NO MORE METH, his cloud finger drifting through the shatter of glass, shaping the shards into letters that shimmered and shone in the new morning sun like mica. Her father's got ALS, Lou Gehrig's disease, and after he stopped being able to swallow and breathe on his own they put him in the convalescent home across from where Teeny works at the Quickstop. She won't tell him about his sliding door. It would just worry him; her dad liked a sense of order to things—used to natter at Teeny if she left that door ajar a quarter of an inch. But he won't be coming home again.

She meant to just crack the glass, a spider web, something obvious enough that the birds would stop hurling themselves into it, thinking it was their ticket to the other side. Four of them last month alone. Every time she came over to check on her daddy's house, water the plants, fetch his Sunday *Times*, it seemed another had flung itself against the glass out of some sort of birdy despair.

Teeny's real name is Martha, which has nothing to do with her nickname. It was her dad who started calling her that, *Teeny Tiny Lumpkin* he'd chant, the trench of his chin dimple gaping like ladyparts, and she isn't tiny at all. He meant it to be *ironical*, he said. Her back and shoulders muscled as a horse, harpsichord ripples of her chest and ribs, biceps prominent as a strongman's, a *really* strong man—she can bench press 200. As an infant she flipped herself onto her stomach twenty-four hours after she shot from her mother's birth canal, two days of hard labor, her mom wailing like it was the apocalypse in there, her dad said, the four horsemen themselves trying to bust out, *then* Teeny decides she's ready to present. Her mother was never the same afterwards, slept a lot, then one day she didn't wake up.

Her best friend Andrea said to try just a *snort* of meth, that it's a whole-body orgasm plugged into a socket, turned ON. Lord knows Teeny wasn't getting many of those unless she supplied them herself, so she thought why not? She'd made it a point to be game; just try things her daddy used to say, though that was more about eating her vegetables.

Ten months later Teeny quits cold turkey, gives her the shakes for days, burning inside like the white bitch (Todd called it that) had been frying her blood, its absence congealing into pockets of slimy grease, such that the AR-15 seemed like a reasonable solution. "Can't have those little birdies committing suicide on Daddy's glass doors now, can we?" she told Todd.

"Well Christ almighty Teeny, you don't blast sliders with a weapon of war! You're lucky the whole damn house didn't implode," he'd said, shaking his head, clumps of his hair thinning on top like leftover spaghetti stuck to a bowl—she's been noticing these things about her husband since he was laid off from his job at the Giant, signposts of loss. Now when he wasn't mopping floors at the old folks home (his hours cut to part-time), he was hanging around the trailer park's garage, building a robot like some lunatic-savant, which Teeny herself was the model for. Not her *essence*, per se, but her arms and her torso, her muscular form. Figured if he could make a robot do what Teeny did, lift her father in and out of his bath, slip him back into bed as if her father's wasted body was light as a basket of fruit, he could make a fortune.

"Yeah," she told him, "they already have *that* robot, it's called a forklift!" As if her husband graduated from MIT or something, she thinks now, heading off to work. Plus he's making it from scrap metal, PVC pipes, parts of this and that he finds at the salvage yard, even picking through the damn dumpsters at Sunshine Acres, the trailer park they manage. Last time she looked the thing had Budweiser cans for biceps! Todd just shrugged, figured if the robot didn't work he'd call it art.

The day is a wash of browns and blues, the sky, the caked-mud ground she's walking on, the Quickstop just a mile down the road from Sunshine Acres so she figured may as well hoof it, save on gas. A car full of teenage boys whizzes by honking and Teeny straightens her spine just a little. Not that she's at all interested, but Andrea said once your periods stop guys quit noticing you, the smell of your pheromones disappear; like hanging out the closed sign on your shop, you're no longer a viable mate. Teeny figures at 45 she must be draining the dregs far as her ovaries are concerned.

Merle who manages the Quickstop winks at her the moment she steps inside, a blast of frigid air, his eyelid cracked and horny as a lizard's. "Think you can cover for me today? Thought I might visit my la*day*; she's got the afternoon off, get a bit of afternoon de-light."

Teeny pins the nametag to her tank top. *Hi, I'm Martha!* it says, but most folks know not to call her that. "You got that air conditioner set at Arctic again, Merle, fifty freeze-your-ass degrees? Got to be out of here by six o'clock, feed my dad."

"Thought he on a feeding tube now?"

"He's not dead, hon. I like to give him at least a taste of something that reminds him of that you know."

"Well close up if I'm not back. It's not like we due for a rush on business. Since the damn state's been dragging its tail on the gas leases the trucks all go down 81 to Pennsylvania where there's work. *Sheeeit*, this region poor as yesterday's gizzards, like we don't need the prosperity new jobs could bring? We get the tourists who think if they're in upstate they should be seeing the Adirondacks. Where those mountains at? someone asks me the other day." Merle shakes his head. "Jesus, don't anyone look at a map? Upstate could swallow New York, Adirondacks just the icing on that big-ass cake. And still the government won't consider them leases."

Yeah, Teeny thinks, gas well explosions, poisoned water, air, what's not to consider? She won't say it. A landowner, Merle's whole life would change if he could lease his acreage to the gas companies for hydraulic fracturing. He's sitting on the shale mother lode, and with *BP* in his pocket he won't be no Quickstop employee anymore, "that's for shit sure!" he said. She and Merle been round that block too many times, fracking and the jobs it *could* bring, Merle insists, versus land poisoned by waste and spills. Far as she can tell it's just a giant cocktail of the same kinds of toxins that went into her meth, only fracking chemicals crack rock whereas meth chews up teeth, and now she's got a dental problem to deal with.

That's Teeny's new goal, implants; have a financial goal, her daddy always said, and not breasts like Todd asked her—dirty old fart. Teeth. Sure she's 45, but that's the new 15, right? "So sue me!" she said when he told her they didn't have money for no implants. She might end up homeless but by god she'll live her remaining years with teeth. The dentist told her she'd need a bone graft, not enough jawbone he said, and that it involved cadaver bone. "You OK with that?" the dentist asked. Teeny figured they'd be clean bones, from some good clean person who lived her life right, avoided toxins like crystal methamphetamines and in the name of philanthropy willed her bones to dentistry. Figured it must be a woman cadaver. Men don't give up bones or much of anything else, in her experience.

Teeny stares out the window over the cash register as Merle roars off, the tail pipe on his souped-up Ford Torino spewing a rope of exhaust, out the driveway to the merge in the roads. "Jesus!" she whispers. Of course he wouldn't worry about fracking waste, Merle whirls about in his own cloud of mess, Pigpen turned AARP. Above on the electric wires a muddle of blackbirds twitter and shuffle, natter at each other, rise then fall on the ground like ashes, then up again in a cloud-like swoop. She's been seeing this a lot lately, flocks of birds amassing. Not like they're planning evil, more like unease— they know something we don't and it's making them jittery. Take those suicide birds, four last month, two the month before, hurling themselves into her daddy's doors. Well at least they won't be expressing their bird-angst there any more, seeing as there's no more glass to speak of. Todd hammered plywood over the gap after yanking out the jagged edges, grumbling and cursing when the plywood didn't fit right and he had to do it again with a bigger piece. "Damnit Teeny!" he snarled. "Like I don't have enough crap to fix around the trailer park so I've got to come to your daddy's for more."

From out of nowhere it seems a man appears in the Quickstop entranceway, no car, where did he come from? All hunched into his hoodie like the day is cold or he's bracing for wind or some sort of weather assault, never mind that it's summer, the air sultry as a laundromat. She can't see his face until he opens the door, jingle of chimes and a swoosh of baked air, then closing it carefully, even though it would shut automatically behind him. Then he doesn't seem to know what to do with himself, peering about, dazed, like he's surprised to find himself here.

"Help you?" she asks, in the casual voice she's perfected, letting customers know she's the one in charge, but not so eager they'd think she takes any of it seriously, or them for that matter. It's a paycheck, *ironical* her dad might've called it. She could've been more, the tone of her voice tells them, but she's here so let's get the show on the road.

"Just looking," he mumbles, eyeing the shelves a little askance.

She sighs. "Hon, this aint Macy's. I assume you don't need gas since you didn't bring a car, so we got milk, beer, coke, two kinds of bread, wheat or white, your usual assortment of artery-clogging snacks, aspirin for your headache and tobacco. I could put on the coffee pot if you want, but it's hot as a mother out there. That about does it for window-shopping. You a smoker?"

He shakes his head.

"OK, one option off the table." She steps out from behind the counter and peers at him closer, the dark eyes and eyebrows under a shortened forehead and hairline, decent enough jaw line. He has an odd smell, like disuse. She reaches out as if to touch him, then withdraws her hand as he steps back, alarmed. She shakes her head. "Sorry, but you look familiar. Weren't you that guy used to live in our trailer park for a while? In fact, didn't you work with my husband Todd at the Giant?"

He looks a little panicky at her identifying him, she thinks, what an odd duck—almost says this out loud, then he points randomly at the shelves. "Women's products?" he asks, stuttering a little on the *s*.

Teeny grins. "Oh, I get it, you've got a girl."

"No!" he says, almost shouting.

She wrinkles her eyebrows. "Sure, you use tampons for nosebleeds or something? Ha ha," she snorts. "Just messing with you. We keep them behind the counter with the condoms. Kids get into these things, not enough for them to do around these parts apparently. Here," she says, slipping back behind the counter then handing him a box, which he takes from her gingerly like it's hot, glances at it and passes it back to her.

"They're assorted sizes, all we got. That do?"

He looks at her perplexed, like she's asked him to work out an equation. "OK," he says.

"What a piece of work," she thinks, ringing up his purchase, placing it in a small bag. He just stands there awkwardly like the proverbial square peg, not even his hand moves to pick up the bag.

She sighs again. "You want anything else?"

"Do you have birdseed?"

"Birdseed! This isn't a pet shop, kiddo. Funny you should ask though. Have you noticed anything strange about the birds of late?"

He looks suddenly alert, the dazed expression replaced by almost a keen interest. A crafty look, she thinks. "There's a new one," he says.

She frowns. "Well they're better be more than *one* new because I'm telling you . . ." Then she stops as a couple blasts in, the girl grabbing a cold six-pack then slamming the refrigerator door, and the guy yanking a twenty out of his wallet for gas, clearly in a hurry. She figured he'd snatch his bag and slip out the door while she rang the couple up, then a beefy, red-faced man immediately after, but he just stands in the place they'd been conversing, like she'd pressed a pause button on him, not moving an inch, making the other customers maneuver around him.

"Isn't your name Jones something or something Jones?" she asks, after everyone has left.

He looks alarmed again and she laughs. "You're a sly one, huh? Like to roam the world incognito? I could nail you in the old trailer park ledgers, you know, no going off the grid these days, we're all computerized. Walk down any street and some security camera's tagged you. They'll catch up with you sooner or later so if you're a drug lord or a serial killer time to start working the exit. If I was *interested* enough, that is, to look you up." She winks to let him know she's not. "I'm Teeny." She likes to do that, introduce herself then stick up her biceps, show them her guns.

He glances at her nametag and she shakes her head. "A decoy, makes people think I'm who I'm not. Where'd you move to?"

Jones frowns, shuffling his feet. Teeny rolls her eyes. "Wow, I'm not going to visit you or something. Just making conversation. When folks leave the trailer park it's usually for better digs, though honestly it isn't such a bad place—we do with what we got. So I was saying about the birds before, they've been flying into my daddy's glass doors in unusual numbers, like they're doing it on purpose, you know? He doesn't stay there anymore. He's in the Crawford Convalescent Home, up the street. Got ALS, a prisoner in his own body. The doctors say it's a miracle he's lived this long—he's seventy-one."

"Is he good?" Jones asks.

Teeny pauses, considering the question. She stares at Jones, who lowers his eyes, but seems sincere enough. "He's my dad and mom all rolled into one. The place is a little depressing, though. Some think the folks living there aren't people anymore, wards of the state since they can't afford private care, three meals if they still can eat and someone to visit them is the best it gets. Frickin Todd is always busy building his robot wife, so it's just me. It's damn depressing to tell you the truth, Heaven's waiting room, people whose bodies have turned on them, trapped in their own skin cells. Still, when my dad looks at me like he wants out I tell him none of that now, you hear? Then I let him taste what he'd be missing, chew up a chocolate chip cookie, his favorite, put a little in his mouth, or even steak when we have leftover from our barbeque. He can't swallow anymore though so I have to take it all back out again."

"You think . . ." Jones hesitates, "he might be ready to be free of it?"

She shrugs. "Well I'm not ready. I'm a *life* science kind of person. Would've gone to college and studied biology, but then my dad got sick and we didn't have health insurance, so guess where my education fund went. I'd have studied the animals other folks don't like, garter snakes for instance. You see them in the summer and they're lone wolves slithering about their business, but when it's cold they hibernate and come spring they emerge in a giant, snake-mating ball, a hundred of them sometimes, a snake orgy! Isn't that crazy?"

His cheeks flame and he starts to stutter some response then quits before the sentence gets going. Teeny laughs. "Did I offend your sensibilities? Sorry, I know I talk too much, like those machine parts Todd monkeys around with—once he gets them started they just keep on running. Guess I've got a battery-operated mouth sometimes. Anyway, I didn't resent it, not going to college. I could still read. My favorite book was *The Great Gatsby*, that surprise you? Sometimes I feel like the girlfriend, the one Karen Black played in the movie. She was my favorite. She lived over a gas station kind of like this one, a blip off the highway between industry and waste, but she was on a mission to get out of there. I imagine her sometimes when I'm working here, waiting for my rich lover to swoop me away for a weekend in the city. We'd have a small but elegant walk-up, you know, a classy, antique-y kind of place, and he'd buy me a puppy. Oh screw the puppy, this is fantasy after all, I'll take the diamond necklace! What I'm saying is I wasn't supposed to be the gal behind the Quickstop counter. Before my dad was my daddy he was a sales rep for a textbook company, traveled all over the northeast, bookstores, companies, colleges, wherever people needed to learn about hotel management and business administration, that was his gig. Kind of clipped his wings when I was born and my mom checked out."

Jones lifts the bag with the tampons delicately off the counter using two fingers and his thumb, like he's afraid he'll injure its contents. "What if I want to get someone a treat . . ." he whispers, so softly it's like a breeze drifted in.

Teeny grins. "You could try ice cream. Everyone loves ice cream."

"I got to go," he says.

She nods. "Yeah, didn't mean to bleed out my life story on you. You're almost like a friend removed, given that we used to live in the same place and you worked with my husband."

Jones pushes open the door, then turns around and stares at her. "Maybe . . ." he starts, gazing outside at the sky for a moment, then turns back again peering at her intently with those dark eyes, eyes the color of nothing and everything, she thinks, no color and every color all soaked into one. "Maybe your dad flies in his dreams. Ever think of that? Like a bird, since he can't move any more in real life."

She snorts, "Sure, so long as he doesn't slam into some sliding glass door!"

Jones shakes his head slowly, almost like he has to figure out which side to go next, left or right. "I don't think they do it on purpose. They're looking to what's beyond. Why would they do it on purpose, they've got the whole sky."

"What, like the sky's the limit?" she smirks.

But he just stares. "No. No limit. That's what I mean."

THAT EVENING AT the Crawford Home, a dull red sunset inching its way through the captain's window over her dad's bed, the thickness of the glass cutting and reshaping the light like a finger-paint smear, Teeny listens to the whoosh from her dad's oxygen mask, the gentle in-and-out hiss of ventilators from beds around his, clicks, clacks and clankings from all manner of machinery meant to keep people going, and thinks maybe Todd's not so out in left field making that robot. Maybe when Teeny dies it will be like she never even left, just plug her in, a squirt of WD-40 in the joints and she's good to go. The robot-wife wouldn't do things like snort crystal meth or blow out sliding doors with Todd's AR-15. She'd do whatever Todd programmed her to do. Yet again, as if she's been having the same conversation over and over with herself (which she has), Teeny confesses the crystal meth was dumb, the dumbest she's done in a very long time. For someone born smart, who could've been someone else, Teeny sure had been dumb. And now she's got the bad teeth and a tremor in her hand to remind her. But she'd blast out that door again if it saves even one bird. She recalls the feel of the last little corpse she picked up off her father's deck, a goldfinch, its glassy eyes, the softness of its feathers so yellow and final. She felt her betrayal, like she was to blame in some weird law of the universe where big trashes small; her dad might've called it evolution but she thought it sucked. Besides, damnit, she kept the birdfeeders full, couldn't that have been enough? Teeny buried it in the shoebox with the others, a mass grave sponsored by Nike, under the planter on her daddy's deck.

Crawford Home smells like burnt meat tonight, along with the usual repertoire of bleach, urine, decaying bodily functions. The building is wooden and old, clinging to its bouquet of odors like a history. Teeny is the only visitor. She wrinkles her nose, then pushes her face closer to her father's, breathing his own acrid scent, the smell, she knows, of his organs slowly shutting off. The hospice worker pointed out his skin was breaking down, crops of bed sores blossoming into full-on abscesses despite Teeny's faithful efforts, schlepping him in and out of the bath, dragging along his oxygen apparatus like a reluctant Siamese twin, and with most of his muscles frozen now, his lungs alternating between bad days with the BiPAP mask that blows air down his airways, and worse days when they threaten to hook him up to a ventilator, he couldn't have too much longer. No tracheotomy! he wrote on his advance directive, when he could still write. He had long since lost the ability to speak, and yet with her ears this close Teeny could swear she heard him whisper something to her. She sits up and stares at him, his eyes beady as a reptile's hooked into hers.

"Nope Daddy," she says, shaking her head, grabbing his hand and squeezing it. "Uh uh, we're not going down that path again. You can't talk with that mask over your mouth even if you *could* speak, so who we trying to kid, huh?" Now she thinks she really is nuts, or maybe it's some sort of meth flashback, because she hears his words like he used to sound, that baritone voice with the chuckle just around the bend from everything he said to her. It's *ironical*, Teeny, his chin dimple flashing.

His one finger that still has some alive neurons firing to his brain, a miniscule amount of muscle control and maybe he's writing it into the palm of her hand, shaping the letters big and loopy like back when he taught her cursive, *Let go* . . . or maybe he's not, just those jerky, messy movements, the last hurrahs of a muscle. Teeny gazes out the small window, glass thick as a fist, like she really could see the shadows of trees, the dying rays of the sun through them. She thinks about Jones, what an odd duck! His unflagging optimism that despite a world where he doesn't seem to even own a car to drive to the Quickstop, where something in his spirit gets paralyzed holding a box of tampons, still the almost beatific look on his face when he told her there was no limit.

Last month as she was getting ready to leave after kissing her father goodbye, Donna, the night nurse, approached her. She's a youngish woman, a CNA with a face like a doughnut, dull and sweet, someone who would get by in the world doing for others, Teeny had pegged her, rather than on looks or brains. Donna had been kind to Teeny's dad, so Teeny tried to interpret her jumble of barely coherent words, and finally she had grabbed Teeny's arm, leading her to a bed where an old woman lay wheezing in and out of harsh, painful breaths.

"Can you do something for her?" Donna whispered. "She's got a DNR on file but no matter how much morphine I give her I'm telling you she's hurting bad. Nobody comes to see her. She's got nobody."

"What am I supposed to do?" Teeny said, but she knew what Donna was getting at. It wasn't the first time she'd been asked, just the first time she didn't immediately say no. It was her strength, she figured, her muscles that set her apart, something repugnant (a daddy-word) yet needed for their stories, maybe, when they spoke of it later—angel of mercy they'd call her. She hunkered down on the bed, took hold of one of the old woman's hands, the skin cold and blue, scratchy like something imitating skin, a fiber for a belt maybe or gloves, and whispered, "What do you want?" Of course the woman didn't answer but Teeny gathered her in her arms, figured anyone who doesn't have family to visit might be glad for the contact, the human warmth, her struggling breaths pushed up against Teeny's ripped chest, and she hugged that dying old woman like a sonofabitch.

Now Teeny reaches into her purse, pulls out the fifth of whiskey, Jack Daniels, her father's favorite. His eyes get brighter, or she imagines they do anyway as she shows it to him. "Just a taste, huh Daddy? A nightcap." She eases him down flat, removes the pillow from behind his head then lifts the mask off his mouth and nose. She knows it's only a matter of minutes without that oxygen forced inside before his lungs seize up. Hopefully enough time to determine her role, dutiful daughter? Angel of Mercy? At least not a meth-head, she thinks, but why is it she never gets to choose her own path? Then again her dad didn't get to choose in the end; his illness did it for him. "I'm not the disease, Teeny," he used to tell her when he could still speak. "I'm not ALS, I *have* ALS." She takes a Q-tip off the nightstand, dips it into the whiskey and places it on her father's tongue. Then she pours a capful and dribbles that inside his mouth, holding his chin so it doesn't run out, so it slides down his throat, its fiery taste bringing his world back to him for the moment.

AT SUNSHINE ACRES after racing the mile back, the night alive with cricket song and mosquitoes doing flybys around her ears, Teeny's rhythmic wheezing on a mindless continuum like some damn watch, she sees the lights blazing in the garage, Todd and his robot-wife. "Screw that!" she spits, rummaging in her purse for her car keys.

The Hideaway is two towns over in Pennsylvania, but the drive through the dark, hilly countryside is cleansing and Teeny takes it fast, plugging her iPod into the radio's speakers, the Stones wailing *give me shelter,* and she's right along with Mick for that particular tune. Crossing the state line she sees the gas wells, tongues of blue and orange flames licking toward the sky, their neon glow flooding the darkness like some radioactive wasteland. How long will New York hold out? It's all about the profit margins, her dad would've said, when he could still say anything at all.

The usual assortment of pickups in the driveway, several Cabot Oil & Gas tankers and the fancier rentals for their workers up from Texas, plus a line of Harleys—old bikers' bar, as in only old bikers can afford motorcycles these days. Begley, the bartender, is a young prick though, who recently fired Andrea on the spot when she came to work high, not even a second chance. "Wasn't halfway gone,"

Andrea said. "Just a couple Xanies to take the edge off quitting the meth." As if it took full consciousness to do what she did, tray perched on one arm trolling for orders, schlepping beers, picking up the empties.

Andrea is slumped over a barstool when Teeny breezes in. "Fill me up, and another for your former bar slave!" Teeny barks to Begley, sliding onto a stool beside her. "You should apply for *his* job," Teeny says. "How challenging is that, draining beer from a tap!

Begley slaps two glasses down on the polished wood surface. "Wouldn't you like to know, Quickstop-girl!" he grins, exposing a glare of bleached teeth, probably brighter than his brain, Teeny thinks. "Oh wait," Begley says, "but *is* she a girl with those biceps? Teeny the Tranny? Muscles on top, but what's between the legs anyone's guess."

"You'll never get to know, that's for sure, *Bagel!*" Andrea snaps her gum, blows a bubble, then removes it from her mouth, sticking it on the bar in front of him. "Awwwe what a shame, nobody to order for cleanup anymore, huh? To think I did that jerk-off once," Andrea whispers, as Begley swaggers to the other end of the bar, ignoring the gum. "He's like a gift box, all wrapped up in pretty paper, Jack diddlysquat inside when you cut the ribbon."

Teeny nods. A coldness is inching through her veins, like someone dumped out an ice tray into a major artery and chunks are sluggishly drifting along, bits of ice not quite cold enough to freeze things, but maybe she wants that, for everything to just stop. *Then* maybe, she could think about the Crawford Home and what it will feel like when she doesn't go there anymore. She grabs her napkin, peels off the gum, tossing it behind the bar.

"I hate my life," Andrea says.

Teeny shrugs, "You got an alternative? Today I told this guy about snake-mating balls, only I left out a critical detail. Up to one hundred snakes in those things, but here's the deal, ninety-nine of them are male! Can you picture those odds, one female and the rest all trying to do her?"

"Probably it takes that many to have a shot, as in she's real picky," Andrea snorts. She sighs, chugs the last of her beer then smacks the glass down. "*I* should've been more picky, that's for damn sure." The bar is all background noise, Mötley Crüe howling from ancient speakers, thwack of pool balls and a rumble of voices, mostly male punctuated here and there by the shriek of a woman's laughter. An odor of spilled beer and sweat permeates whenever the air conditioner blower cuts out. Andrea rubs her eyes. "I'm losing it all, Teeny. Found out today. Ryan gets the house, kids, I don't even have a fuckin' job to *rent* a place to come home to. It's all about the drugs, just that *he* was never caught. What else I got, huh? I ask you, what else the hell I got!"

Teeny stares at her, her dank, blond hair twisted into a greasy bun, no makeup, her damp, tired-looking eyes, too old for the forty-odd years she's been using them. Then at Begley in his linen designer shirt, swiping a rag over the bar, pretending to look busy, chatting up some well-fed biker encased in a body stocking's worth of leather, a belly hung so low it needs a sling, and two Cabot manager-types with their expensive company haircuts and their slow, Texas drawls. Like talking through a mouth full of jellybeans, she thinks. Her own face in the bar mirror stares back, solemn, not beautiful, but that glint behind her pale eyes—*the thinking look* her daddy called it—a face that by today's stats for women might be the dead-middle of its mortality curve (Teeny saw this in one of her dad's magazines, *Business Week* or *Fortune*, the hours spent reading to him, "Life Table" it's called), but she had a hunch those figures were more about Cabot wives and female execs, their Teflon lives, not a Quickstop cashier whose husband is building her mechanical replacement out of Budweiser cans in the garage. She sees her hairline inch back and her chin slacken, boobs droop then soon enough the discs in her spine slide together like dominoes. Do they calculate *this*, a body shrinking from its own frickin façade? A vision of her dad's body stunted by disease, but still that spark in his eyes; he went out with the lights on.

"You ever want to fly, Andrea?"

"What, like in a plane?"

Teeny shakes her head. "Nope, not a plane." She slips off her barstool then crouches down beside Andrea's stool. "Climb onto my shoulders, kiddo."

"Huh? You crazy?"

"Just do it, I can support your weight; I can bear anyone's damn weight." The room grows quiet as Teeny rises with Andrea perched upright on her shoulders like a human totem pole.

"Hey!" Begley calls out. "What the hell you two think you're doing?"

Andrea giggles as Teeny swoops around the bar, knocking over chairs, slamming into tables, pushing aside anyone that gets in her way. "Watch out, Bagel, bird-woman coming in for landing!" Teeny shouts. "You were wondering about my muscles, little prick? Check this out!" Mugs crash off shelves in splinters of glass as Teeny hurdles the bar, Andrea grabbing and whacking at everything in her reach. The room erupts into a roar of commotion, but mostly laughter at the diversion they've created, Teeny figures, lives so boring a strongwoman with another one anchored to her shoulders has got to be a welcome sight.

"You're *sure* you won't reconsider hiring me back? Andrea shrieks. "Still want me to suck dick?"

"I'm calling the police!" Begley snarls. "You two chicks are cooked."

Teeny hesitates, knowing what she said to Jones earlier was true—this whole scene is being captured on security cameras and it'll be played over and over, just like she warned him. Maybe it'll even hit the news and Donna from the Crawford Home will call her the Angel of Mercy, and she won't mean it *ironically*. Then Jones sees it and maybe that encourages him to get his own shit together, whatever it is making him so jumpy and secretive. Though why she'd even think about that odd man while she's busy chalking up jail time for herself she couldn't say. Funny how some folks do that, just get under your skin somehow.

"Duck your head!" Teeny orders Andrea, riding atop her shoulders yelling *whoohoo, giddap*, and she flings open the Hideaway door, inhaling a huge breath of air because she can, because though the gas wells shimmer in the distance, right now this air is good. The darkness is alive with pulsing stars, as if even the sky is breathing; like there really *is* no limit, that space between breath and none.

Things Blow Up

I

In 1955 Kīlauea erupts for eighty-eight days sending fountains of boiling lava high into the air, burying twelve homes and evacuating Puna. I'm four years old and attending Busy Bee nursery school where all morning long a boy named Carl Craft pulls my hair if I don't show him my "deviled eggs." At story time I jingle my charm bracelet with its little silver bells in his face and he and I are ordered out to the lānai, where perched beside him on the *lau hala* mat I slide down the straps of my sundress and let him peek, but he keeps pulling my hair anyway. When the day is over my brother and I pile out of the Bee-mobile, a big orange station wagon packed with screeching four-year-olds, into our mother's long arms. She's a vision, waiting for us at the door of our Kailua house in her green-and-white, polka-dot halter-top and Bermuda shorts. We are relieved to be home. This is the year the Korean War ends, with over ten million people killed, and a Korean War novel is published called *The Dead, the Dying, and the Damned.*

Three years later, August 1, 1958, night becomes day at 1 A.M. as the US explodes a nuclear bomb above neighboring Johnston Island, a brilliant white flash followed by glowing colors like the northern lights. But this isn't Alaska. This is Hawai'i, not a state yet, but they do it, with two more nuclear bombs dropped above Johnston Island. Each explosion is like one million tons of TNT, fifty times more powerful than Hiroshima, just seven-hundred miles away from where we sleep in our beds, dreaming of the tidal wave spawned when the earth rocks, wailing sirens and police knocking on our doors to evacuate, all the while inhaling poisonous sulphuric gasses from the volcano (that years later will be named *vog*), fueled by the nuclear wind. What did we have to fear? It was the 1950s and labor unions were being infiltrated by commies, our father said. Communists are dangerous, we're told, particularly the ones in Cuba and Russia and Red China. We practice crawling beneath our desks at school, head between our legs and our hands over our ears to protect them from an atomic blast. This year Jeremy and I are in the same class (we were periodically subjected to conflicting views on educating twins: they should always be together or they should never be together), and we hold hands discreetly under our desks, preparing for our deaths together, though in our above-the-desk lives we wouldn't be caught dead doing this. In 1959 Hawai'i becomes a state and Kīlauea Iki erupts with fountains rising 1,900 feet into the air, the highest recorded in Hawai'i.

These days you can stare down into the tunnels of former tree trunks the scalding lava burned away, where humans have tossed their litter, cigarette butts, candy wrappers, Primo beer bottles, and a Diet Coke can. My favorite is one where a live 'ōhi'a tree is growing on the lava-rock side of the empty space. Casting its roots all the way down to a soil base, it clutches the rock with its long, willowy root fingers. Moss and ferns grow through the lava sides of another tree mold, and maybe 'ōhelo berry? My grandmother would have known. She could name every endemic plant. But she's gone now and Jeremy is too. Mauna Loa above, blue as an ache in the early evening light.

2011 AND THE summer air abuzz with the drone of insects, heat a white-hot blade. The homeless pick through the garbage leftovers of the open-air markets in Honolulu's Chinatown for slightly bruised fruits, and discarded carrots, competing with the pigeons, the mynah birds, the mourning doves. All night in the airport hotel the jets roar from the runway, and the inspectress checks for taken things: alarm clocks, towels, remotes for the bolted in flat-screen TVs, face cloths, hangers, pillowcases, anything that can't be nailed down. She slips into the rooms like a shadow, like a file through a lock, recording the wrongs, her white-gloved hand inside a suitcase here, a pair of pants thrown carelessly on a chair there, pockets gaping open like a mouth.

This morning I said goodbye to my mother, sitting beside her nursing-home bed where she was being entertained by little boys in white shirts, girls in plaid dresses, a woman giving me a massage, supposedly, and her friend, the wife of a lawyer, now dead. Reaching her hands out to them, she saw us sitting in sewing circles, city parks, and restaurants. "The waiter is here," she'd say. "What will you have? I think I'll have a hamburger," she'd say, and she'd pretend to eat it; or maybe in another world, the one inside her head with its wild, uncombed Einstein hair, and her eyes (which can't see much these days anyway) mostly shut, she really was eating it. "Jeremy's here," she said when I kissed her goodbye. I looked up for a moment expecting, what? My brother floating above her, his big shit-eating grin, a splif in one hand and flipping me off with the other? "Fuck you!" I whispered. I'm not about to let him see any more tears.

Later, on the jet flying to where I live now by the Susquehanna, something nasty in the plastic container of nuts and dried fruits, a bitter taste, and worried about the salmonella peanuts from that Georgia plant (*fifty-two sickened, seven dead across the freakin' country and Congress drags the marshmallow-faced, peanut-plant president into a hearing where he keeps pleading the fifth; Did you know there were maggots and you let them go anyway into candies, cookies, snacks for kids?* "I respectfully decline to answer," *he says— about the little blond boy with the million-dollar smile, dead from eating those peanut-butter crackers*), I barf peanut-flavored bile into the metal airplane sink then head back to my seat. The jet lists then rocks like a cradle in the darkening sky.

I CALL RUTH from the airport parking lot. "You were supposed to pick me up!" I whine to her voicemail voice, crisp and certain and not there. ("No place to run anymore," she said when I left, our drive to the airport, going back to Hawai'i without her—a commentator on the radio announced there'd been a development in the case of a missing teenage girl and Ruth switched it off. "What now?" she sighed.) I tell her voice I may have eaten one of those poisonous peanuts the fat CEO let go into packages because he didn't want to spend money to get rid of the bad ones, which means I may be dead. A sound like a little girl sobbing into the phone, and gazing around the near-empty lot I think how I won't tell her about the loneliness—my mother who didn't recognize me and the jeweler on Maunakea Street who did, who asked me to model his diamond balls, the necklace, with nothing on underneath. Later in a soccer dad's minivan, the moon grinning into the window, his hand in my pants and I'm holding onto his like a lifeline, going *come on, come on, come on.*

Before leaving Hawai'i I went to the big island to where my grandparents' house is caving back into the land, the land reclaiming its wood, its air, its formerly inhabited spaces, and I rattled the front doorknob like someone was home to let me in, begged them to come back to me, bring me back to a past still hopeful of a future that hadn't happened yet, as certain in its unnamed possibilities as their house being repossessed by the weeds, the birds, screens dangling like broken arms, the window where she used to wait for us, our grandmother, her silhouette with that long dark hair piled on top of her head. Later I took a hike around Kīlauea Iki following a kalij pheasant, its blue-black feathers the lip-smacking color of licorice, that stayed just a little ahead of me and did not fly away, not even when I approached it, hand out. "My grandfather has been reborn as a pheasant," I said, and he didn't deny it.

II

EACH TIME YOU come back to this island you imagine running into the man who taught you how to give a blowjob—he's been living here for some thirty years now and how big can an island be before one day, in The Volcano Store maybe, you're buying your nonfat soy yogurt and vegan grainy things and he's got a manapua in his hand, that toothy grin, wandering the cluttered isles. Still the long dreads but, realistically, maybe not so much on top. You feel the clerk's contempt, 'ukus nipping under your skin, her eyes crawling over you—fuckin' haole, she's thinking. She's Japanese, not even hapa, not a breath of Hawaiian in her and you know she feels she belongs here and you don't. You can remember back when this was the Hongo Store—can she? It was the only game in Volcano for years. Otherwise you took the old Volcano Road with its collapsing shoulders and puka ferns—hāpu'u ferns with their hairy long roots concealing giant tubes in the lava, a rift zone with cracks going down twenty, thirty, even sixty feet ready to swallow you up—for the hour-plus trek into Hilo for groceries.

Now there is the Volcano Highway. Now there are several of these little stores—open-air style with their wooden floors, dried seed Li Hing Mui and cuttlefish, Nā'ālehu milk, five dollars a gallon—and a lot more tourists these days poking through. You want these tourists with their Midwestern accents, their fish-white, jello thighs, to know you are not one of them, but you can't speak pidgin anymore and there's your freckly Scottish skin. You're appalled to find your childhood treat, the Stone Cookies that you could only get freshly baked from the Mt. View Bakery a couple towns away, are being sold here now. It used to be an outing, the family piled into your grandfather's Pontiac, fins like sharks, Tuesdays, cookie day, burning rubber down the old Volcano Road to purchase these hot from the big stone ovens. You include one with your other checkout items—I mean regardless these are not to be resisted—asking her when did *this* happen (while glancing surreptitiously, could it really be *him*)? She just shrugs. You read the ingredients and note they have trans fats in them but you don't mention this, because now you see he's in the beer isle, reaching for a Primo to wash down his manapua. You remember drinking beer with him, hot blue days in his catamaran off Lanikai, sailing to the Mokulua Islands where it's just you, him, and the frigate birds, *'iwa*, man-of-war birds. He didn't know you were only seventeen (he's twelve years older), and when he found out he said don't tell. He isn't the one who shoved your head down between his legs brandishing your ponytail like a whip. Not this one. Patient, graphic, technical instructions like you might find in a manual, *Fellatio for Dummies*. First, place organ in right hand. Now, insert into mouth opened wide like eating a banana. Caution: do not bite. Tender little licks work best.

Later you'll see his face in the landscaped bank of the rental cottage, two chunks of lava for eyes and the mulch is his beard. You'll remember the tickle of this beard, his head bobbing up and down like one of those car puppets between your own two thighs. You are glad not to care about these kinds of things anymore, at least not with this man, though once upon a time you could've sworn your life was over when he confessed to you he was getting married again, to his ex-wife. For years you were envious of this wife and by association all skinny women with long kelpy hair, until it occurred to you being married to someone who gives blowjob lessons to teenagers may not be such a desirable thing.

YOU PICK HER up by the side of the Volcano Highway hitchhiking, long black hair usually so carefully braided or trapped in a bun now flying out on either side of her like bat wings. She's got on a backpack big enough to carry a small house. Bring her up to Volcano and she is Pele, you decide, volcano goddess minus the little white dog. As the tale goes you pick up either a beautiful woman and her little white dog or an old hag hitchhiking and she disappears the minute you get close to her home, Halema'uma'u crater. It's your lucky day. She's a beaut.

Are you Pele? you ask her. You don't go anywhere near Halema'uma'u, which is erupting, just in case. She smiles her smile, gives you that deep-eyed, goddessy look, though maybe it's the vacant stare of a person who lives on the streets. "I'm hungry," she says. When you get to your rental cottage you fix her a roasted-pepper sandwich and a shot of gin. One must always give Pele her gin or she may play a trick on you, command her lava to bury your house or make it rain for thirty days—although that's if you pick her lehua blossoms. "What's your favorite flower?" you ask her. She just rolls her eyes.

Later you watch her strip. Layers of the streets coming off in clouds of silt, smoke, and grime and then her bare skin the color of a finely polished wood. You consider offering her a bath, though of course if she's Pele, why would she seek water? Keeper of the flame.

That night you dream you and your grandfather are standing at the rim of Kīlauea crater, and he tells you sharks have been known to cannibalize in the womb, the strongest fetus eating the weakest, natural selection at work. The vog is thick, a wind switch from trades to Kona blows it over you in a gray mist only it's dry, stinks of sulfur, and scratches your throat. Around you ferns are brittle and curled from its acidy breath. You inhale, cough, the viscous taste of the vog on your teeth, your tongue, the roof of your mouth, turn toward your grandfather but he's vanished. You wake shaking and empty, a sense of your brother having been here, though maybe not. Maybe you're back in the womb again and you do what the firstborn twin must, be alive at the expense of the weaker. The volcano night in a shroud of fog, a cold wet tongue of it slurping at the hāpu'u ferns and you close your eyes, pray for a dreamless sleep.

The next morning is bright and sunny and peering into her bedroom you half expect to see just a pile of ashes—you had checked for your wallet too, just in case. But she's there and you hand her a steaming cup of coffee. You made sure to get it very hot, a spin in the microwave after pouring it from the Mr. Coffee, just in case. You don't offer lukewarm beverages to a fire goddess. "The thing we have to do this morning," you tell her, "is go up to my grandparents' house. They've been dead for a while and their house is being sucked back into the land. I'm charting its progress," you say.

You drive the three miles or so up to their road and before even turning into their driveway you can spot plants like little trees growing out of the gutter, ivy crossing over the front-door stoop, and the window where your grandmother stood and waited for you, silhouette of her big hair in the dining room light, is cracked, its curtains in tatters. Your stomach roils, head hammers, chest aches; you feel like you're being turned inside out with the old grief. "I'm afraid of it," you tell her, "this dying." She snakes her bony wrist against your cheek, the back of her hand like she's checking you for fever.

That afternoon she's gone and you pack a picnic, put it into your backpack and climb down the Halema'uma'u trail into Kīlauea. In the distance Pele's sluicing her fires, a red cloud over the crater and all manner of poisonous, sulphuric gasses, and you perch on a ropey piece of pāhoehoe eating your pepper sandwich, the wind reeling hot as a breath, and a scarlet-feathered 'apapane singing like there's no tomorrow from an 'ōhi'a tree that managed to thrust its way out of the lava cracks, not unlike the weeds waving triumphantly from your grandparents' collapsing gutters.

III

Ruth, the woman I live with, knows all about things that blow up. She knows about explosions, eruptions, beyond what even

Jeremy knew, and at one point he was thinking about being a volcanologist. For instance, Ruth will tell you: *December 8, 1941 the day after Japan bombed Pearl Harbor the U.S. snagged Kaho'olawe and the military bombed the island continuously until 1990, for target practice. Kīlauea erupted in 1983 and is still going great guns, its lava having added more than five hundred new acres of land to the big island, destroyed two hundred Kalapana homes, caused more than $60 million in damage, and buried Kaimu beach and the Queen's Bath; breathing its sulphuric vog has killed at least fifteen people along with acres of native plant life. And in just one day, November 29, 1975, Kīlauea erupted spawning the biggest earthquake in a hundred years, causing $4 million in damage and creating a tsunami that killed two people.* That was also the last day she saw her father. He kissed her mother on the cheek, patted Ruth's head, and walked out.

We belong to a kind of club, a group of people who get together because they're missing other people. We're united in our losses, though we have little else in common—just that we can't seem to move beyond what we're missing. After Ruth's father disappeared, leaving over $100,000 in credit-card debt, their house was foreclosed and her mother and Ruth became homeless. Because of this she lives in our home like any day she could wake up and it's gone. Her suitcase is packed and ready at the door. Coolers are there too, ready to be loaded with all the extra food she keeps stocked in the fridge, just in case, and four luggage carts are in our basement that can carry this stuff out onto the streets if need be. These are already somewhat packed as well, a sleeping bag for both of us, and two plastic makeup bags filled with such necessaries as alcohol wipes to wash our skin in lieu of a bath, bug spray ("You can't imagine the amount of crawling, biting, sucking insects that attack people who have no homes," Ruth told me.), and the kinds of containers you get from hotels, miniature bottles of lotion, shampoo, toothpaste, etc. She's got our big beach umbrella ready for when it rains, and various plastic tarps to cover it all, bungee cords and electric tape to hold things down. Boxes of canned goods and a can opener, and even a few bottles of wine. "We can trade the wine for other things," she said. "Bartering is currency on the streets. You only think your home is secure," Ruth said. "Only if you're a turtle and the thing is attached to your back. Otherwise like everything else it can be taken away." A Hawaiian who had never before left the islands, she inherited the Susquehanna house from an aunt she never even knew she had.

Ruth gets the little bottles of hotel lotions and shampoos and conditioners because she works as an inspectress at the Holiday Inn, inspecting the jobs the housekeeping staff does, going into each room after one of them is done, then rechecking the room after a guest has checked out to make sure said guest hasn't left with anything that's supposed to remain in the hotel. She has a list of items posted on each bathroom wall, with the price that will be charged if it is removed from the room: Wash cloths, four dollars; face cloths, five dollars; bath towels, seven dollars; shower heads, twenty dollars; night table lights, thirty dollars; night tables, fifty dollars; TV remotes, ironing boards, irons, pictures off the walls, bedspreads, sheets, pillows, etc.—pretty much all the stuff Ruth has made sure we won't be without when we lose our home, minus the night tables and the pictures and the TV remote—we won't need those on the streets.

Once when we were back in Hawai'i, driving the Hāmākua coast, its one-lane bridges, the twisting, looping road weaving past waterfalls, drop-dead stunning coastline, and the neat little tin-roof houses of the former plantation workers, Ruth glanced up and saw a sprawling McMansion in the middle of what was once a sugarcane field, its panoramic ocean views, and at the side of the road a skeletal cat. She shook her head, her long black hair yanked into a tornado-shaped bun pointing out like an arrow, and glared at me like I had done this thing, built myself a house that could shelter a town then abandoned a little cat to starve in the streets.

DID YOU KNOW, Ruth said, that ninety percent of all methamphetamine labs are discovered when they explode? A memory, where was it? Not here, not now. The mainland. A pond so scum- and trash-covered the baby ducks popped their tail feathers up, their heads whizzling in and out of the muck like mini dolphins, needing to breathe. And then the men in the white suits came, all of them leaching out of a big steel truck, masks, eyes to the side like flounders. Breathing apparatus attached to their backs, black trash bags, and canisters filled with some kind of spray that sizzled across the water leaving an aqua slime like a line of glitter. Next day the ducks were gone.

Meth cooks dress like this too when they make the stuff, maybe not the white suits but the gas masks. Pure poison, don't you know. Red phosphorous makes phosphine gas when it's cooking. A few breaths of that and you don't have to worry anymore about explosions, greenhouse gases, rising seas, starving cats, animals and plants, all manner of life forms just gone.

Across the street from that pond a woman hosed down her yard, her feet anchored to the path in pink chenille slippers, right arm bracing herself on the handicap railing where a common white cabbage butterfly landed and she shooed it away. The hose, cigarette poised carefully between two fingers in her other hand, the one clinging to the railing, her vacant stare, the dampened grass, each blade shining wetly like little, green knives.

Scientists believe over a hundred different species of animals disappear every day. Butterflies among them, fragile, their lacy wings flitting out a story if only we would've listened before it's too late. When Jeremy and I were kids we played with them in their caterpillar stage as they grazed on the crown flower bushes outside our house. Plopped them when they were ripe, big black and yellow wormy things, into glass peanut-butter jars, a sprig off the crown flower bushes inside each. "Maybe when I grow up I'll be the guy who studies butterflies!" Jeremy said. He was always speculating about who or what he was going to be. Me, I just wanted to be a journalist, and if that didn't take, a teacher. We punched holes in the tops with a bottle opener, watched the caterpillars spin their cocoons and when they hatched into butterflies we set them free.

IV

Whales grieve the deaths of their own. They strand themselves on beaches after suicidal dives down so far to escape the navy's sonar that they rise up with the bends, bleeding around their brains, ears, lesions in their livers, lungs, kidneys, nitrogen bubbles in their tissues. The pain of of the sonar a jolt in the brain like getting electric shock therapy over and over and over (imagine car jumper cables plugged into your head!). And still they forgive us, gray whales almost exterminated at one point approaching boats in Baja where they birth their calves, snuggling up for a pat on the head, a gaze at us out of huge, ancient eyes, flukes still bearing scars from the harpoon's intent.

Who was that little girl crying? "You, Janis," said Ruth.

Ruth's been thinking a lot about death, and she gave me a table with printed out stats, said she got it off the Internet in one of the Holiday Inn rooms. "Somebody left a laptop," she said. I noted the sleek black case beside her suitcase, lined up for speedy evacuation at our front door.

Annual Causes of Death in the United States
> Tobacco: 435,000
> Poor Diet and Physical Inactivity: 365,000
> Alcohol: 85,000
> Microbial Agents: 75,000
> Toxic Agents: 55,000
> Motor Vehicle Crashes: 26,347
> Adverse Reactions to Prescription Drugs: 32,000
> Suicide: 30,622
> Incidents Involving Firearms: 29,000

Homicide: 20,308
Sexual Behaviors: 20,000
Illicit Use of Drugs: 17,000
Anti-Inflammatory Drugs Such As Aspirin: 7,600
Marijuana: 0

I STILL COME across my brother's e-mail, my computer still auto-selects his address when I type in J. Even technology will not acknowledge Jeremy's disappearance from this world. Last time I looked there were 287,000 websites for fraternal twins. "They don't share any more genetic material than regular siblings," said one, "but there's a special bond between them. Perhaps because they share so many of the same experiences growing up," it speculated.

At a Teacher's Day meeting Michael Donahue, World History Grade 11, collapses from a massive heart attack and his girlfriend Tina Chang, Media Specialist 9-12, pounds on his chest shouting, "Breathe, Michael, breathe!" Something so automatic that when we were children my brother and I obsessed over it; what was it we did that made it happen, this breathing, and what would happen if we stopped doing this thing?

Breathe, Jeremy, breathe!

Though my brother didn't simply disappear, at least not in the missing person sense, here today gone tomorrow. He dwindled away, that last year of his life, his hair, his skin, his teeth, the weight of him in this world, his heart, his happiness, and then the hemorrhaging in his brain. So I guess he did in fact go missing, a shell of what he was before, a cob, a husk, the beautiful golden kernels of my twin having been eaten away. Crystal methamphetamine cannibalizes the body, so toxic that the body, programmed from the get-go to be a survivor, steals from the lesser—hair, skin, teeth—to feed the greater, liver, kidneys, lungs, the heart.

Blood exploding in his brain like a dam released, a rush and a roar and maybe the sound he hears is the whooshing of rain on the tin roof of our Kailua home, or Maunaulu when our grandmother took us to see it erupt, the pop and gush of liquid lava. In that moment between breath and none, did he remember our promise, clasping hands under our desks while the world fell away?

Every time "Knockin' on Heaven's Door" comes on, regardless of who's singing, I hear Bob Dylan and a grinning, freewheeling Jeremy and me in Drew Griffen's old T-bird, borrowed for this day, with its slick metallic fins like two marlins cruising, radio blasting, spiraling down the highway between Boston and Sturbridge Village where we'll be meeting our grandmother and her friend Hattie. Grandpa's gone and though strike-three breast cancer lurks, Grandma's still feeling pretty good, enough to take this trip. Jeremy's hitchhiked from Ranger School in the Adirondacks, his two semesters there (this the year he thought, maybe a forest ranger!) to where I am a graduate student at Boston University, working toward my master of education degree. For Thanksgiving I'll visit him at Ranger School, bleak and snowy, the campus deserted except for Jeremy and me, too far from home to go home, and Dirk, the nerdy chemistry postdoc I'm sleeping with, who unveils some homemade acid dubbed *Dirk-do-you-good*, which we sample, staggering about the frozen woods like maniacs, and back again to scribble poetry all over the concrete dorm walls—looked like a World War II bomb shelter—whose present occupants hadn't anything more expressive to scrawl on those barracks beyond a plaintive I'm Horny!!! Then into town we'll jaunt to a diner, the only place open for Thanksgiving dinner, where we try hooking up Jeremy and the waitress with the peach-colored hair, leaving his phone number on a five-dollar bill.

But for now it's autumn, the leaves are on fire, and we're spinning down that highway with Dylan, *Knock knock knockin' on heaven's door.*

Aftermath

"A changing climate leads to changes in the frequency, intensity, spatial extent, duration and timing of extreme weather and climate events, and can result in unprecedented extreme weather and climate events."
—Intergovernmental Panel on Climate Change, The United Nations

SEPTEMBER 2011

TJ said there's an alligator in the Susquehanna from god knows where, not around here that's for sure, what tropical swamp creature sets its sights on New York? So they prodded him with sticks to make him crawl out of it, TJ said, but he just shot deeper in. A damn grenade, one minute his head poking up like a log, those flinty eyes then the next, boom, he's in the middle somewhere and TJ and Josh still drifting near the shore like dumbasses in Josh's fiberglass rowboat. Was supposed to have been a good fishing day but then the sky opens up and the rain doesn't quit for a whole seven hours, nine inches of it pummeling the boat like bullets. Yesterday the rain fell all day too, and the day before that; the creeks are overflowing and they could feel the swell of the river under their butts. Josh snarled, "Screw this! We'll need a goddamn ark."

Stella's more worried about the silver coyote; the alligator can ride it out, she figures, the Susquehanna rising over its banks like a tide of molasses, all seepage, gummy and brown. A strip of woods between the river and their house, the coyote living somewhere in between, so if the water comes up and drowns those trees, where will he go? What happens when there's no more middle?

The river's rise seemed slow at first, like a massive spill, moving languidly in an ever-expanding puddle, fingers of it pooling around houses, settling in the parks, downtown storefronts. A public golf course becomes a lake. Streams snake down sidewalks, claiming the streets with the right-of-way of water, not mindful of stop signs, blowing right through the red light, vast liquidness capable of sinking it all. But so tranquil, it seemed, not the crackling eruption of fire, or a twister carving its chaos of blasted-out buildings, no earthquake seizure fracturing the land. It's like the river was meant to do this, splay itself out in the middle of things, demanding what was.

Police pound on doors, sirens wail. *Evacuate, evacuate!* SUNY Events Center turned Red Cross Shelter, hundreds of cots in rectangular rows, solemn angels with Red Cross armbands floating in between, distributing fleece blankets wrapped in plastic, plastic-encased pillows, hands fluttering like wings. One of the volunteers, a young girl with challenging green eyes, wearing a new blue cardigan (Stella can see a price-tag poking out at the back of her neck), has stripy marks on her wrists like bands of kelp had wrapped around them. When she sees Stella staring the girl shrugs, tells her it's because she was tied up. "Aren't we all," Stella drolls. The girl scowls, shakes her head, her long hair yanked back into a braid so tight it bends in on itself like a comma. "For a *really* long time," she emphasizes, like she's daring Stella to one up her again. Stella thinks how she could tell this girl about Rosie, hers and TJ's daughter who's forsaken everything for the streets of Santa Cruz, and how sometimes their lives seem so pointless now. Instead Stella says she has a daughter in California and could be she's tied up too since she never calls. Pointing at the girl's wrists she says, "Your scars look like a lei."

Stella asks TJ, "Where will the coyote live now?"

Two nights later they go home to a soundless world. Route 17 with its parade of cars, trucks, wail of the semis' horns, screech of brakes, tires, accelerating motorcycles all silenced when the river broke out of its banks and pushed over the highway, the eternal whine of the traffic like an electric saw, *rrr rrr rrr*, stopped. Stella can hear wind ruffling the pine trees, and at first she thinks the round yellow eye over the neighbor's sunken second story is a solar light, or maybe one of those Japanese O-bon lanterns they have in California—Rosie told them about these back when she still told them anything that meant anything at all. But it's the moon. After a deluge from a sky the color of pavement, you might have figured the moon would never appear again, emergency sirens still moaning in the distance, a night sky settling into some kind of normalcy after all. The quiet so eerie, like they'd been transplanted to some other place, far away from here.

The next morning you can see it, a world defined by what the river left, TJ and Stella standing stupidly in front of their mud-splattered house, which the water mostly spared—just the basement had taken on a few feet. A layer of sludge to wade through, but at the Jenkins' house a couple properties down, the Susquehanna still laps at their living-room windows and ducks sashay by, squawking.

Watermarks reach clear up to the shelves Stella displays family pictures on; luckily she had thought to grab their most recent of Rosie, police beating on the door—the one where she's still smiling, still theirs, standing on a long wooden pier gazing out at the Pacific Ocean. Her needle-straight hair the color of pepper—she got that hair from TJ, who doesn't have his anymore either, shaving it in some kind of warped solidarity after she razor-chopped hers. Rosie had scrawled on the back of the photo, *Santa Cruz!*

At its peak the river had taken out most of the neighborhood, except for their house, perched high enough on its own little hill (the *mound*, TJ calls it) to be mostly spared, the rest stinking to high heaven, acres of mud and sludge like a sticky coat of rancid paint. Clusters of mold, little pricks and buds blooming into full-blown bouquets all over their basement walls. TJ and Stella in knee-high rubber boots staunch in the mess like something rooted, and Stella thinks about that mold, born of human waste and animal carcasses, leached chemicals, decay, whatever else was carted by that river into their basement. She can picture its tiny iridescent spores blowing through the heating system like dust, sucked into their lungs. Stella shakes her head. "No way am I sleeping in this house!" she says.

Luckily their old, canvas, four-person tent, an LL Bean purchase from way back when, had been stored in the attic. TJ reluctantly helps her pound the pegs into the ground. "This is nuts, babes! Our house was mostly spared. It's a sign, damnit, a good deal. You got to figure things are looking up. This house was saved for something, can't you see? It's a goddamn miracle; maybe we should become missionaries or something."

Stella rolls her eyes, tugs at her ponytail, hair the dull copper of an old penny. She used to frost it but after Rosie didn't come home she figured why bother? What are glossy highlights in a life where daughters mow their own locks like so many weeds, opting for bald on the streets? "The world is a dirty-enough place, Sir" (she calls him this sometimes, not out of respect), "I draw the line at breathing poisons in my own home. Think of all the old factories that leaked crap in that water, tech businesses, car repair, asphalt road run-off, golf course weed-killer, the sewage plant for pity's sake. Our town's history is borne by that water, a VOC banquet and on top of all that you and Josh go fishing with a 12-pack and pee in it!"

The tent perches beside what remains of her mud-drenched garden, anchored to yards of industrial sheet-plastic to diminish any contact with contaminated ground. Bathroom access through the back door to the kitchen when the woods won't do, minimizing having to walk through the main part of the house where two large vents force air from their polluted basement into the living room. Stella uses their kerosene-fired hot plate for cooking her coffee and oatmeal, cans of soup or Dinty Moore stew, like when they used to take Rosie camping in the Catskills, back when life was the three of them. She's even hung curtains off the plastic window flap, cheerful checked ones she found in a bin at Target marked clearance for folks who lost things to the flood. Stella didn't lose much. Having a daughter on the streets meant you did your losing well before any flood could take more. But she ached for the ones who did, whole homes sunk into the muck, shops shuttered, businesses trashed, and livelihoods in this part of the state weren't booming even before the river stole the rest away.

Water waist high, roads trucked under its weight, storm-drains overflowing with filth, a school destroyed, markets closed, even invincible Walmart surrounded by five feet of river, mud-caked sidewalks, sludge-covered steps to destroyed homes, a slime of muddy footprints, lifetimes hauled out to the trash. There's what you can see, then what lurks behind the walls, mold growing secretly in the wet wood. And the stench! Sewer in the living room, gasoline in the dining room from someone's exploded furnace, kitchen, bedrooms, the toxic muddle. Mountains of debris, and in one neighborhood someone's stuck an American flag on a colossal pile of wasted furniture, ruined carpet, mold-spangled linens, dishes, books, CDs, clothes, children's toys, pillows—the flag waving like an act of defiance, or maybe a kind of perverse patriotism, like that shot at Iwo Jima; we'll gut the sucker then build it back, studs to studs.

OCTOBER

TJ USED TO call her Stella Luna after the book they read to Rosie, *Stellaluna*, a big beautiful fruit bat. Only TJ said it was Stella's *mouth*, her big beautiful mouth. OK, so she's got a mouth at times and this is one of them. *What are you up to in that house, TJ!*

Then the tick burrows into her belly, refusing to be coaxed out with a smear of Vaseline, lighter fluid, even bargaining with the thing—"If you withdraw I won't obliterate you!" Its little legs dangling and wiggling about, its mouthparts dug into her flesh like some long-lost stalker boyfriend, distracting her from whatever it is her husband's up to—though damnit she knows it can't be any good. Since the flood, some things still damp and the stinking, dried-out, sludge-coated fields and lawns, the insect population had gone berserk. Fleas, flies, ticks, mosquitoes, and Stella, in her tent, vulnerable to them all, especially the damn ticks, like she's some kind of tick whisperer—forget the neighborhood dogs, the bloodsuckers make a beeline toward her. First she amputated its legs with tweezers, then tried to dig out the rest with a needle, little black tick-bits flaking off like crumbs, its mouth still stuck in her, clamped on like the jaws of death. A doctor gave her a megadose of antibiotics to ward off any threat of Lyme disease, told her to leave the mouthparts intact. "Can't hurt," he said. "It's deader than dust"; that her body would eventually absorb it.

But Stella swears she can hear it talking to her sometimes from its attached little mouth, late at night inside the tent, pattern of leaves on the canvas ceiling, a dangling branch off their dying elm waving at her through the plastic window. *What's that husband of yours up to?*

There's a particular loneliness that comes from living in a tent, pitched in a yard outside the house where you once had an acceptable-enough life, such that a legless tick chatting you up in the middle of the night could even be company of sorts; middle of your life and here you are in a tent, the middle-aged mother of a 25-year-old daughter homeless on the streets of Santa Cruz.

Well Rosie must've had her reasons, the tick offers. *And furthermore, who would've imagined you'd be a middle-aged woman with zits on your face, zits AND wrinkles!* the tick without an iota of tact points out.

Stella jabs at her stomach where what remains of the tick is stuck. "You will now shut the *eff* up!" she tells it. Grabbing her compact mirror off the lawnmower box she uses as a table, Stella ponders her face in the harsh light of their battery-powered lantern. Red bumps on her chin and the squiggles of lines around her mouth, no wonder TJ doesn't call her Stella Luna anymore. *But what is he doing in that house?*

She's seen them slip inside late at night, the door leading into TJ's workroom, the one he's been keeping locked. TJ shuts off the light so they're only silhouettes, but she's counted as many as four of them. *Commerce,* TJ called it when she confronted him, and "No I'm not profiting," he told her. "Christ almighty Stella, you think I would? I'm giving the proceeds to people who need it to get back into their flooded out homes. This house was saved for the greater good, babes."

"Proceeds from exactly *what?*" she snapped.

TJ shook his head. "Classified, revealed only to those sane enough to live inside."

Stella wasn't having it. This was her husband's manipulative way to get her back at it, cooking his meals, washing his clothes, and she's still the breadwinner with two damn jobs.

But he's up to something, she can tell, the spirally way his eyes went when she asked him. And isn't he looking a bit thinner these days? There's his occasional marijuana binge but this makes him hungry, devouring everything in sight. He'd have the body of a potato if she condoned *that.* Last night after consulting the tick (and a mug-full of merlot for resolve!), she decided to take matters into her own hands and snuck into their house when he was asleep, getting Russell, the neighbor's fourteen-year-old albino kid, to assist. He's big for his age and up all night anyway since daylight hurts his eyes, so she paid him to help her haul TJ out to the tent, trussed up like a pot roast with her extra-long bathrobe tie and a macramé belt from way back when. "It's an intervention," she told TJ, but then she was unsure what should happen next.

"Untie me, damnit!" TJ howled. "Are you out of your mind? You can't have an intervention in a goddamn tent! What's the matter with you, Stella!" So they brought him back inside.

Russell's mother who had recently turned Buddhist said the tick was probably an ancestor who couldn't let go and that Stella should light candles and pray for guidance. "Make an offering of some sort", she suggested. Tonight Stella fires up a whole box of sage-scented kitchen candles, but she can't think of what to offer a tick other than her own blood. "Next time you propose an intervention, how about clueing me in what the next step is!" she tells it. Stella needs a shower but is too embarrassed at last night's aborted abduction to go back inside their house. Then the wind picks up and the tent catches fire from all the candles while she's peeing in the woods (nothing the garden hose can't handle but the toxicity from the smoke damage makes it uninhabitable), and before the night is over she's back at the Red Cross Shelter with cots lined up like fiddlesticks, specimen cups filled with shampoo and antibacterial soap for her shower.

The next day TJ buys her a small nylon tent. "A cheap one," he says. "Don't even pretend it's a peace offering." The town picks up the remaining piles of flood refuse off the curbs in front of their neighbors' houses, the ones that don't have a big orange X on their doors, the lucky homes deemed habitable enough. The police take down the road-closed signs and the neighborhood is theirs.

NOVEMBER

DAYLIGHT STUNTED, THE slant of the earth tipped toward a sun that only *looks* warm, lighting what shriveled leaves are left on trees with the heat intensity of a flashlight. It wasn't much of a fall this year, leaves turning a dull gold instead of the usual brilliance of yellows, reds and oranges. Something to do with the flood, no doubt, but what exactly Stella couldn't say. She's been hanging out in the town park after work, a short drive from their property, power-walking its perimeter to avoid the thin, nylon tent, which is colder than death, even though they've yet to have the first snow, and only enough frost to finally zap all those damn bugs. She considered buying herself a better tent but figured that would piss TJ off even more. He still hasn't forgiven the *midnight shenanigans*, he called her attempted intervention, conveniently bypassing any discussion about whether there is, in fact, something to intervene. Last week she drove to the walk-in healthcare and a nurse practitioner excised what remained of the tick out of her stomach. Ancestor or not, its advice sucked.

Stella knows by now the air in their house is probably fine—they had cleaned out their basement throwing everything away from inside the storage room (mostly Rosie's from when she was little, mold-speckled dolls, stuffed animals, a crochet set, Monopoly, a Game Boy, and random plastic pieces to god knows what), and from the TV room they tossed out their couch, pillows, an overstuffed chair, knickknacks, even the ancient analog television. TJ tore out the contaminated drywall and slapped up new, spraying killer mold spray between the walls—"Look Stella, now you see it, now you don't! No more mold." But it's the principle of the thing, and besides there are still those sporadic shadowy figures sneaking into the house late at night—she can hear their laughter, smell the smoke from their cigarettes. What if they're doing something *really* crazy, like cooking LSD in the workshop (TJ was a bit of an acidhead back in the day, OK they all were but Stella grew up!) or worse, crystal meth. There's a lot of that going on around these parts and TJ was always so good at chemistry. The fumes from either of those suckers would be much worse than mold. At least mold wouldn't make you hallucinate and drool in the corner, or waste your brain huffing Drano.

She figures whatever they're doing is another one of TJ's fast-cash schemes (last year's was an earthworm farm in the downstairs bathtub, loony at best!) to preoccupy him so he can ignore what's happening with Rosie. "I don't want to talk about it," he says, when Stella tries to get him to do just that. He refuses to mourn Rosie but she can't help it; she's their daughter, a creation from their loins when said loins were pretty damn hot, hers firm, supple, and how she had loved seeing his when he undressed, his muscular thighs hard-packed and shapely as a frog's. God if she wasn't so dried up now she could get wet just thinking about it. They'd been crazy about each other and Rosie the proof. When lust began to fade, replaced by a routine of household chores, mind-numbing jobs where you barely broke even, that greater need to stay afloat, they had Rosie to come home to.

So what happened to her? A trip to Santa Cruz for her college graduation present—they could only afford her ticket, Stella insisted (though she secretly hoped TJ might argue to send her along as chaperone). Rosie's degree was in marine biology and there was an ocean institute out there she was itching to explore. They had been so proud, the first to finish college on either side. TJ had two semesters at a technical college, Stella three years at SUNY toward some kind of humanities degree, which was part of the problem; she could never nail it, what she wanted to be when she grew up. Then she got pregnant and after Rosie was born Stella stopped asking herself what she wanted to *be*.

Now she was stuck with her teller's job at a local bank, a glorified McDonald's window, doling out cash instead of fries, and when things were tight and they needed a little extra, she'd pick up waitressing shifts at the Red Door Inn. TJ was a professional assistant—plumber's assistant, electrical assistant, but with the economy the way it is, they mostly don't need him to assist. "I'm history," he told Stella. "I can do any of the stuff as good as any of them but I don't have the license and now there's all this software you're supposed to be an expert in. Christ, why would anyone care when their toilet is plugged, if the guy unplugging it is updated on his iPad?" His *schemes* were designed to take up the slack, but usually they were more bother than income.

Then the phone call—Rosie wanted to stay in Santa Cruz for the rest of the summer, would find work, a guide maybe on a whale-watching boat, she'd pay her own ticket back. The summer became the rest of the year then the year after that. The phone calls became emails became Facebook posts became nothing. Days, weeks, a month went by, Stella chewing her nails down to bloody nubs, then they got the engraved card with no return address: Rosie was delighted to announce she was "engaged" to be one of the brides of Bobby Brick, a cult leader, far as Stella could tell, not even a Mormon. "We call him Swami the Large," Rosie said, when they finally got her on the phone. "Don't call again—Swami says we must renounce technology"; that she would be donating her phone to the soldiers in Afghanistan.

Stella remembered how when Rosie was little she would play "bride" and parade around their yard in Stella's white nightgown, a tablecloth of lace on her head, tangle of dandelions she picked from their lawn in her small hands. She never made up a groom, as if being a bride was something she could go at alone. Stella thought about hiring one of those reverse brainwashing experts but in the time it took to Google this a Facebook update appeared. Rosie was not only renouncing technology, including her laptop— this would be the last posting, she wrote—but was giving up Bobby Brick, her worldly goods and the roof over her head, and would reside on the streets as a "research project," documenting what little one needed to stay alive.

"Has she gone completely mad?" Stella shouted, wondering if TJ's family DNA had spawned a mentally ill ancestor lurking in the closet. TJ told Stella to calm down, that it was out of their control. "She's an adult," he said. "With a bachelor's degree," he added, like this was some license, a line of defense against crazy. "Or maybe she's really still a kid and this is just a phase?" he shrugged.

'Right!" Stella screeched. "And you figure she'll *grow out of it*? Twenty-five years old?"

TJ sighed, "I wonder what happened to Bobby Brick?" Like this was the thing that mattered.

But it was enough of a quest to put Stella on that plane; she'd be damned if she'd let TJ cajole her out of it. A few years back she

let him dissuade her from her own father's funeral in Colorado—
"He's dead, Stella, he won't know the difference." You'd think they'd
be rich the way she and TJ went on about money, but it was because
there never seemed to be enough. Now Rosie was choosing to live
without any of it.

It wasn't hard to find her, near the Santa Cruz Wharf. If you
went any further you'd fall into the ocean with the otters and sea
lions and whatever else was cruising around in there. Rosie would've
known. A gaggle of homeless teens and young people, their scraggly
clothes, knotted hair, a few strumming guitars, playing harmonicas,
like this was some kind of festival, a celebration, others panhandling
for change, bumming cigarettes. Rosie, slightly apart from the rest,
sprawled on a beach mat in a grassy patch back from the curb,
Monterey Bay winking and gleaming behind her.

She smelled like sun-baked tar, underarm sweat, and unwashed
socks, and Stella willed herself not to mention it or crinkle her nose,
or do or say anything that might make her daughter not listen to
her. She tried to appeal to her innate logic. *You have a bachelor's of
science and you're living on a beach mat?*

Rosie just gave her a distant smile, still those good teeth, three
years in braces; Stella had waitressed weekends at the Red Door to
pay for them.

After an hour of inhaling clumps of sea air like it still had things
swimming in it, forcing herself to breathe, *breathe*, Stella knelt in
front of Rosie like she was praying to her daughter, stroked what
remained of the beautiful hair Rosie had razor-cut, patches of fuzz
on her scalp like dust balls (Stella read that lice get into the hair of
the homeless so pervasively it's better to shave it off), and asked her
if she was happy.

Rosie stared at her mother, then slowly nodded her head. "This
is what it looks like," she said, closing her perfect hazel eyes, and
wouldn't meet Stella's gaze again. Stella shed her sandals and slunk
through the sand until her feet touched the water. She remembered
Rosie telling them her first summer here how she was learning to

scuba dive, and to get her license she had to dive sixty feet down to where it was frigid and dark, sharing air all the way back up with an eleven-year-old boy. When she saw the bubbles grow lighter as they rose to the surface, Rosie had said, she believed there could be a god. That ocean was so cold Stella's toes burned.

Maybe it's because there was no doctor at her birth. Stella in heavy labor at 3 A.M., and she guessed that doctor must have wanted to sleep or something because he kept telling TJ on the phone she was fine, no need to go to the hospital yet, so that by the time they got there, Stella screaming from the back seat of their Honda Civic, Rosie was born in the hospital parking lot, blue and not breathing. Maybe she's still trying to catch that lost breath.

DECEMBER

IT SNOWS A couple times but it's the ice, finally, that will drive Stella back into her house, pelting the nylon tent like explosions of glass, like it wants to slash its way in. When she steps outside the tent to pee, still clutching the flap, she immediately slips on the ice-encrusted plastic tarp pulling the tent down on top of her. She figures if nothing else she'll finally know what TJ is up to, those late nights when she hears the laughter, smells the cigarettes and God only knows what else; maybe the only way she'll know for sure is to be inside and catch him at it. The Red Cross Shelter has closed, most either back in their refurbished homes or their homes abandoned or condemned. The rest in their drowned neighborhoods have put up holiday lights, glistening and twinkling in the cold.

First night back in their bed when TJ crawls in, paperback in hand (he'll pass out after reading one page, Stella knows his habits), she accuses him of not caring that their daughter is sleeping on the streets in the middle of winter. TJ snorts, "What middle! Winter's only just begun." She knows he's joking with her, trying to make light of it and she doesn't appreciate him making light of *this* and tells him so.

"She's in Santa Cruz, babes. No ice storms, no blizzards, and it's not like this is some big city where a lot of crime happens. If you're going to be on the streets it's the perfect place. Location, location," TJ grins, chucking her gently on the cheek. "If I could start over I'll tell you what, it wouldn't be here with the river at our backs."

Stella thinks about the ocean at Rosie's back and how she was drawn to it, the Susquehanna never enough, it had to be the ocean— the thing they couldn't give her in upstate New York. They'd take walks alongside the river in the winter, ice skate its shallows, and afterward Stella made her daughter hot chocolate, didn't she? It's like she can almost remember, but not quite. Sweetness, the warmth of a cup in their hands, soggy squish of the marshmallows. Isn't this what a good mother would have done, one whose daughter would think back to these moments from her childhood and appreciate its comfort and security? The reason folks cling to a belief in the American Dream, even as they grow poorer, even as it's swallowed in the one-hundred-year flood that happens every two years now, the sanctuary of a home? So why can't Stella remember?

At one point Rosie stopped requesting *Stellaluna*, wanted only fish books, books about whales, things that live in the sea. "I'm going to be a marine biologist," she said, and they believed her. Stella worries about that sea now, some rogue wave that could rise out of its darkness one night and crash down upon her daughter asleep on the adjacent sidewalk. She wonders if Rosie has a tent, since it's December and colder, even in California. Stella decides she'll send the nylon one. Not that Rosie has any kind of an address, but maybe if she mailed it to General Delivery, Santa Cruz? Maybe if the tent belongs to Stella it wouldn't have to be discarded as a *possession* from Rosie's *research project*.

That night she dreams about the fish angel, the river rising and it's riding the crest, a magic fish who can grant wishes and Stella asks it to call back the waters. "No more floods!" she tells it. In the morning she determines the fish was an eel; she remembered seeing one in the Monterey Bay Aquarium after trying to bring Rosie home. Failing at that she couldn't bear to fly back right away, knowing that doing so would sever proximity, the last sure connection she had to her daughter. She went to the aquarium thinking if maybe she could learn about the sea, learn to *love* the sea, know and appreciate what came from it, there would at least be that between them. Standing behind the glass she watched a moray eel rocking lazily to some water-rhythm only it was aware of, its long shimmery body dipping and swaying from the coral that was its home. She had marveled at its jaws, a bite so strong it could amputate a finger, now satiated and powerless behind the glass. *Morays are often thought to be bad tempered and vicious*, the information plaque announced; *in truth they would rather flee than fight.*

JANUARY 2012

IN THE PARK Stella is witness to a miracle, or something like one, a flock of bluebirds! But how can this be, middle of winter and their dazzling blue feathers flash through a tree's naked branches. Where are they going? Where have they been? Surely not stuck here through it all, the devastating flood, toxic cleanup, a solstice darkness with bone-cold temperatures? The color of their wings reminds her of the tropics and she imagines for a moment she is one of them, flying to somewhere brighter.

A few days later they get a postcard from Rosie, of a California sea lion sunning itself on a rock. *Washed my shirt today then napped on my mat in the sun while it dried.*

Stella thinks their daughter must be at least a *little* mentally ill but TJ says she sounds content. "How many get that?" he says. "A nap in the sunshine."

Stella scoffs, "Hallelujah! She has a college degree for chrissake! There are people around here still fighting to get back into their flood-destroyed homes and she's *choosing* to sleep on a mat in the street? Where did we go wrong!"

"What if it has nothing to do with us, babes? What if she saw there's no jobs, or maybe for her it's an adventure of sorts; what if she doesn't know why she's doing this so she has to goddamn do it to find out!" TJ inhales a breath, stares straight over Stella's head like he's looking for something past her, shifts his gaze onto her forehead then back into her eyes. Stella shivers. The awkward boy she went to high school with, who was supposed to amount to something but was an *underachiever*, the teachers used to say; even then Stella thought she could love TJ, even when she hadn't a clue what love really was, how bloody taxing it can get, how sometimes it doesn't even look like itself.

"What if..." TJ hesitates, "there just aren't any answers, Stella?"

"An *adventure*? What the hell happened to rock climbing or skydiving! Or even being lowered in a damn cage where sharks feed; I guess that would qualify as an adventure in some people's minds. But *this*, she shakes her head, I'm sorry but I can't live with it."

TJ grins, "Of course you can, you're breathing, aren't you? Look at it this way, at least you're not the mother-in-law of Swami the Large!"

ONE NIGHT STELLA wakes up and she hears them below her, those middle-of-the-night voices, chaotic bursts of male laughter, cigarette smoke curling up through the heating vent from the dining room. She hears TJ trying to hush them and she wrinkles her nose at the stink, slips on her bathrobe, checks her face in the mirror for anything scary—no dabs of desiccated night cream, trails of sleep drool or stuck-up sleep hair, then sneaks down the stairs ready for a fight.

And there they are, huddled around her dining room table, four middle-aged men playing... cards? "What the hell!"

"Hey Stella, want in on a hand?" Josh asks. "It's mostly straight, five-card draw or seven stud, but we can do black jack if you'd like.

The ladies seem to go for wild cards but we got a rule about that, only one-eyed jacks!" They snort.

Poker? She stares at TJ, her eyes narrowing into bullets. "All this time? You're playing poker? Thought you said you're no good at cards. Thought you said something about commerce!"

He shrugs. "I'm not good at cards, terrible in fact, I never seem to get the winning hands. But it's fun, and we give the pot to United Way for the flood victims. That's the commerce part." He grins at Josh and Josh grins at the other two, all of them avoiding Stella's gaze.

"And speaking of *pot*, what the hell, you've got cigarettes burning gangbusters in ashtrays and I saw that joint, Josh, the one you're clutching behind your back, don't think I didn't. You lit bloody cigarettes to disguise the smell, huh?"

Josh looks at TJ who looks at Stella, shrugs. "Well babes, you don't like me smoking marijuana now do you?"

"Not particularly but what kind of idiocy are the cigarettes? Marlboros are a hundred times more toxic than joints, you fools, all of it just idling away, poisoning the air—and don't think I won't recognize my eggcups you're using for ashtrays!"

"Diek gets a medical dispensation to purchase it legally," TJ says. "It's all on the up and up, but I knew you didn't care for it so just figured we wouldn't get you worrying, keep things spic and span."

"How very thoughtful of you!" Stella hisses.

"Ahem!" Josh pumps his fist on the table then stubs the remains of the joint carefully into an eggcup, beside the burning cigarette he also extinguishes. "We were talking about the river, Stella, before you came down. We were saying we think it's changed since the flood." He pushes his cap up on his forehead then whips it off, his head with its sporadic tufts of hair like an old onion, Stella thinks, wrinkled and warped.

"Yeah," says the other guy—she doesn't recognize him but they could all be a set—"I think it's changed. Totally. It's like it reversed its direction or something, expanded its horizons, places getting river what never had it before."

"Yup," Diek nods, his hangdog face, chemo-sleek physique. "No question about it. Killer earthquake in Japan takes out a nuclear reactor, twisters in the Midwest leveling whole towns, and now our catastrophic flood where nothing happens. May as well figure that's the way things are going to be."

Stella stomps back up the stairs with TJ at her heels.

"Babes, be reasonable! I didn't tell you because I thought you'd be mad if I lost. The money and all, and you've asked me not to smoke pot so of course I didn't want to broadcast that either. Just a couple times a month, doesn't make it a habit."

"*Of course*! Jesus!" she sputters, back inside their bedroom, slamming the door to give the others a not-so-subtle hint to get the hell out of her house.

"Well, then what did you think we were doing?"

Stella snorts, "I don't know but didn't figure any good could come of it. Making crystal meth?"

TJ's gray eyes pop. He rubs them then scratches his naked scalp viciously, yanks at his earlobe, staring at her like *she's* the insane one. "You can't be serious! Are you serious?" He flops down on the bed, dragging her arm toward him, starts to laugh then frowns. "Why in God's name would you even think a thing like that?"

"You hear about it," she shrugs. "Plus there's your little fast-cash ventures, we're about ripe for another one of those. Folks a lot dumber make money at it. You were always good at chemistry. So maybe you found a way to make it less toxic, a 'light' or 'organic' version. You could've been a chemist!"

"Could've been a lot of things, babes, but drug dealer was never in the cards. That's a joke, Stella. Get it, *cards*? Christ, I'm nowhere near that stupid, or crazy when you come right down to it. What's gotten into you? Just because I don't have a regular job doesn't make me some psycho loser who'd cook up a combustible illegal concoction because he got an *A* in high-school chemistry! We just wanted to have a little fun while doing our part. Call it survivor's guilt. Our house was saved and everyone else suffering, didn't seem right. Like I said, I didn't tell you because I thought you'd be worried about me losing money, you worry about things, Stella. Seemed a perfect time with you insisting on staying in that tent, we got on a roll and just continued, is all. I figured someday you'd catch us at it and here we are. What on earth has gotten into you?" TJ repeats.

She'd have to wonder, slipping off her bathrobe, lying down beside him. And maybe even wish, just a little, that they *could* be that crazy, at least in the abstract. If Rosie could *adventure*, couldn't they? Check it out: married to a sexy drug dealer, like on a television show, like someone else's life, somewhere where shops weren't closed-up, jobs gone to India and the river didn't swallow what remained. A place where daughters stayed put.

"Why do you really think our house was spared, TJ? Answer me straight, like our marriage depends on it."

He sighs. "Because we live on a hill, Stella. We had the good luck to buy a house on a goddamn mound." TJ tugs the covers over them both, shuts out the light.

Stella presses up against his back, wrapping her legs tight around his. "You think I still have decent loins?"

"Best in show," he says, poking her thigh like he's testing it for doneness.

"Liar!" she whispers. She thinks about the Susquehanna, how it was here long before humans and will be here after they've gone; how it will claim what they've built and what they've wrecked, meandering into its future, polluted or not, while everything that's now passes into history. Amazingly enough, this doesn't depress the hell out of her. In fact, she thinks it's kind of smart.

She rubs her arm where TJ grabbed it hauling her toward him, and remembers the girl from the shelter, the one with the scars draped around her wrists. From being tied up, the girl had said. Some time later Stella learned that she was the girl who'd been abducted from a parking lot and everyone had given her up for gone. The man who did it was someone Stella went to high school with. She remembered having felt sorry for him back then, he was so painfully shy, with his mess of dark hair, those uncertain eyes, almost more animal than human, and that halting way of speaking—the other kids were cruel to him. He looked ill at ease in his own skin, but it wasn't *bad* skin, just somehow not the *right* skin, not like the others. She remembered him asking her to walk into the woods with him, stuttering the invitation, couldn't even look her in the eyes. She was falling in love with TJ, but he didn't know it yet and Stella wasn't sure if she *wanted* TJ to know it, and so she said yes. Did anything happen? Stella didn't think so or she would've remembered.

The girl didn't press charges (*he let her go!* she'd said), which Stella figured must've been that Stockholm syndrome—she'd heard about this, where the victim develops empathy for her captor, mistaking his not hurting her for something like love. Stella wished she hadn't said that thing about her scars and would've liked to tell her how brave she was, but when she returned to the shelter that second time the girl had moved on—out of state, another worker said. Still, Stella thinks now, the scars were good, like battle wounds, marks of having survived. Besides, she remembers learning in anthropology or cultural studies or some such class that leis could mean both hello and goodbye—that girl has her bases covered!

When TJ's breathing grows deeper, settling into sleep, Stella closes her eyes and imagines she's on a paraglider—she read about this recently, a sport called parahawking where they follow a trained hawk's flight, a combination of falconry and thrill, the article said. They were in Nepal, where the money for the paraglide was donated to help Nepal's disappearing vultures, threatened by a drug fed to livestock that poisoned the birds when they ate the carcasses. Stella thinks how some folks seem to muck things up, but then others come along and set them right. Maybe that's what she can hope for Rosie, who felt the wounds of the world enough to withdraw from it, that at some point she'll become someone who does something to fix it.

On the updrafts of air, catching the thermals, Stella wheels higher and higher until she's a speck the size of an eyelash. The river below is a moonlit trail heading neither here nor there until she can no longer see it, and there is only the wind, the infiniteness of sky, and Stella, soaring.

Epilogue

The Hoodie's Tale

Its journey began in a Beijing factory, assembled, crated, and shipped to the American manufacturer where it was inspected, its label sewn in, *made in China*, then on to a Target warehouse to be sorted and boxed and trucked once more to *their* Target, where it sat on a shelf in a stack of the others just like it, size medium. Its color was what attracted the mother, guava, she thought, remembering her own mother coming home with these in the summer sometimes, cutting them open, that rosy effervescence like the GMO version of a basket of strawberries meets cotton candy then bred into a dense, pulpy fruit. Pretty, the mother thought, on the daughter whose hair is the color of nutmeg.

The daughter thought so too and wore it like a second skin.

Its pockets were filled with Bonnie Bell's Lip Smackers Dr. Pepper lip gloss, used Kleenex, loose change—two nickels, a quarter and a dime—a smooth pebble the girl had found two days before she and the hoodie would part company forever, flat and speckled with mica, to skip in the river shallows where she and the boy snuck off to sometimes, smoking a joint on the bank, the boy insisting only *guys* could skip stones, and her intent for this pebble was to challenge that; and a thin chocolate mint wrapped in shiny green paper from the Olive Garden, where she and the mother had pasta and salad the night before, nothing in the fridge and the mother too tired to shop—the one bit of edible matter that might have attracted the dogs who dragged the hoodie out of the woods, and because of this mint it would end its journey bagged and tagged in a forensic file at the local police station—but that's not what this tale is about.

Its pockets filled with her innocence, the hood and neckline scented with her shampoo, a Rite Aid buy, green and herbal; the sleeves at the wrists smelled like Fritos, the last thing she ate before removing the hoodie in the boy's car. This was her offering, like peeling an onion—the next layer for him, her bony shoulders, her bra points with their still developing breasts poking from the tank top she wore under it.

After the girl disappeared the boy tossed the hoodie into the thick woods on the other side of town where it lay under a majestic white pine on a pine-needle bed, which in the rainy spring became a mud-slicked hole, and the sultry summer a dry, caked earth; in the winter the hoodie was entombed under a foot of snow. Above it the pine rustled and bent in the wind, songbirds nested and woodpeckers bore holes into a leafless branch, the forest alive with its patterns and routines, its scents and weather and the creatures it fed, sheltered, living and dying in their predictable ways that had little to do with the world the hoodie had been part of.

Its owner was a *good* girl, a girl filled with an innate goodness. The mother knew it, the man who held the girl captive knew it, the boy who hurled her hoodie into the woods knew it and suffered remorse that he was somehow implicated in her vanishing. Even their community knew it at some level and felt a quiet despair that such a girl would be lost among them. And if the hoodie could know such things it would have felt this truth in the warm press of her flesh and mourned its absence while it lay in the forest that had no recognition of it, nor the hoodie of this forest.

For weeks after the girl didn't come home the mother curled up every night in the girl's closet thinking how good this girl was, and if any essential goodness remained in this wrecked world, she would be saved. The mother rocked and thought these things, her head between her knees, face down, eyes shut, visualizing the girl in the guava-colored hoodie, her nutmeg hair, her thin face beneath the hood, pictured her showing up one day in the little, gray house as if she'd never been gone, and the mother would make her a guava chiffon pie like her own mother used to make, the guavas from Chile no doubt, or Ecuador, but she would tell the girl they were from Hawai'i, a tropical world where the sun always shines and the sky is cerulean, and with this her promise: they will go there, the mother, the daughter.

As the seasons passed the mother found a new job and went to it daily like it was her duty to do this, to *move on*, as her friends pleaded. When the hoodie was extricated from the jaws of the huge black dog, the mother identified it at the police station and still she didn't give up, though her friends, her coworkers, all stared at her with that drowning in their eyes. No, the mother thought, this is proof of her daughter, this hoodie she loved and wore like her skin. The mother imagined the girl deep in the forest perhaps, beyond where the hoodie was found, and it didn't frighten her to think it.

For this is a staunch and resolute land, impervious to the human drama on its outskirts—caring is for the humans who damage things and are then compelled to care for what's been ruined. For thousands of years the eastern timber wolf roamed this land, the chorus of its cries would have filled the cold nights like a symphony, until the colonists began to clear the land and in their fear slaughtered them all. Now there are coyotes, much bigger than their western cousins and recent studies bear witness to a new species, the "coywolf," a coyote that has bred with the Canadian gray wolf and is social, sentient, one of the most intelligent, adaptable animals in North America, scientists claim, monogamous, protective of their young, with larger stature and beautiful wolf-eyes, howling mournfully—or perhaps joyfully, who knows?—into the night. A land where things can still evolve is a land where there is still some hope, and the sun paints its hills a deep blush at sunset and the leaves of its trees green in the summer, red and orange in the fall, none at all in the winter, its trees vital and waiting under the snow.

One night when she came home from work, the mother curled up in the girl's closet again on the frayed beige carpet, lingering among last-year's corduroy coat, the flung-about sweaters, thin summer tops hung neatly in a row over the mother's head, a pair of jeans draped across the peg the girl left them on, the pair she didn't wear that day. Hunkered down among her shoes, crawled into one of them, *Chuckies* the girl called these, a rich brown canvas the color of ale, the color of her hair. Inside the scent of her foot still lingered, muted but unique, the arch high like the mother's, remembering how she counted her baby's toes after she was born— *you did it! She's all here.* The mother had glanced out the window in the birthing room, holding her swaddled daughter in her arms for the first time, and noticed an unusual bird with a golden head and throat perched on a tree branch. *Look!* she told her daughter, the infant's eyes half-opening at the mother's voice, a squint, her furrowed, crinkly brow. The bird preened its feathers then cocked its head as if listening to an unfamiliar sound, its gaze intent on something in the world beyond what their window revealed.

Jaimee Wriston Colbert is the author of *Shark Girls*, a finalist for the ForeWord Magazine Book of the Year and USA Book News Best Book of 2010 awards; the linked story collection, *Dream Lives of Butterflies*, a gold medal winner of the 2008 Independent Publisher Award; a novel in stories, *Climbing the God Tree*, winner of the Willa Cather Fiction Prize; and the story collection, *Sex, Salvation, and the Automobile*, winner of the Zephyr Prize. Her stories have appeared in numerous journals, including *Gettysburg Review, TriQuarterly, Prairie Schooner, Tampa Review, Connecticut Review*, and *New Letters*. Originally from Hawai'i, she is professor of English and creative writing at SUNY, Binghamton University.

CPSIA information can be obtained
at www.ICGtesting.com
Printed in the USA
FFOW03n2213140617
36726FF